ROY

A ...
Towards Victory

from the Granada Television series
created by John Finch

GRAFTON BOOKS

A Division of the Collins Publishing Group

LONDON GLASGOW
TORONTO SYDNEY AUCKLAND

Grafton Books
A Division of the Collins Publishing Group
8 Grafton Street, London W1X 3LA

Published by Grafton Books 1989

First published in Great Britain by
Mayflower Books 1972

ISBN 0-586-20922-0

Printed and bound in Great Britain by
Collins, Glasgow

Set in Times

A Family at War: Towards Victory

Life, like a dome of many-coloured glass,
Stains the white radiance of Eternity.
SHELLEY

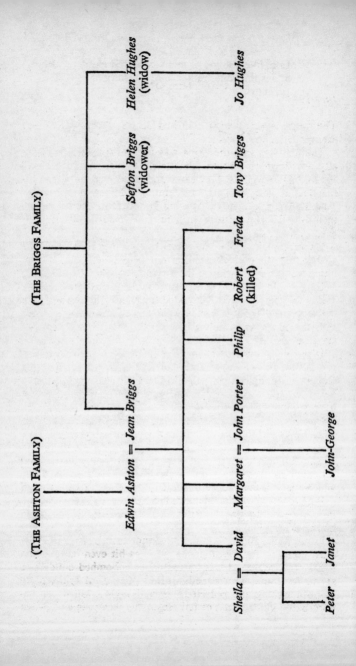

(THE BRIGGS FAMILY)

(THE ASHTON FAMILY)

Helen Hughes (widow)

Jo Hughes

Sefton Briggs (widower)

Tony Briggs

Freda

Robert (killed)

Philip

Edwin Ashton = Jean Briggs

Margaret = John Porter

John-George

Sheila = David   Janet

Peter   Janet

CHAPTER ONE

June 1943

The warm spring which followed Jean's death was a grey aftermath for the Ashtons.

The first sign that the worst was over was when Edwin finally got down to writing "that letter to your Aunt Helen." He told Margaret, as she cleared the table, that he was commandeering the living room "until midnight if necessary. And if Freda and her chattering friend Doris come in, tell them it's 'Do Not Disturb' in here. I can't put it off any longer."

Margaret smiled. She knew how many times he'd tried. She wished him "Good luck, Dad, give her my love," and left him biting his pen and staring at the virgin notepaper.

How could he explain to Jean's sister? His cable telling Helen the terrible news had ended up "Letter Following", but the more he'd tried to decide what to say and what to leave out, the more he'd thought "less said the better". His pen stayed poised over the paper.

It did no good now to go over it all. Jean had never forgiven him, to her last breath, for his signing the paper for Robert – still under age – to go to sea. It proved to be Robert's death warrant; Jean went to her grave believing that. Did he have to tell Helen? Just because she was her sister?

His thoughts delved further back in time. Before the war, when they used to take the children – Philip, Margaret, David, Freda and Robert – to the seaside; everyone laughing and larking on the sunny sands. Before Helen had married and gone out to Australia. And she'd lost her Jack since then; which made it even more difficult to write about happy days.

But Edwin knew that if he didn't make a start somewhere, he never would write the letter at all. So he decided to begin on the bright side.

"I suppose, Helen, we should count our blessings. There must be many families that the war has hit even harder than it has ours. Margaret was buried under a bombed building in an air-raid, and she escaped without permanent injury." He stopped writing and reflected: even though it killed her unborn baby. No. Better not tell Helen she was pregnant, when

7

John had been missing all that time. Or he would have to explain about Michael, the baby's father. Helen didn't have to know that.

"David is still on flying duties and seems to be the only one in the family in direct danger. Margaret has gone back to teaching, now her husband John is back and surely never going to have to endure more than he's gone through. He is bound to get his discharge. Our Philip is teaching, too, his desert experiences are being used to train others. And Freda is really grown-up. You'd never recognise her."

Edwin paused. What else? Without harking back to Jean. "Poor Sheila seems very low these days: she worries about David on bombing raids, and sees very little of him. Or of their children, evacuated with Mrs. Thomas in Wales. Two lovely grandchildren I should be thankful for, Peter and Janet. Jean spoiled them too." Edwin's pen stopped again: was it Robert's death that broke Jean's heart? Could she really have believed Edwin allowed him to go to sea, knowing he would be killed? The war was to blame. And still it went on. "The Desert War is over but Europe is still in the power of Nazi gangsters and has to be liberated by invasion one day.

"It's a difficult letter, Helen, and you must forgive me going over what is past and done with. No, it's not done with, is it? It echoes into our lives today. And will tomorrow.... And the next day. And the next."

A very different letter, addressed to Flying Officer Ashton, had been just as difficult to write. David knew the Welsh postmark, recognised the writing. Mrs. Thomas always did the envelope when Peter wrote to him: and the "postscript" was always in Janet's infant-school printing.

But this was from Mrs. Thomas herself. "I'm sorry to have to write to you about money." David didn't think his payments were behind. He was vague on the practicalities of life. He always looked as though they worried him, but they didn't really. Oh, the number of times Sheila had complained about that.

David couldn't even remember if he'd paid back the last fiver he'd borrowed from Frankie, who'd kindly picked up his letter with his own mail. He had? That was a relief.

Flight Sergeant Frank Cox was due for his commissioning leave soon; immediately after the last op of the tour, in fact. Perhaps it was something of both events that made Frankie wonder if the law of averages would allow him to make it. So many of their mates had bought it. Over Cologne or Frankfurt or....

"Don't recite the list, old boy, we know it by heart," said Peter Bryant, Frankie's pilot.

"By sight, most of 'em," cracked David. "In the dark, too." It was the usual ploy to get anyone off a subject that didn't bear examining. "What's it like on the receiving end? That's what's beginning to get me. Once we've pressed the button and turned for home. What's it like for them down below?"

It wasn't that Frankie didn't sometimes think about that, too. But at this moment, "Well, you see Dave, I'm going to get married on leave, and naturally, it makes you wonder.... Well, will I ever make it?"

"Course you'll make it, mate. Who's the lucky girl?"

And when Frankie said it was Chrissie in the W.A.A.F. parachute store, David and Peter jumped at his invitation to celebration drinks in the Turk's Head. Then David remembered he was on a Forty-eight hours Pass. That was okay, Frankie understood. He'd feel the same when he and Chrissie were well-and-truly hitched. David didn't bother to explain that he wasn't going home to Sheila.

Sheila Ashton was washing up; Colin Woodcock was drying for her, and telling her about a girl he knew in Preston. He took her to this play he didn't really want to see. Sheila said he must think a lot of her to do that. No, this girl wasn't the reason he hadn't been here recently. It was the way it worked out. "I can't just pick and choose where my jobs come up; there hadn't been any in Liverpool. Simple as that."

Colin didn't like to have to refer to his civilian work. Sheila knew he was a conscientious objector. But he couldn't help wondering what she felt about it. David might at any time be reported missing or killed. And yet, he, Colin went about his job as a draughtsman almost as if the war didn't exist.

He got off the subject. Anyway, what he'd called about: was she on at the N.A.A.F.I.? And if not, he'd call back when he'd finished for the day.

Sheila said something about thinking of going to the pictures. So Colin offered to take her. But if he wasn't back by seven, she'd know he couldn't make it. "Well," said Sheila, trying to sound as though she didn't mind either way, "Don't put yourself out, Colin."

9

Grace Gould's Kensington flat was the antithesis of the meagre rooms David had left Sheila to cope with in Liverpool. The look-what-money-can-buy decor epitomised Grace's facility for forgetting the war was on. In fact, war was to her advantage. Charles Gould, like so many husbands, was away from home most of the time. Nearly all the time in fact.

"Well, if it isn't the boy David. Surprise, surprise." It was so long since she'd seen him, she could just about put a name to his face. David was annoyed at her reception. "All right, I'll go if you want me to."

No, he needn't take that attitude. She treated him like a little boy. "Just say you're sorry and we'll pick up where we left off. I'm easy, you know that." So David said he was sorry and she began to undo his tunic buttons. "That's a good boy," said the look on her face. David didn't notice. This is what he thought about when the flak was thickest: when they turned for home "Bombs gone". Like Frankie wanted to come back to Chrissie, with him it was Grace. Well, at present it was.

Tony Briggs was spending a brief shore leave at home. He rarely came back to Liverpool without visiting the Ashtons. His cousin Freda was on about her friend Doris's everlengthening list of American airmen. The chatter stopped abruptly when Tony asked what about Freda herself – hadn't she been smitten by the love-bug yet? Her answer was rather more than he'd expected. "What is love, Tony? Does anybody round here know? 'Cos I don't." Was love the rift between her brother David and Sheila? Or her sister Margaret having Michael's baby, thinking her husband had been killed on active service? John Porter is back and recovering but poor Margaret's still not able to tell him what the whole family knows. Is that love?

Freda realised she was going on a bit and switched the conversation to asking about Tony's girl-friend, Jenny. And when Tony admitted he was no longer seeing her, he realised it only added point to Freda's question: "What is love?"

Ian Mackenzie chose that moment to call.

"Who's he?" asked Tony after Edwin had contrived to leave Freda alone with him in the living-room.

"Lived just round the corner for years, grew up there. We didn't get to know him until Freda took up nursing. He's a doctor at the hospital – specialist, I believe. Given her a lift home once or twice. I'll never forget him when Jean died. Tower of strength to us all, he was."

"Seems a nice chap, Uncle. Is it ... developing? Between them?"

"Don't ask me. I'm only her father."

The book passed from lender to borrower. "It's anatomy. Quite good. Might be useful with your studies."

Freda looked suitably grateful. "How nice of you to bring it round. Thank you, Mister Mackenzie." She flipped through the pages without really looking at them.

Wasn't it time she called him "Ian"? They joked about the "doctor-and-the-nurse" cliché. They searched for other mutual interests. Music? Freda liked the Max Bruch Concerto. Tennis? He'd seen her pass their gate on the way to the local club. There was a tennis court at the back of their house, why don't they play there? Well, he mustn't interrupt any longer....

They'd run out of excuses for his staying. Freda thanked him again, and as soon as he'd gone, Edwin and Tony appeared in the hall. "Maybe the war's going to do someone some good, after all." Edwin smiled approval.

Freda ignored their teasing. "There's absolutely nothing in it."

Sheila was doing her best to clear up the mess when Freda and Doris arrived. They thought, for a moment, that a bomb had fallen nearby. But weren't those days over? Sheila told them some missing slates had caused it. She'd been on to the landlord, but without a man about the place, what can you do? The landlord knew she was on her own and expected you to be, you know, grateful.

"Grateful?" Freda queried, as she and Doris helped mop up and get things tidy again – if Sheila's design-for-living could be called tidy. "Oh I see, that sort of grateful. What a liberty."

Colin had done several man-about-the-house jobs for Sheila, but the roof-slates were too big to tackle. She'd never even dared ask him.

"You and Colin serious, then?" Doris never beat about the bush where boy-friends were concerned.

"Colin says he wants to marry me. But there'd be all that dreary business of divorce. Takes ages. Not to mention what it would cost. Colin says he'd wait; and wouldn't mind having

11

to take on Peter and Janet. Then the next minute he's talking about this girl in Preston. She's single; he's got no complications with her, I'll bet."

Freda saw Sheila's face was full of doubts. Were they both thinking the same? If David had never gone in the R.A.F., would it have come to this? If there'd not been a war? What a big "if" that was.

There was a massive raid that night: droves of bombers lumbered across the coastline with full bomb-loads, heading for big German towns. Peter Bryant – Grace's brother – and Frankie were in it; their Wellington running into flak bursts as soon as they were over enemy territory. Peter kept the kite weaving in an attempt to fool the guns' range-finders. But it was still sheer luck if you got through; and home again.

If Grace Gould was giving brother Peter a thought at that moment it was soon pushed from her tiny mind. Kensington was a different world. Her flat door was opened by the one man who had a key. Charles Gould was home on leave.

Grace was very cool. She lit a cigarette and inhaled before she said. "Not the most considerate time to arrive, Charles, dear. I have a friend here." She indicated their bedroom.

"Oh, have you? So sorry not to have telephoned. How inconsiderate of me."

Grace had explained to David when Peter had first introduced them. She and Charles arranged their affairs – in both senses of the word – so that they went their separate ways. But here was Charles suddenly arriving out of the blue and saying he'd missed Grace and he really did love her. Grace found it a bit sudden to say the least. And not quite to their rules.

"Darling, I love you too. But let's not get serious about it."

Freda was shocked by the stark announcement on the radio. The brilliant actor Leslie Howard, one of the heart-throbs that made the war more bearable for women of every age, had been killed in an aircraft shot down on the way back from neutral Madrid.

Edwin looked over his half-moon spectacles. "The war's no respecter of persons. Perhaps the first war that isn't." Would it be the last war ever? The war to finish wars for good? There did seem some sort of a look towards a peaceful future now. Margaret and John were picking up the threads

12

of their marriage – although with a secret that had to come out one day. John was recovering nicely and would be well enough soon to go back to his old job at the Town Hall. Freda didn't like to hear her father philosophising. "Oh, by the way," she suddenly said brightly, "Mister Mackenzie, you know, from the Crescent, will be calling for me in the morning."

She turned her father's questioning look aside quite flippantly. "There's nothing in it, dad. I told you. He virtually passes the door and you know what the trams are like these days. Why shouldn't I accept a lift? Anyway, I'm not interested in marriage, after what I've seen of it."

"Oh? And what's that supposed to mean?"

"Well, look at David and Sheila. He never comes to see her. And don't tell me he doesn't get leave, 'cos everybody does, some time or other. One of these days Sheila's going to see just what a dance our David's led her. And if she leaves him for some other chap, I'll be the first to tell her she's done the right thing."

Edwin wasn't surprised at her outburst. "I wouldn't blame her myself, love."

David had dressed hurriedly and came out of the bedroom wondering how violent a reception he would get.

"Charles, darling, this is David Ashton. He's in Peter's squadron. My husband, Charles."

"Hello, Ashton. Grace tells me you've called to collect a tennis racquet for Peter. Give him my best, will you?"

David now saw what a marvellous take-off Peter did of Charles. Just as he was here, looking down his nose from his slightly-superior rank – in a different arm of the service, too – and almost giving him orders. Just the sort of bloke Grace would marry.

"Yes, all right, I'll pass it on to him for you." David decided not to push his luck. Better than a punch-up. After all Charles was her husband, they were married. Come to think of it so was he. He didn't think of it these days, that was the trouble.

Colin didn't get much of a welcome when he called to apologize to Sheila Ashton. He was sorry he hadn't got back that night for the pictures. The job had taken longer than he had expected and now he was off back to Head Office. He thought he'd be in the Liverpool area again next week. Maybe they could make up for it then.

13

Sheila made it sound as though she was thinking of Colin's own good. What was the point of him hanging around a married woman with two young children to bring up. If he took her advice, he'd go for that girl he kept talking about – in Preston. Marry her.

Sheila seemed mad at him. He didn't know what to reply. "I've got to put my job first, Sheila. So ... should I pop in? Next week?"

"See how you feel. When the time comes. If I'm in, I'll be here, won't I. If I'm out ... Well, that's it, isn't it?"

As soon as David got back to his Station, Peter came to his room. David got in first. "Who d'you think walked in? Bloody Charles Gould. Didn't bother me, really. That set-up's a bit too cut-glass for me. I'm thinking of ..."

As he said it, David noticed Peter was drawn, his skin pale. And his arm was bandaged under his jacket.

"You get that last night?"

Peter didn't know where to begin. It came out in spasms of words. "We took a smack on the way back. Flak knocked the rudder out. Doubted I'd get us home. Crew in crash-positions, it was that dicey. But we scraped through. I got this on landing. Bashed her up quite a bit. Well, to pieces really. When I came round I'd been thrown clear. Yards away from the kite. She was ... just a heap. And then ... she went up ... Just like that. Fuel, ammo, the lot. One big bang."

David's mouth went dry; he spoke huskily. "Frankie? The others?"

"The prang must have trapped them. They all bought it. All my crew."

They used "prang" and "bought it" to try to cloak the horrors of crashing and dying. But the euphemisms didn't help David's feelings.

"Chrissie's been told, I suppose?" was all he said, and turned away without waiting for the obvious answer.

Sefton Briggs had called on Edwin to see if he had any problems over Jean's will. There were times when Sefton, the hard-headed businessman showed a soft-centre. Not often, but it could happen. At Jean's funeral he had seen his sister's husband and her children in the same trough of unbearable grief as himself. And he had felt very close to them.

Sefton told Edwin that if he wanted any additional advice

he'd put him in touch with his own solicitor, George Askew. Edwin thanked him, he'd remember that. And as he closed the front door behind him, the telephone rang. It was David.

Edwin immediately sensed something wrong. Had he been drinking? Was he crying? He was vaguely saying something about a mate of his.... Had his Dad seen anything of Sheila recently? ... He'd just been on a forty-eight and should never have gone. It was all ... a mess ... a bloody mess.

"What's wrong, lad? ... Tell me what's wrong?"

"Nothing's wrong. Nothing. Everything's fine. Except ... I keep thinking about mum.... You know, as if she's still there with you." He was crying, Edwin was sure. But what could he do at the other end of a telephone line? He felt helpless.

"I miss her too, lad. We all do."

CHAPTER TWO

July 1943

The early morning routine at the Ashtons always had an air of urgency. There was never time to breakfast without keeping an eye on the clock. Edwin wanted to get to the printing works before the staff clocked in. Freda was invariably late down. And Margaret had to see they were fed before they rushed off.

But this morning there was apprehension as well as urgency. It was John's first day back at work.

He came into the kitchen conscious that they would all look at him. He put a finger inside his stiff white collar; he smoothed the lapels of his grey suit. Not that they needed it; Margaret had pressed the creases out with loving care the previous evening. He hadn't felt so conscious of his clothes since the first time he put on battledress. This suit was the uniform of the white-collared brigade.

Margaret smiled approval, pulled out his chair and put bacon, egg and fried-bread before him. Edwin and Freda joked at his being favoured. But, on this day, no-one expected Margaret not to make a big effort.

Edwin could see John still lacked confidence. It had been a hard climb back for him. When he was invalided out it had

15

looked as though Margaret would have him on her hands for a very long time. Even now.... Well, perhaps it's better he makes a start, it might even help him, thought Edwin.

John couldn't eat; his knife and fork clattered to the kitchen table, and he got up to go.

"Don't want to be late, first day."

"Bags of time," reassured Freda.

Margaret concealed her disappointment at his not eating the King's breakfast, and saw him off. The others made parting shots intended to break John's tense face into a smile. They failed.

By the time Margaret had returned to the kitchen, Freda was scoffing the bacon and egg. No good to anyone cold, she excused her hoggishness. Margaret reminded her of the ration per person, and that Freda did all right eating at the Hospital.

Freda hit back; she knew what was making Margaret so snappy these days. Edwin could see the drift and counted himself well out of it as he left for the Printing Works.

What was Freda getting at? Margaret demanded to know. Why doesn't she come right out with it.

Freda did. Why on earth didn't Margaret come straight out with it. Tell John what happened whilst she thought he was dead, somewhere in Belgium. He was bound to find out eventually.

Margaret really wanted to tell him; how she wished she could get it over with. It was going to be a shock, to learn his wife had had a baby by someone else. But he still wasn't fit enough to take it. Not yet, anyway. Not quite. She'd be the one to know when. She didn't need any prompting from Freda, or anyone else, thank you. She would know the right moment, when it came.

"No doubt you will. But supposing John finds out from someone else first." Freda looked at the time and dashed out as she heard Ian's car arrive. And all the way to the hospital she regretted bringing the subject up. If only she wasn't so blessed impetuous, she kept reprimanding herself.

Ian smiled without taking his eyes off the crossroads ahead. "Penny for them?"

Freda came out of her thoughts. "Oh, just telling myself off for being a bit stupid." But she didn't explain.

Mr. Temple looked up sharply. The desks in the Borough Treasurer's Office were arranged so that he could see every clerk. He watched John arrive and walk towards him. He glanced at the clock as John stood before his desk.

"Good morning, sir. My name is –"

"I know who you are, Porter. Glad to have you back." There was no offer of a welcoming hand-shake.

Mr. Temple had been a clerk himself when John left for the Army in 1939. His promotion must have been accelerated by all those above him going to the War as well. He knew John was returning that day from a memorandum on his blotter. He seemed to be addressing the name on the paper more than the man in front of him.

John had noticed his glance at the clock. "I'm sorry I'm a little late. I didn't quite know where to come."

"The office hasn't moved, Porter, just because of the war. We've managed to keep going. Of course you won't know everybody."

John didn't know anybody. They seemed very young; or, like Temple, very old.

"I've even managed to arrange for you to have the desk you had before. Isn't this it?"

John didn't greet it as an old friend. He had no happy memories of their previous association. Hardly any memory at all, in fact.

"I hear you've had a bit of a rough time, Porter, so I'm putting you on your old work – Public Health accounts. It'll soon come back to you. There's a stack of the old forms, it's roughly the same lay-out as before; except the paper is poorer quality, of course. So better make a start; there's plenty to do. We're still short-staffed, you know." Temple turned towards his big desk. "And don't forget it's nine o'clock we start. Not three minutes past."

John spent the day working through the old forms, doing the same sums, making the same old ledger entries. It was as if the war had never started, let alone dragged on for five years. He found it hard going; but he'd expected that.

What he hadn't expected was how difficult it was to concentrate. His thoughts fled from the papers on his desk to Belgium. In a cellar, assembling a radio of sorts, a basic mishmash of wires and valves on a board. He could hear guns and bombs not far away. The other clerks, particularly young Haydon who sat opposite him, noticed his day-dreaming.

"You all right, Porter?" Haydon whispered with concern.

"Yes. Thanks. Just thinking. Not quite used to credits and debits again yet."

"Temple's just left. That means we can go, too."

"After five? Is that the time?" It wasn't that the day had flown for John. He just hadn't had any idea of time at all.

After their meal Margaret watched John mooch around, not knowing what to do with himself. She suggested he took the girls for a drink. She meant Freda and Doris, but not herself. Doris was the sort of friend who fell in with any suggestion. "Yes, that's a smashing idea. Come on, John, how about it? Freda? Margaret? I'm game."

Margaret had a load of John-George's washing to do. "You go. Maybe I'll come on, if I get through early enough." But she knew she wouldn't.

As John set down three drinks on the pre-war beer mats, a strong Welsh voice said, "Remember me, then?"

He'd been at John-and-Margaret's wedding; Philip's friend, didn't they remember Gwyn Roberts? Freda only remembered the scene he made; but didn't say so. She didn't encourage him to join them, and could have died when John said, "Oh yes. Philip's home on leave, didn't you know? He'd have been with us if he'd been in. You must pop round to see him."

"I'd like to. Get that one down. The next one's on me." Gwyn Roberts took the fourth chair at the round table and plonked his tankard on the glass top.

"This is going to be one of those evenings that goes off; very quickly," Freda's expression said.

Sefton never came to see Edwin without a specific purpose. It was about Jean's will; again! It still worried him that she'd left her shares in Briggs and Son split up in such small portions. Why she'd bequeathed each of her children a five per cent share and her husband only the same, he hadn't been able to fathom.

"I never took it for granted, Sefton, that she'd leave her twenty-five per cent entirely to me."

"Well I did. And it would've been a damn sight better to keep control of the Works in a few hands. Yours, mine, my sister Helen's – even though she is the other side of the world. Instead of this mess up. Too many people to ask, when you want to take big decisions."

"What you mean is you could've got your own way with

18

me. And Helen would give you carte blanche, wouldn't she? What big decisions are in the offing then?"

Sefton realised he'd said enough. "Oh, nothing particular. But something might crop up, couldn't it? You never know."

Edwin looked hard at Sefton. He never gave anything away until he wanted to, didn't Sefton. He was quite right, you never do know.

John stared blankly at the bedroom ceiling. He lay very still, so as not to wake Margaret, who was breathing heavily, exhausted from the day's chores.

What was Gwyn Roberts going on about? And he did go on, didn't he. Nobody else hardly spoke.

"Talks a lot, doesn't he?" Freda had said on the way home.

"I thought he'd never stop," Doris added. "A load of drivel, if you ask me. Gift of the gab worse than me. I'm not in the same street. At least you can understand what I say, can't you?"

John hadn't understood all he'd said, either. Not at the time. But it was beginning to make a sort of sense. He'd hated Gwyn at first. Now. . . . Somehow, he'd begun to feel sorry for him. All right so he's a conscientious objector. So what. That's what he believes in, honestly and sincerely. Why despise him for that; why look at him as if he wasn't quite human? Wasn't there something to be admired about a man who stands out against everyone else? Takes some doing. Courage, that's what it takes. The girls found him aggressive, trying to make trouble, pick a quarrel. But, somehow, John thought of him as lonely; the lonely one out of step. Or could he be the only one in step? The rest of us could be on the wrong foot; who knows?

Then he drifted into the Belgian cellar again. "Oh God, no. No." He didn't know he'd said it aloud until he realised he'd woken up Margaret.

"What's the matter, love? Nightmares again?"

"No. Just thinking. Trying not to; more like."

"Would it help if you told me, John? Maybe then you wouldn't think about it so much."

Gradually he began to talk, almost as if to himself, his eyes fixed on the ceiling.

He'd lost contact with his Unit in the chaos of the retreat to Dunkirk. What a mess they were in. Their transport had been bombed to hell. Communications were gone. In the mist rising from the plain he'd wandered across a road and been hit by a truck. Could have been one of his mates for all he ever knew. He lay in a ditch until Marcel found him, and took him to this place where the cellar was. They bandaged his arm and leg, and fed him. They were armed and Belgians; but were they German agents or collaborators or what? He'd never heard of the Resistance at the time. He refused to tell them anything. Or to work with them.

So they'd imprisoned him in this tiny cellar, windowless walls running with damp. They found out – he must have let it slip – that he knew something about radios. And they desperately needed a new transmitter. So they'd forced him to work on their broken one, and kept bringing him bits of other equipment. From where he didn't know, or care.

He decided to pretend to work at it, but never finished it. So they could never use it. After a month or two – he lost track of time – they rumbled him. And they started . . . trying to force him.

Margaret wondered why he hadn't told her of this before. There seemed no reason why not. But she said nothing.

One day Marcel only just stopped him from smashing up the work he'd done on the radio. He hit John harder than he'd bashed at the radio. Marcel came back with one of the group; a girl, young, pretty. He'd said something to her which John couldn't understand. Like an order. She nodded in reply.

John said no more until Margaret asked. "What was she told to do?"

"She kissed me; put her arms round me; undressed me; fondled me. I could only think it was so I'd want her again. They . . . You see they'd tried denying me food and water. This was the next trick."

"This is why you've not told me before?"

"She couldn't make me make love to her, Margaret. Not when I didn't want to."

John's voice was adamant. Margaret tried to say it didn't matter. Whether it happened, or didn't, or whatever happened no longer mattered. But she couldn't say it. John hoped he'd convinced her, wanted to desperately. Because in spite of his protestations, he knew, remembered more clearly than anything else in that cellar, that it did happen. He did make love to the girl. But he couldn't say that; he couldn't bring himself to.

Maybe if Margaret had been able to say it didn't matter, he would have been able to tell her.

Margaret kissed his cheek lightly, lovingly. "Try to sleep. Now you've told me. Let's forget it."

"Met a chap in the pub tonight who reminded me of that cellar. He was locked up, too. In his own mind. Doesn't seem to make contact with anyone he talks to. Conscientious objector; that takes some doing. You're some sort of outcast, traitor. Whilst everyone else is doing their bit in the war."

Margaret felt her heart beat stronger. Michael was a conscientious objector. Could John have accidentally met the father of her stillborn child?

Now they were both staring at the ceiling. Thinking.

John Porter lay awake most of the night. No wonder he scraped into the office only a few seconds before nine o'clock, out of breath after running from the tram-stop.

Haydon grinned, "Don't worry. Temple isn't in yet. Sometimes he calls at the hospital on his way. Never tells us when, of course. Treatment for his back, getting past it in my opinion. Be damn glad when he goes for good." Haydon grabbed somebody's Homburg hat and did a take-off of Temple's routine on arrival, fussing, hanging up his hat very precisely, frowning at the staff as he strutted to his big desk. He affected a passable mimicry of Temple's voice, his "good morning" as devoid of greeting, as he eyed various clerks. The laughter was overdone in escapism from the stacks of paperwork they knew would clutter the next eight hours of their lives.

Haydon spoke with Temple's pomposity. "Now I want a great improvement in the work, gentlemen. From every single one of you. I will not tolerate —"

But as he sat in Temple's desk what it was that wouldn't be tolerated flew from his mind and his face blanched. The laughter died the same instant. Mr. Temple stood at the door glowering at the performance.

In silence Temple walked the length of the office. Haydon had got up from his desk intending to go back to his own as if nothing had happened.

"Stay where you are," Temple rapped out. "Haydon. You will not spend another minute wasting my staff's time whilst you await your military service. Collect your cards at once. You are fired."

21

John watched with growing anger as Haydon walked towards the door, knowing there was no point in arguing.

"Mister Temple, I'd like to put in a word for Mister Haydon, please." John found himself a focus for all eyes.

"Would you, Porter. Well, you'll have to wait until you've passed your exams, and are fully-qualified; and have attained a sufficiently superior post of responsibility. Then you may offer suggestions with regard to the employment of staff. Fortunately for me, by that time, I shall no longer be here to have to listen."

"But the whole thing's ridiculous." John stood his ground. "It was just a ... a joke. We were all laughing. We're all to blame. We should all be fired with Haydon."

Haydon was wincing; he could see Porter joining him even if nobody else did. Having done him no good at all.

"That could be arranged too, Porter. Or those who try to justify Haydon's nonsense might have to join him."

"I'm not justifying it. In fact ... well, I think Haydon should apologise. But that should be the end of it."

"I don't suppose he has the decency. Or the strength of character." Temple believed he had destroyed Porter's argument.

Haydon was very quick. "I am sorry, Mister Temple. No offence, honest. None intended."

Temple saw the opportunity to look magnanimous. And remembered his staff-shortage problems.

"Oh. Well, in that case ... Get back to your desk and get on with your work. The matter is closed."

Haydon reached his desk quicker than he'd ever done before, and looked at John as if he was some sort of saviour. As soon as he knew Temple wasn't looking, John winked at him. Haydon was not to know how much better John felt, too.

Margaret looked worried when she brought Edwin's tea after his evening meal.

"Oh, by the way, dad, I bumped into Uncle Sefton today. What d'you think? He asked me if John was interested in a job."

"We couldn't use him in the printing works. He hasn't got a trade."

"No. In the shop. Serving I suppose."

"Mm. That's not to do John any favours, Margaret. Sefton needs shop-staff badly. But when the war's over, what happens when the chap whose job he's got comes back? What's John say about it?"

"I haven't told him yet."

Edwin stopped drinking, noticing her worried look. "Why not, love? He might as well look into it with your Uncle; something for him to think about. What's the matter?"

Margaret sighed deeply. "It isn't that. John's taken Philip down to the pub. They're meeting some chap John was talking about last night. He's a conscientious objector."

Edwin knew what was going through her mind. "Oh. I see. And there aren't many of those around, these days. That it?"

"Yes ... It could be Michael they're meeting. Michael Armstrong. Couldn't it."

John listened whilst Gwyn Roberts and Philip locked each other in perpetual argument. As they often had done before the war. "Can never be the same again, between you and me Phil, boy. You've sold your soul, you know that? You of all people. Letting 'em teach you to kill. You should be drenched in shame, boy. You should've revolted against it. Like I did."

Philip told him that there would be no freedom to revolt if they sat back and let Hitler walk in. Gwyn wanted us to win the war, course he did. So Philip accused him of not doing a stroke towards seeing that we did. John interrupted, not to contribute to the argument, to excuse himself to the "Gents".

Philip used John and Margaret to make his point, without mentioning names. "It affects everybody, Gwyn. I know someone who thought her husband had been killed, right? She had an affair with a man she thought she was going to marry and –"

Gwyn held up his hand. "Oh, don't give me that one, I've heard it hundreds of times. She has his baby, and the husband turns up and it's all hearts-and-flowers. Irrelevant to the argument, all those hard-luck stories, boy. Nothing to do with Thou shalt not kill? There's no proviso, you know; except in certain circumstances, such as going to war, then you can kill as much as you like. Doesn't add that, does it?"

Philip saw John was returning and quickly switched the argument back to generalities. Unfortunately John invited Gwyn back. "Come and meet my Margaret. She hasn't seen you since the wedding. Have you got time?" Gwyn had time.

Margaret was relieved to discover he wasn't Michael and smiled a welcome.

23

"This is Gwyn Roberts, Margaret. Remember? At our wedding? What a day that was."

Philip had had enough of Gwyn, and joined Edwin and Freda in the Front Room. Edwin also remembered Gwyn's performance at the wedding, so they stayed put.

Both Gwyn and John showed signs of the beer. John's speech was slurred; Gwyn was getting even more talkative.

John became drowsy, only half-hearing Gwyn's rhetoric. Margaret was a captive audience, listening politely until Gwyn got onto the change that had come over Philip, as he saw it. "He used to argue so brilliantly. He's nothing like the free-thinker he used to be. Nothing like. You know, tonight he got right off the point in the argument. Right off, he did. Going on about this girl he knew whose chap had gone off to die for his country. At least she thought he was dead, that was her big mistake."

Margaret interrupted quickly. "What time's your train?"

John inadvertently helped. "Heck is that the time? You'll miss the last one, Gwyn, if you don't go now. I'll get your coat." John went out into the Hall.

Gwyn carried on as he got to his feet. "Where was I? Oh yes, Philip's lady-friend had someone else's baby. As if that mattered. I mean, she probably sleeps around; you know, anybody's."

Margaret was on her feet too. "Get out of this house."

Gwyn looked at her. His jaw dropped as the truth dawned. "Philip's . . . sister. Not his friend. You. I didn't know. Believe me, I didn't. I'm sorry."

As they undressed for bed, John wanted to talk about Gwyn Roberts again. "Funny chap, Margaret. He talks a lot, I know, but a lot of sense."

"Not to me, he doesn't. I was glad to see the back of him. And I'm too tired, if you don't mind."

It was a miracle that John wasn't any wiser. But it made Freda's point. She must tell him before someone else did. She was too weary tonight; after all that.

Almost exactly twenty-four hours later, Philip trudged up the Ashtons' path and let himself in. The girl he'd met lived over the other side of Liverpool and it was one of the hazards of war that it meant a long walk home because public transport went to bed early.

Edwin was still up, looking at Jean's photograph. His mind was in the past. "We weren't very close at the end, Philip; your mother and I. Whilst you were in the Desert, our differences grew ... more and more. Robert's death put the final kibosh on it. She never forgave me. But now? I'm beginning to miss her, you know. Things that were part of our lives; some of them just routine. Where she'd put things of mine; what she always said at certain moments. We shouldn't have let anything come between us. We should have risen above it, as they say; yes, even Robert. I should have talked to her about it; worked at it. Until she realised why I'd let him go to sea; because he wanted to. I'd no right to stop him. I didn't do it so he'd be a dead hero. When you marry, Philip, think on. Learn by our mistakes. Because it's too late to learn after. I know that now."

John was already in bed. Margaret slipped down beside him trying not to disturb him. But he was awake.

He began talking about Gwyn again. How he made enemies of everybody. He talked at people, that was his trouble. He'd even upset Margaret, he could tell that. "I'm sorry I brought him home, love. But I feel sorry for him, too, somehow."

The more he talked the more Margaret silently thanked God that he hadn't found out. But it could happen, just like tonight. She must tell him about Michael. Now. She'd put it off another day.

She was about to begin. Where, she didn't know, that was what held her up; just those few seconds considering, during which John looked at her and then kissed her.

"I don't know what I'd do without you, Margaret. I really don't. Oh Margaret."

"John ..."

But she couldn't tell him. Not at this moment. The worst possible time to tell him; the best time between them. In spite of everything.

CHAPTER THREE

October 1943

The disintegration of Sheila's relationship with David was not her only worry. Young Peter and Janet were happy enough, evacuated at Mrs. Thomas's in Roslyn, North Wales. She did visit them as often as she could afford the rail-fare. She knew that David sometimes went to see them, too. At different times from her visits, of course.

But she was their mother; Liverpool was their home. Mrs. Thomas was marvellous with them, but the more she mothered them, the more Sheila worried. Throughout the whole train journey she never took in the significant headline on the newspaper of the man seated opposite her: "MONTY LANDS IN SICILY". Her thoughts were miles away; but in a cottage in the Welsh village she was headed for.

David Ashton was preparing for a raid that night; putting on his flying-suit and smoking more heavily. The more ops you did the more the mental thing built up as take-off approached. You always thought you'd get more used to it. But David didn't.

He never knew that nearly all air-crew felt the same because no-one talked about it. And when Peter Bryant flung open his door and said "Tonight's off. Don't ask me why, I'm only one of the pilots, old boy," the immediate relief was stifled, too. Under a feigned grumble of disappointment, David uncoiled his wound-up tensions.

"Oh, that's great, isn't it? Wait until we're all set and then they tell us."

"There's a spot of leave, David. I'm going up to the big City; just 'phoned Grace. She's expecting you too, if you want to go." In fact, his sister had told him to invite David for her.

"Oh. Great. Well ... tell her thanks but I think ... I'll go home. For a change. You know, I haven't been for ... quite a bit."

"Made it up with Sheila, old boy? You didn't tell me."

"No. No, it's not that." David was only deciding as he

26

talked. "Er ... Think I'll go and see the kids. Or they'll be forgetting what their dad looks like. Yes, that's what I'll do."

Sheila always found it a tentative meeting. The awkward first greetings had started her worrying. The kisses, hugs, near-tears were lovely; but then came the awful moments of "How are you, then?" and "School all right?" and "My, you've grown." Then listening like a stranger to excited young voices recounting what they'd been doing. All that was happening in their growing-up, which Sheila had to be told, because she wasn't sharing it. And Mrs. Thomas interjecting, because she knew her children better than their mother.

Until inevitably: "Where's dad, mum?"

"Well, you see ... He couldn't come this time, Peter."

"Mum. You never come together." Janet complained from her heart.

Mrs. Thomas, too. "It's a long time since he's been at all, Mrs. Ashton. Terrible it is, the way the war divides loved-ones, you know."

Did she suspect? That was another worry Sheila had to cope with. The pretence that all was well. To Mrs. Thomas as well as to Peter and Janet.

Peter said Dad had sent him a postcard. Then added, not realising how it would hurt his Mum. "From London it was. Dad was in London."

Janet showed her letter from Daddy. A love-letter to "My Darling Janet". Written in the hand that once wrote "My Own Darling Sheila." A long time ago, it seemed now.

When the children were in bed, Mrs. Thomas damped down the fire. "Why don't you and Mister Ashton make a big effort; you know, to arrange the same weekend off. And meet here, see? You know, you could have the big bed, no trouble, none at all. You've only got to say the word ..." Her Welsh accent made the invitation so warm that Sheila was no longer able to keep up the deceit. The confession on her face made words almost unnecessary.

"I haven't seen him for over a year now, Mrs. Thomas. We only keep it up for their sakes: Peter's and Janet's."

Mrs. Thomas was dismayed. "Well, I have been wondering. I couldn't help, could I? Oh, it's a shame what this war's done. It's a cruel shame, a cruel shame."

Janet was making sure the day would be her day. She was

first out of bed, wakened everybody, reminded them she was now ten, not nine any more, accepted the "Happy Birthdays" and the presents with wide-eyed excitement. And there was a card from Daddy. "Sorry I can't be with you, darling. All my love to you and Peter."

Mrs. Thomas had shopping to do. Sheila tidied the cottage for her. Janet tried to help chattering away all the time. "Mummy, why can't Daddy ask for a holiday? If he told them it's my birthday, wouldn't they let him come?" Sheila was trying to think of an answer which would satisfy her when there was a knock.

She opened the cottage door to David.

They looked at each other speechless as Peter and Janet went into raptures. "Daddy." "Daddy's here." They grabbed him and pulled him in. "Dad. What you brought me? For my birthday. Where is it? Where is it?" Janet was feeling deep into the pockets of his greatcoat.

"Er ... well, you see, I've been pretty busy. And living on an aerodrome I don't see the sort of shops where you can buy something for a grown-up young lady of ten. Now do I?"

All the old charm-talk, just like he used to give me, thought Sheila as David took out a pound note and gave it to Janet.

Sheila had to play along. "Daddy wants you to choose for yourself. Maybe something to wear; you'd like that, wouldn't you?"

Janet had never had a pound note in her hand before. "Ooh yes, Mummy. Thank you Daddy. Thanks a million."

Mrs. Thomas came in and nearly dropped her egg-basket in surprise. "Oh, Mister Ashton, if only I'd known I would've arranged the beds ..."

"Sorry I couldn't let you know. They sprung it on us, and I took a chance. As it's this young lady's birthday."

Janet had worked it out very quickly. "S'all right, Auntie. I can sleep with you and they can sleep in my bed."

The adults exchanged glances and then David said, "No, we don't need all that switching round. I can get them to put me up at the pub ... I'm not sure I can stay overnight anyway."

Peer and Janet protested in chorus. "Aw, dad. No. Stay. Please. Yes."

David looked at Sheila. There was no plea in her eyes, even to stay at the pub.

Peter and Janet were in their element. They had no little

28

old bridge over a fast-running brook in Liverpool. They could stride and hop between the stepping-stones whilst the stream cascaded from the waterfall under the wooden arch and bubbled around their feet.

David and Sheila sat on a dry-stone wall, watching them; both noting how happy they were, oblivious of the world's troubles; and their parents'. Whilst they watched they talked. Just about. Without making contact.

"You shouldn't get any more air-raids up here now. Hitler's really got his hands full. What with the lads moving up Italy a treat. And the Russkies advancing west. Not to mention the pasting we're giving Hitler on his home ground. Bit of their own medicine. Lots of rumours about a Second Front. Won't be long, I'll tell you."

It was calculated to keep away from anything personal, but Sheila didn't let him get away with it.

"It's not because of the bombing I leave them here, now. I can't do my work at the N.A.A.F.I. and bring them up as I should. I have to work, you know. Or didn't you know?"

"Good for 'em here, anyway. Healthy air, great open spaces, places to play." David could always get off the point when it suited him.

"I'd still like them with me, though. At home. If it were just up to me."

"Look Sheila, I don't want 'em back there with another chap about the place." David got up and threw a stone into the water petulantly.

"That's a rotten thing to say. You've no right to say it anyway."

"It's true though, isn't it? I bumped into him, didn't I? Your bad luck. Just leaving you when I arrived on that forty-eight, remember? And I don't suppose you've packed him in just because I found out. For a minute."

"Colin and I are not living together, if that's what you're suggesting."

"Expect me to believe that?" David called the children. "Peter. Janet. Come on. Time to move off. Birthday tea coming up."

"David." Sheila had little time to reply as the children started running to join them. "I want a divorce."

"On the grounds of my adultery, of course, not yours."

"You admit there are other women, don't you? You can't do anything but."

29

"I'll admit it, if that's what you want, okay."

Peter reached them first and flung his arms around his dad. Janet, not all that far behind, grabbed Mummy lovingly.

The argument had to cease.

The birthday party went beautifully. Everyone tried so hard. But when the children were tired out and ready for bed David dropped his bombshell, as lightly as he could. "If you get into bed quick enough, I'll have time to tuck you in before I go."

There were howls of protest and Mrs. Thomas said, "You'll only just catch that last train if you go right away. Why not stay over?"

She didn't fancy her chances as peacemaker but oh, how she wanted to succeed.

"No. I've got to get back. Thanks just the same."

Sheila knew he was lying, but said nothing.

He tucked in Peter and Janet. He kissed them. He turned to Sheila when they were alone at the cottage door. "It was when I came home and saw that bloke, that I went back to this girl I'd met. I thought we were finished, you and me. For keeps. So I took off with her. I thought I loved her. Yes, I loved her. And she had my baby, if you want to know."

"I don't, thanks." Sheila felt her hands icy-cold on her cheeks. "One thing kept me faithful, David. All the time I've hung on thinking that in spite of everything you did love me. You couldn't have destroyed that. I thought. It's not possible. He still loves me."

"I loved you. I loved her. Love isn't a monopoly, Sheila. You're not entitled to have it all, you know."

"You saying you don't love me any more, then? I mean I might as well hear it from the horse's mouth."

"Gotta go. I'll miss the train."

When Sheila closed the door, the tears refused to be held back any longer.

30

CHAPTER FOUR

January 1944

Harry Porter had made such an elaborate explanation as to why he had arrived without his wife, that Margaret sensed something was wrong. "You see, Celia announced this morning that she was coming to Liverpool this afternoon to do some shopping. Things she couldn't get in Chorley. So I came along myself and gave John a ring at the Town Hall. From the Station."

"He's not allowed private calls," Margaret told her father-in-law.

"Yes, so they told me. Unless it's a matter of life and death or something. I've got an hour or two to kill. I see the Americans have made a beachhead at Anzio. That's good, isn't it."

Margaret explained that Edwin wouldn't be coming home from work. He'd gone off that morning to see his cousin in Castleford. Harry Porter didn't seem to mind; gave no indication that it was Edwin that he'd hoped to see, particularly.

It must be something to do with Celia, Margaret thought; how could Harry continue to live with her? To get away from her whining voice on the slightest pretext must be worth any effort. And yet ... there was something more. She could sense it. And she was right.

Celia Porter wasn't shopping. She was drinking tea at a marble-topped table in the station buffet when her son came in and joined her. John anxiously asked what was the matter. "Is it Dad?"

"No, he's all right, of course. They wouldn't put me through to you so I had to say a close relative was sick. They just don't care, officials, these days. Think you belong to them body and soul, don't they? Well you don't. Tell them from me."

"Mum; why didn't you let us know you were coming? We could have met at home, couldn't we? Instead of here. Dad is all right, isn't he? You're not just saying that for my sake?"

"Right as he ever will be. Inhaling that muck all those years. I kept telling him that powder-filling job was all wrong. On and on at him I was. But you can't talk to him. Never listens to a word I say. Never has."

"I'll get a sandwich. Want one mum? Or another cup of tea?"

Margaret tucked in John-George. "What d'you think of your grandson?" she whispered so as not to wake him.

"Does he always go off as quick as that?" Harry was impressed.

"He certainly does not. Showing off for his grandad, that's what that is."

As Margaret flopped into a chair in the living-room a long sigh escaped her.

Harry looked at her searchingly. "I take it you haven't told John yet? If you had, you'd 've told me how he'd taken it, by now."

"About Michael you mean? No. Not yet. Not yet I haven't."

"You can't make the excuse he's not well enough any more. He's come on a treat, recently, you know."

"I know I must tell him. I really must. Freda was onto me about it. Trouble is, it gets harder, doesn't it, the longer you leave it. And things are going so well for us ... I just don't want to mess it all up. It could ... so easily. Don't you think?"

"You think he might not forgive you, Margaret, that it?"

"And he might not forgive me for keeping it from him all this time."

"With the best of motives, Margaret."

"But will he look at it like that?"

Harry spoke huskily, but firmly. "You've got to tell him. And soon. You see, for all I know, that could be why Celia's come to Liverpool. And you can't risk her telling him. Can you?"

Margaret now knew the real reason her father-in-law was here. "I know. You're right."

"You see ... if you don't ... Celia's going to beat you to it. Then what?"

Celia had promised Harry she wouldn't tell John, but only because he had threatened to leave her if she did. There had been a big row about it, here at the Ashtons. Margaret remembered it all too well.

"You know what his mother is. She still talks about the way

32

she found out about it. That Christmas Eve. The letter from ..." Harry nearly said "her lover" but changed it to "... Michael, wasn't his name? And I'm afraid she no longer believes I will leave her if she does tell John. Unfortunately she's right. She's determined John should know, and she's working up to telling him. I know her."

"Yes. I must tell him. I must. Oh, I've something on the stove." Margaret escaped to the kitchen.

At last John had reached the front of the queue and returned to his Mother with a curled sandwich on a thick plate monogrammed "L.M.S."

"Is that instead of your meal? Surely it isn't?"

Celia had never accepted that John's well-being was no longer her responsibility. She rambled on, John listening politely as he didn't want the few occasions that he saw her to develop into fractious arguments. They would have but for his efforts. The natural link was almost all they had in common.

When she'd married Harry Porter she'd been quite a catch. Everyone had said he was, too, coming out of the First War a full Major. Of course, men stay younger don't they, and he had an eye for a pretty girl, John didn't know that, did he? Yes, there was another thing she'd had to put up with. Other women.

When John asked what proof she had, he was relieved to find she had none. She was trying to blow up something out of nothing. She really wanted something to beat his father with, mentally. Yes, that was it, he told her censoriously.

Celia quickly changed the subject. "One sandwich is nothing for a growing lad. I'll buy you another one."

What was all this leading up to, John asked himself. Something, that was certain.

John-George had been crying and Margaret came downstairs again to find Harry had resolved to say something he hadn't intended to.

"I didn't come with Celia, Margaret love. She said she was coming over. So I caught an earlier train, to warn you."

"Then thank God she can't get past the Town Hall switchboard either. He should be home any time now." Margaret left the room to make sure John's meal would be ready the moment he got in.

Celia made no comment when John didn't eat the second sandwich. She'd made her point in buying it. John looked at the clock.

"I'll have to go soon, mum. It's my night-school class. I must ring Margaret or she'll wonder why I haven't been home."

"Yes, you must let her know, mustn't you? Don't keep anything from her. You met your mother in the station buffet, she's got to be told that, hasn't she? No secrets. Not from her, anyway."

"I don't know what you're talking about. She's expecting me. What are you going on at Margaret for? What's she ever done to you?"

"Not what she's done to me. What she's done. That's more like it. What has she done, indeed."

"What's that mean?" John was confused.

"She's never told you, has she. No, I can tell from your face she hasn't. She's never told you about that man, has she? She wouldn't, of course, would she?"

"Man? What man?" The colour was ebbing from John's face.

"The man she slept with. That man; while you were missing. I always knew you'd come back, never lost faith in you once I didn't. But she took it for granted you were dead and gone. Didn't she?"

"You're making it all up again, aren't you? Like you were doing about dad?"

"Making it up? Can I make a baby up? Yes, she had a baby. By him. This other man. Dead, fortunately, when it arrived. All the family know. You're the only one who doesn't. There. Now, I've done my duty."

"Margaret? Had a baby? Whilst I was ...?" John couldn't believe it possible.

"At least someone's had the courage to tell you. What you had every right to know."

John got up as if in one of his bad nights. He walked subconsciously towards the buffet exit. Celia rose to call him back; but she was in a public place and everyone was watching her, she thought.

In fact, nobody was.

Harry took down his coat from the hall-stand. "Well, I'm sorry I missed John. But I'm glad I got to you first, anyway.

Maybe Celia thought better of it and didn't come, after all. Hope so."

"I think John must be working overtime. Then going straight to his class."

"Well, give him my love; keep half for yourself." Harry kissed her cheek and she kissed his.

Alone, Margaret tried to decide how she would tell John. To cause him the least hurt. He was bound to be hurt however she did it. She was still thinking about it when the door opened, and he was there.

"What about your night-class?"

"Giving it a miss for once." John looked at her. She looked no different. Still his Margaret. Was she his alone?

"I'll get your meal then. It'll be a bit –"

"No thanks, I'm not hungry. I fancy a drink." As he spoke he got Edwin's whisky bottle from the sideboard.

"Whisky? You?"

"Not under age or anything, am I?" Margaret detected the edge in his voice.

"I know you're not, love. Only you don't usually ... That's all. I've no objections." Margaret changed the subject. "Your father's been here."

"Oh. What did he want? Couldn't he wait to see me?"

He was in a bad mood. Margaret wondered why.

"Well, we thought you weren't coming home ..."

"Been talking about me, have you?"

"No, not at all. Well, yes; of course you came into the conversation. You're my husband; his son."

"I suppose so. I'm not sure of anything any more." John, near to tears, dashed out and up the stairs.

Margaret was puzzled for only as long as it took her to realise that John must know. Celia must have met him from work. As she reached the foot of the staircase the doorbell rang. She let Harry in.

"He's upstairs. I think he knows."

"He does. I happened to see Celia sitting in the buffet, waiting for the same train I was catching. She's outside in a taxi. Is there anything I can do, love? Anything?"

Margaret was very down. "No. Thanks just the same. It's too late now. It's all my fault, I know."

Margaret grabbed hold of Harry and pulled herself to him.

"Yes. There is something. Let her wait. I need ... somebody around. Please stay a bit."

The front door was pushed open from ajar; Celia came in. "How long d'you expect me to sit out there?"

"We're not going yet. There's another train." Harry went to pay off the taxi.

Celia walked past Margaret into the living room and Margaret followed her. "You might have waited until I told him myself."

"You? When would that have been? Tell me that."

"You're trying to split us, aren't you? It didn't really matter that he didn't know."

"It's for John to decide, not you. Now he knows the truth." Celia spoke as if right were entirely on her side.

Margaret heard John-George cry and flew upstairs as Harry came in again.

John was cuddling their child when Margaret walked in.

"John. You shouldn't have wakened him."

"I didn't. He stopped soon as I picked him up. Sh. He's nearly off again."

"I was going to tell you. Believe me, I really was. Soon as you were ... really well again. Then when you were, the more we picked up the pieces and ... things were going so well, it became so ... so much to risk ... to lose. I was scared what might happen if you didn't ... understand what happened."

John laid John-George, out to the wide world, in his cot again.

"Both of them. Your Mum and Dad."

"I'll get rid of them. I don't want anyone in the house with us."

Margaret made to go down with him.

"No, you stay here. I don't want any arguments between you and her. Stay with the baby."

Celia had been preparing Harry for John's reaction. John would be coming back with them. He wouldn't stay one more night under the same roof as that wife of his. But John's first remark surprised her.

"I don't want you here. Take her home dad. Please."

Celia stood her ground. "Well, what did she say? She can't deny it."

Harry was exasperated. "Celia. Leave things alone. Please."

"You can come back home, John. I always said the door

was open. Didn't I always say that? I must have been psychic. Well, it's still open."

"Celia, for God's sake."

"Mother, Margaret doesn't deny it. Does that mean I should walk out? Without giving her the chance to tell me why it happened?"

"Oh, she'll have made up a good story, after all this time. Don't worry about that. You can bring John-George. She shouldn't be allowed to touch your child after the way she's behaved."

John was trying to control his anger, but without success. "D'you think it's all one-sided? D'you think I'm perfect myself; your blue-eyed boy? Because I'm not. You wouldn't believe what happened to me in Belgium. I made a radio, out of bits and pieces. It meant so much to them, you know what they gave me in return? As a present? A girl. A girl who gave herself, too. Who undressed me and undressed herself for me to –"

"Stop it. Stop talking like that. It's dirty." Celia was disgusted.

"Oh, it was dirty all right. Because you know what else she gave me, besides herself? She gave me V.D. You know what V.D. is mum? It's a nasty disease which I'd 've passed on to my wife, if I'd made love to her when I first came home. I had to pretend there were other reasons. And to make excuses every time I went to get treatment. You've no idea how much I wanted to make love to her, after all that time away. And I couldn't. Not until I was cured."

"Stop it! Stop it! I don't want to hear."

"Course you don't. But it's true. I missed Margaret like she missed me. And when I was tempted I was unfaithful; when I knew she was here and alive! At least, she could be forgiven because I was dead."

Celia had closed her eyes as if to prevent John's words conjuring up pictures she didn't want to see. "I'm going home. I don't want to hear this filthy talk."

Harry's eyes met John's. He tried to say something. But there was no need. They had never been so close in their lives.

Margaret was still sitting on the bed, watching the sleeping baby when John tiptoed in.

"They've gone?"

"Yes." John said it as if nothing had happened, and sat beside her on the bed.

37

"John. I've so wanted to tell you. I want to tell you now. Everything."

"I want to know. I'd like to know." John took her hands. "But on our own bed. We don't want to wake him, do we?"

John-George didn't wake up all night. What with talking and then loving, John and Margaret hardly slept at all.

CHAPTER FIVE

May 1944

When his sister Helen came back from Melbourne, Sefton Briggs invited her to stay as long as she wished. It seemed a kind gesture. But Sefton had been concerned about the ownership of Briggs Printing Works ever since his mother had died. And even more so since his other sister, Jean Ashton, had died bequeathing her share-holding in what he called fragments. "As a result, everybody in the family has got to have a say, before you can take decisions that affect the business. Bloody ridiculous situation, that is."

He scribbled out the "present position" on the arm of his favourite chair, on an old envelope that he could burn afterwards. He didn't want anyone to know he was even considering the problem: let alone what he had in mind to do about it. George Askew listened with a solicitor's ingrained diplomacy.

"Just look what a messpot it is, George; a right old pickle. I own thirty per cent, Helen's got twenty-five. My lad Tony holds ten per cent. Helen's young Jo has got ten."

"She hasn't come back with her mother, has she Sefton?"

"No; Jo wants to stay out there; a young country for young people, she says. Where was I? Yes, well, since Jean died we've got all the Ashtons to contend with, all of 'em. Just because there was a bit of needle between Jean and her husband – something to do with Robert's death, you know, she took it very badly – she left her twenty-five per cent not to her husband, but split-up equally between Edwin and their children. That's –" Sefton seems to press the pencil-point harder at the thought – "Philip: five per cent, David: five. Margaret: five. And Freda . . . all five per cents. Well, it's ridiculous. You can't run a family company like that, without a lot of unnecessary bother."

Askew was professionally tactful. "I take it you've ... something you want to push through? For which you need majority shareholding support?"

"That's my point, George. I have, between you and me. The printing side of the business is nowhere near as profitable as it should be. Oh it's not Edwin's fault, he manages the works well enough. It's war-time restrictions in paper, the need for licences to print stuff, difficulties in getting replacement-parts for machinery ... it all cuts against profit, you know. I've thought about it a lot recently. And I've come to the conclusion we should keep the shop. But sell off the works, lock, stock and barrel."

"And with it, Edwin's livelihood? You have thought of that, I presume."

"That can be taken care of. We'll stipulate whoever buys the works takes Edwin with the deal."

"Supposing it's someone Edwin can't stand. Like old Pringle, for instance?"

"Aye. Well, I must admit it's Pringle I've got interested in buying. But you can't be too choosy in this world, George. We all have to put up with things we don't fancy, from time to time. Have another? Not a bad whisky that, considering."

Wild horses wouldn't have got the senior partner of Askew's to enquire where Sefton bought his whisky, when it was so scarce. "I don't mind, thanks."

Sefton poured another for himself, too. "I'm throwing a bit of a welcome-home party for Helen. You'll come, won't you? Bit sweet on her once, weren't you? She's fancy-free again now. Her husband died out there, did you know?"

"Er ... yes. Very sad." Askew changed tack. "Of course, if Helen were to back you, in favour of selling, that alone would give you a straight fifty-five per cent majority. Just you two."

"Ah well, yes. We have. But ... it might not be quite as simple as that. I've passed a few broad hints, but she's quite a mind of her own, has our Helen."

Askew smiled. "She's a Briggs, Sefton."

"Aye. She is that. Very much a Briggs." Sefton didn't add that because she was staying with him he had time to work on her. And he was a Briggs, too.

John and Margaret were dressing for the welcome-home-Helen party; Margaret realised that something would snap if he didn't get out of that job. He had not the slightest interest in it, none at all; that was the top and bottom of it. She was glad to be able to give him some hope.

"Oh, by the way, John, when Sefton rang to ask how many of us could come to his party, he asked me if you might be interested in working in his shop. Would you?"

"Don't think so. Why, has he a vacancy?"

"Well he has, but the trouble is, it's temporary; until the regular staff come out of the Forces. He didn't say that, of course; then he wouldn't, would he? But I got that impression."

"You know, Margaret, I sometimes imagine what it would be like having a business of my own. You know, doing something I liked doing. And the way I think it should be done. But you need capital for that. Which means it's out so far as I'm concerned."

Margaret tried to give him more hope. "I could sell the shares Mum left me in the Printing Works. I don't know how much they'd fetch, but I could find out from Uncle Sefton tonight. He may even offer to buy them himself."

"No, Margaret, don't. I was only talking; just something to say, I suppose. I haven't a clue what I'd like to go into, to be honest. That's the trouble."

Ian Mackenzie's 8-hp saloon ambled through suburban Liverpool towards the Briggs' party. Freda was looking forward to the event. More to being there with Ian, than in anticipation of Uncle Sefton's hospitality. Going together to a family function seemed to bring Ian closer.

Ian's mind was on something else. He was convincing himself that this was as good a time as any to tell her. Their relationship was now such that.... Well, he must tell her, however much doing so didn't appeal to him.

"Uncle Sefton's parties aren't usually up to much, Ian, so don't expect anything special, will you?"

"Should we go somewhere else then? I don't mind."

"No, we've got to go. Least I have. For Aunt Helen's sake."

Ian plunged straight in. "There's something you don't know about me, Freda. I would have told you before but ... it hasn't been ... well, necessary."

"But it is now? Oh. Something nice?"

"Well, I leave you to judge.... I've been married."

"And you're divorced; yes, I know. You can't live in a

Nurses' Home and not hear gossip about the doctors. D'you want to talk about it?"

They were nearly at the Briggs house. "Well, there isn't anything to talk about really. It's history now; but I thought you ought to know."

Ian turned the car into the gravel drive, pulled on the noisy handbrake, turned to smile at her.

Freda smiled back. "Thanks for telling me anyway, Ian."

They kissed, gently, lovingly. As their lips parted Freda opened her door.

"Come on, this is no place to smooch. I mean, that's what it'll look like if anyone's watching. You know what they are."

Sefton made a speech; he'd created a tradition at his parties. He wasn't bad at it, Edwin whispered to Philip; the trouble was he thought he was damn good.

Sefton called for "hush" and waited until he'd got it.

"Ladies and gentlemen, members of the family. I hope you've all had enough to eat, that's the first thing. We've done the best we can. Considering. And it's not a bad best, though I say it myself." Murmurs of agreement. "I'm sorry our Tony couldn't be here. Nor your David, Edwin. But then somebody's got to finish the war off, and the Briggs and the Ashtons have been doing their bit towards it for four-and-a-half years of it now, and that's a long time. We keep hearing rumours that we're about to invade Europe and it's got to come, soon, mark my words. The Allies are making good progress in Italy, the chief stumbling block's gone now that Cassino's fallen. But er ... I've lost my train of thought, now."

Over the ripple of laughter, Edwin said, "I think you were welcoming Helen home, Sefton." The laughter grew.

"I was coming to that. Leave the best to last, that's the way to make a speech. Yes, Helen love, it was just a little idea of mine to get the family all together, as far as we could, to say welcome home. So all be upstanding, will you?"

Helen was touched as the glasses were held out towards her, and the warmth of "To Aunt Helen," "Welcome home," "Lovely to have you back" made it a moment she was unlikely to forget.

"There's one more thing, though." Sefton continued as the others sat down. "As we're all gathered here and we so happen to have Mister Askew with us, we might as well take a look at the family business."

41

Edwin had suspected that they didn't just "happen" to have Askew with them. Knowing Sefton, he had been invited for a purpose. "We don't want to spoil the party by talking shop, Sefton, do we?"

"We won't spoil it; just by a few minutes discussion. We've got so many shareholders these days, how often do we get the opportunity?"

The party was virtually over from that moment. As soon as Sefton broached the possibility of selling the printing works Edwin was on his feet. Everyone else sat glumly listening as the personal battle was engaged. And went on and on; mostly going over the same ground.

Askew, silently totted up the fors and against. Edwin Ashton would oppose the sale whatever the pressures were. His children would probably support him. Would Helen put her twenty-five per cent in opposition too, or would she back Sefton? That was the crucial question. He got some idea of the answer as she helped him on with his coat.

"Nice to see you again, George. After all these years. Although it could have been under pleasanter circumstances."

"Yes. Not much chance to talk had we. You haven't changed a bit, Helen."

"Nor has Sefton, has he? What's the object of all this, for heaven's sake? Break up the family?"

"Not really. He believes in the old adage that there's no sentiment in business. If he thinks the printing works isn't earning its keep, not bringing in the income that you could get from investing the money a sale would realise, then the business should be sold. Irrespective of any emotional considerations. That's Sefton's philosophy."

"Irrespective of selling Edwin with it, you mean? As part of the fixtures and fittings he was talking about? Irrespective of any feelings any of us may have about it?"

"That's Sefton's way, Helen. I've looked after his legal affairs so long, I read him like a law book."

Helen was very firm. "Well, it's not my way, George. And he's going to find that out."

Edwin mooched around the house, not hiding from anyone that he was very worried. It seemed to him that Sefton was in a position to sell the Works over his head. And what was worse, to sell out to Pringle, whom Edwin knew from experience. He would never work for a man who hired-and-fired

42

like Pringle did, acted against his staff like Pringle would. Never.

But then Helen arrived "to discuss what Sefton's up to." And the more she said, the more he realised he may have been worrying unduly. "Just a minute, love, let me get a piece of paper and we'll work it out. That's the best way to look at it."

Edwin wetted the pencil-point on his tongue. "Right. You've twenty-five per cent Helen and we've all got five per cents. That adds up to exactly half the shares, right? Now let's look at the enemy. Suppose we take it for granted Tony will give his ten per cent vote to his father. Sefton will have got at him long before this."

"And put my Jo's ten per cent on Sefton's side. Because I don't doubt he's been crafty enough to send an Airgraph to her, asking for her support."

Edwin was somewhat relieved. "So. Looking at the very worst he can do, it's fifty-fifty. Which means he can't force a sale through without our agreement, right?"

"Provided one thing, Edwin. We're presuming all your children are against selling. Have you asked them?"

"There's no need, Helen. None of mine would do a thing like that. To their own father? What d'you think they are?"

Sefton showed David Ashton into his lounge, wondering why he'd come straight to see him. He'd never done that before when he came home on leave.

David fiddled with his R.A.F. cap. "I'll come straight to the point, Uncle. I'm a bit short of the old ready, to be honest. And I wondered. . . . Just thought. . . . Knowing what they are at home, all the fuss they'd make, you know. If you could let me have a bit of a sub. Just 'til I'm over the hump."

"Living it up a bit, are you, David? Well, we're only young once, I'll give you that. Yes, I think something could be arranged." Sefton's mind was running ahead; where money was concerned it came naturally to him. He never missed an opportunity like this presented.

"That's very nice of you Uncle Sefton. I'd pay interest, of course."

"You'd find that very expensive, David. D'you know, for instance, what a bank charges? No. I've a better idea. What about er . . . what about the shares your mother left you; in the business? You can't 've sold 'em, otherwise I'd 've known. As Managing Director."

"Oh no, I've not sold those, Uncle."

"Have you not thought about it? Now you're a bit short. If you realised your five per cent holding you wouldn't have to borrow; and you'd have no interest to pay, would you?"

David considered the possibility for the first time. "I've no idea what they're worth. Or whether they'll be worth more if I hang on to them."

"Or worth less, David. Nobody knows that about shares; and I don't believe in crystal-ball stuff. But I'll say this, without fear of contradiction: you'd be better off selling, than getting yourself into debt. That's my advice, if you want it. I can't see your father being very pleased with me, if I help you to live beyond your means. You see the point, don't you lad?"

"Well, that's why I came to see you first, Uncle. I'd like to get something settled."

Sefton played it as if he was doing David a favour, and putting himself out. He stroked his chin. "Mm. Well, let's see. I've already got a fairsized holding of Briggs Printing Works shares, as you know. But I don't suppose a few more would overload me. Supposing I helped you out, by taking them off your hands? It's just a suggestion. It's up to you, of course."

David brightened. "Would you, Uncle? That'd be great. Solve all my problems."

Sefton tried not to show his pleasure at the thought of his personal holding creeping up to over a third of the total shares. "I don't see why not. It's no skin off my nose. I'll give George Askew a ring. Tell him you're coming round; to have a transfer-deed ready for your signature. I'll get him to give you a cheque for, say, half their market value. We can work out the exact amount later and settle up with you. That's the best I can do, I'm afraid."

David shook his Uncle's hand warmly; it was a marvellous best. And when he'd gone Sefton rang Askew, knowing that the sale of the works could go through now whether Helen and Edwin objected or not.

After going through the legal rigmarole at Askew's chambers, David decided he must go and see Sheila. Remembering the last time they met at Roslyn he knew he would get a cold welcome.

Sheila was caustic as she pushed her unkempt hair from her

face. "What have you come for, David? See if you can catch that feller on the premises again?"

"No. Just to talk things over."

"What about? He's married now, Colin is. A girl he knew back in Preston. He never did come round much, you know. Only when his work brought him this way. I know you don't believe me, but there was nothing in it. Not what you think anyway."

"I mean talk about us. About getting the kids back here."

"To this dump? Don't be daft, David. You'll never grow up, will you? Not one bit."

"I mean get a place fit for them to come back to. Where we'd stand a real chance of making a go of it. You and me, Sheila. Get you out of this hole, too. I'm talking about a house, a proper house."

"Oh yes. A house would be great; what do we use for money?"

"Well, I've got a bit. You know, Mum left me some shares. ..." David wanted to pull Askew's cheque out to show her. But he didn't want to have to explain that some of it was spoken for. That he had debts to pay off.

Sheila had heard him go on like this before. Many times. She didn't want to show the slightest chink in her armour by letting him think she was prepared even to listen any more.

"Look, don't explain David; I'll believe it when it happens. If it happens. When you prove you really mean it by making it happen. That's the only time I'll start believing anything you say, David. All right?"

She made it sound like the end of the discussion. He knew she really meant it. The days of sweet-talking her round were well-and-truly gone for ever.

David's next call brought another cold douche. He hadn't been with his father more than five minutes before Edwin said. "By the way, lad. There's a bit of a rumpus blowing up. About the works. There's a move afoot to sell up. You wouldn't be in favour, would you? If it meant I'd be out on my ear. Or have to work under new management, like, say, Pringle?"

"No, course I wouldn't dad; but nobody's going to ask my opinion, are they?"

"You do have a five percent say, like the rest of us. It's not much, but it is a twentieth of the whole shooting-match, never forget that."

"A twentieth? No wonder my shares were worth more than I thought."

"Were worth? When did you check what they were worth?"

"This very afternoon. I've sold them. I needed the money, dad, badly. A couple of the lads back at the station have my I.O.Us. And one pressed me so hard I had to give him a cheque, and it would have bounced if I hadn't –"

"Then why didn't you ask me?" Edwin's voice betrayed his alarm.

"And we'd 've had another row, you know we would. Look, all I did was ask Uncle Sefton for a loan. And he –"

Edwin hit the ceiling. "Sefton! You've sold your shares to Sefton? You've not signed anything, have you?"

"Yes. Askew's have fixed it all up. I had to have the money, Dad. I had to."

David had got another chilling reception when he returned to ask his Uncle Sefton to let him buy his shares back.

Sefton Briggs showed his sincerely-held philosophy. "Business is business, David. Never forget that. Family doesn't come into it, not one bit. In fact, nothing comes into it, except your word, your signature, your promise to pay, to sell, or whatever. You can't go back on it now."

"But mother left me those shares and I don't think she'd 've ... I mean, you see, I've had time to think it over. ... I don't think she'd like me to sell."

"What you mean is, David, your father's told you it gives me a controlling interest. My thirty-five per cent, Jo's ten and Tony's ten, makes fifty-five per cent in favour of selling. That's what he's told you, hasn't he? And I don't suppose he likes it one bit."

"Well ... yes. Dad did tell me. But I've thought it over, too."

"Aye, well, that's life, David. We all think of things too late at times. It's a hard school, the school of experience. I got most of my own education there, I don't mind admitting."

There was no change out of Sefton Briggs.

David went back again to Sheila, believing that when he told her what had happened she might take pity on him. But that ploy no longer worked for him either, although it had

46

many times in the past. As soon as he began to explain the transaction, she could see it was only the same old story: excuses for why things didn't work out his way; or why it wasn't working out for them. She'd had thirteen years of excuses and told him so emphatically.

David gave up. He decided to go back to his Station, cutting short his disastrous leave. Apart from being able to settle his debts, he wished he'd never come.

After a "Well, I'll be getting back, then" and a "Yes, you do that, David," he walked out of the scullery door, onto the stone-flagged yard. In the gloomy dusk, he bumped straight into Colin Woodcock.

"Oh yes?" jibed David. "I thought you got married?"

"I have. Thanks."

David was sarcastic. "Looks like it, doesn't it?"

Colin got tough. "Now look. I left some shoes behind. Sheila said she'd put them in the outhouse for me to pick up."

"And I'm waiting for a train to Siberia."

"Now look, Ashton, you're all wrong about Sheila."

"You've just come here for your shoes; yes, it's all very innocent."

"If you want to know, I'd 've married Sheila if she'd 've had me. But she turned me down. Because she was still hoping it'd work out again with you. I told her she was wasting her time but she wouldn't listen. She would hang on. You don't deserve a girl like Sheila, you know that?"

David swung his fist at Colin's mouth and missed. Colin swung his in reply and their forearms clashed painfully. The difficulty of keeping their feet on the greasy flagstones prevented a punishing fight ensuing.

Sheila had heard the anger and rushed out to step between them, physically and vocally.

"Stop it. Stop it. Both of you."

The antagonists steadied themselves, glowering at each other.

"What d'you think it'll solve if you fight each other. If you've come for your shoes, Colin, they're in here."

David watched Sheila get them from the outhouse.

"Thanks, Sheila. Thanks." Colin took the shoes and with a look of hate at David, he was gone.

"Sheila love. I –"

But Sheila wasn't waiting for still more excuses. She turned back into the scullery and left him facing a closed door, listening to the bolts slotting home.

Helen let in Edwin. The look on his face as he barked "Where's Sefton?" told her to take him straight into the lounge, without asking what had happened. Only her presence prevented a major row developing immediately. Helen kept the emotional temperature down by trying to get down to the practicalities.

"All right, Sefton," she reasoned, "supposing you have enough support to sell out. Why be so insensitive to Edwin's situation If he doesn't want to manage the works for ... Pringle is his name?"

"There's no law says Edwin has to work for Pringle or anyone else. There are other jobs, you know. I'll help him look for something ... suitable. Never said I wouldn't, did I?"

"Printing's the only trade I have, you know that. And I know my craft. I take a pride in the work we turn out at Briggs. Why should I throw that skill down the drain, after all these years?"

"We'll work something out. It's in my mind to, don't worry. But we can't let things drift on as they are. We've all got money tied-up in that Works, and it's not going to be worth much unless we sell. And sell soon. The business isn't doing well, as you know. Oh, I'm not saying it's your fault, it isn't. It's due to the war, and we can't do anything about that, can we? I know I'm right. You can argue till you're blue in the face. You too, Helen. My mind's made up."

Edwin stood his ground. "So's mine. And I say you're not selling out without clear majority voting, Sefton. That's flat!" Edwin made to leave.

"I've got it, haven't I? I've an airgraph from Jo saying do whatever I think best. D'you want to see it?"

Edwin stopped at the door. "You needn't bother."

Helen was thinking quickly. It would be as well to know what the position was between Sefton and Tony. "But doesn't that make only forty-five per cent. And you need over fifty. How sure are you that you'll get Tony's support, too?"

Edwin backed up her question. "He's more like his grandfather Briggs than his father; and he was a print man. How do we know Tony isn't against the business going out of the family?"

"He'll see it his father's way, don't you worry about that.

When I discuss it with him. Give him all the facts. And I intend to do that. Personally. Very soon."

"Is he coming on leave then?" Helen realised how determined Sefton was.

"No. I'm going to see him. Where he's stationed."

Edwin doubted. "I thought you didn't know where he'd been moved to. With the security black-out."

"I'll find out. Don't you worry. Come with me if you like, Edwin. Put your side. I only want to be fair."

Edwin considered. Tony's decision, in effect, would be the casting vote. It was important that he should hear both sides of the issue before he made up his mind.

"All right, Sefton, I will. If you can find out where he's stationed. Which I doubt."

CHAPTER SIX

June 1944

Lieutenant Tony Briggs R.N. was officially stationed "somewhere in England". Slightly more precisely, somewhere on the South Coast. His ship, a converted trawler, waited, as he did, for the invasion of enemy-occupied Northern France. Like thousands of other Naval personnel, Tony knew that D-day was very near; only a few days now, a week at most. Their preparations were so advanced, it must be very close.

The German defences across the Channel knew it, too. Even though security had never been so strict.

Sefton wrote to Tony "c/o G.P.O. Home Forces" asking where he was but Tony replied "Sorry, father, we're not allowed to say. The Navy's very strict about it."

In the event it happened the other way round. It was the Navy that told Sefton exactly where to come: urgently, as Tony's next-of-kin.

Tony was good-looking even without the glamour of the uniform. The combination really got the girls, a phenomenon Tony hardly discouraged.

Barbara lived at the village local, "somewhere on the South Coast". As she sat with Tony in the sand-dunes, talking inevitably of "when this war is over" they noticed a middle-aged couple, walking near a stretch of sand, forbidden by barbed-wire. They held hands like teenagers as they passed the "Minefield – Keep Out" signs. Death hazards had been buried when invasion had been imminent in the opposite direction, just after Dunkirk; a threat which ended when Churchill immortalised the comparatively few pilots who had repelled German bombers and fighter escorts until they gave up; mercifully for this Island.

Barbara told him that all the village knew the couple's story. The slim white-haired man was a retired Commander, beyond the age of recall to even chairborne Naval service. The handsome woman, some years younger, was the wife of "a local bigwig" (as Barbara put it) on active service in the Far East. "I've not seen him since war broke out."

It seemed just a little war-time romance. Two lonely people thrown together. "When this war is over" they'd never see each other again.

Suddenly Tony broke off their surmisings in alarm. The Commander was holding down the barbed-wire to allow his companion to step into the area where mines were buried haphazardly, unseen. Tony jumped up shouting, "Hey! You can't go that way!" Barbara, equally worried, said "They must know what they're doing, they must."

They did; they were deliberately walking out into the mine-field, their arms intertwined, their hands clasped tightly; putting their feet down steadily and firmly as if hoping to activate an explosion beneath them.

Tony ran madly towards them, shouting frantically "Come back!" They looked over their shoulders towards him once, then ignored his calls.

Barbara ran after Tony, but was several yards behind him by the time he reached the barbed-wire. He crossed over it at the point where the couple had entered the minefield.

"Tony, come back! You'll be killed!"

But Tony walked on, carefully measuring each step into the foot-prints in the sand, hoping to prevent blowing himself into unidentifiable pieces. He had seen it happen more than once; he knew what a land-mine could do to its victim.

Barbara stood petrified as Tony progressed across the mine-field, gradually getting closer to the couple, who still ignored his shouts.

The explosion shattered her ears and flung her backwards to the ground. When she recovered enough to look at the pall

of smoke, she could just make out Tony's still body, like a
heap on the sand, his uniform in shreds. The tragic lovers were
somewhere unseen in the smoke; if they still existed at all.

Tony's only serious injuries were in his leg. From his hospital bed he told Barbara that he'd had D-day; the doctors
knew that much for certain. She told him of the village's
mourning. Of two quite separate funerals. A woman Barbara
believed was the Commander's widow had attended one. The
"bigwig" had flown back from the Far East for the other.
Barbara wondered if they had met? Did they know each
other's pain? Would it have been any comfort to know? Or
would it have twisted the knife? Tony recalled surmising
on that fateful day; they had died for something more than
"a little wartime romance".

It was a very different bedside conversation when Sefton
and Edwin sat either side of Tony's hospital bed. A Naval
telegram advised Sefton of the address of the hospital and
he'd asked Edwin to come with him. They noticed that the
damaged leg and its trappings bulged the bedclothes; but Tony
made light of it.

"They won't keep me here long, father, don't worry. All
these beds are standing-by for casualties after D-day."

Edwin picked up the inference. "It's that close then, is it?
The invasion"

Tony's voice fell to a whisper, "Close? I can't have missed
it by more than –" Even at a level they could barely hear, he
stopped short of any real information. He need not have bothered. The first airborne troops had landed at 00.20 hours in
the small hours of that very day.

Edwin had suggested to Sefton that they didn't bring up
business matters, it would hardly be the time or place. But
Tony's opening remarks had given Sefton his head.

"You're nothing like as bad as we were expecting lad. I'm
pleased to say."

"I'll have to walk with a stick they say; maybe for a month
or two. No permanent damage, thank goodness."

At that moment the first casualty from the Normandy land-
ings was wheeled in. A Captain of Sixth Airborne Divisional
Signals, Tony learned later from the Sister. He was laid in the
next bed but one, more bandaged than not, his head completely
swathed. He never recovered consciousness.

51

They stopped talking whilst screens were put round the bed; then Sefton whispered, "You reckon this is the end of the Navy, for you, Tony?"

"With a flesh wound? No, it's not over yet, father."

"I know, but you don't have to be so eager now, you know. You've done your bit; how long have you served now? – I mean, you've got to look ahead, too. To what you see yourself doing when it's all over."

"Uncle Edwin, has father come to talk business?" Tony knew the signs, from experience.

"I don't think he has, Tony; that is to say, we ought not to, Sefton."

"Father. What are you up to now?"

"What are you, is more to the point, Tony. I hear this girl you're knocking about with has a baby. Father's some type in the Army that won't wed her."

His blunt broaching of the subject did not throw Tony. "You get the wrong idea from pub gossip. Barbara's a nice girl." His eyes burned with conviction.

"And has a nice baby. We've seen it. Brought it into the Saloon Bar, didn't she, Edwin?"

"Yes. Yes. She . . . made no bones about it being hers."

Tony was adamant. "Whether she's married or not is her business."

Edwin corrected him. "Well it'd be yours as well Tony, if you got serious. And you never know."

"I do know. It is serious."

Sefton looked at him in amazement. "What? You've thrown over a girl like Jenny for someone that's already . . . had someone else's baby?"

"It's been over with Jenny for a long time, father. I liked her, but I didn't love her."

"And you're saying you . . . love this one?"

"I'm seriously thinking of asking her to have me, yes."

"You'd marry her? With an illegitimate baby?"

"Why don't you say 'Bastard'?"

Edwin tried once more. "Your father and I were talking about grandchildren on the way here, Tony. He's envious of David's Peter and Janet, and Margaret's John-George."

"Is that it, father? The baby! Won't be of the blood? Not a Briggs? You're still living in the days of the Satanic mills."

"We'll talk about it when you're on leave. You are getting a spell, aren't you? Due to this?"

"Oh yes. Let's talk then. By all means. But I intend to ask her before I come on leave."

Sefton was resigned, but tried to show how much he was hurt. "I see. I'm sorry. I'm ... very sorry, Tony."

"It's not that bad, Sefton," Edwin tried to reassure him. "There might be other children, wouldn't there Tony? Your children?"

Tony smiled. Even Edwin went along with the blood-ancestry tradition. God, how strong it persisted in their generation. "Well, as I haven't yet asked her to marry me, we haven't discussed babies. Wouldn't it have been a bit premature?"

Sefton nearly snapped back "Not in her case, it wouldn't," but Edwin sensed the jibe was coming and coughed just in time. Sefton changed his reply to: "Think on what I said earlier, then. If you're going to take on unnecessary responsibilities, it's all the more reason to think about your own future."

"I don't know yet if she'll have me, do I?"

Sefton couldn't resist "If she'll have you? She'll grab you."

"Father. We'll talk about my future, and whatever this business is that affects me, when I come home. And when I know whether Barbara is going to marry me or not."

Tony leaned on his stick and Barbara's arm as they walked slowly along the beach path towards the minefields. He'd resolved to propose to her on his first day out of hospital, but her refusal hadn't really surprised him. She intended waiting until Stevie's father came back. Hoping he would change his mind and want to marry her. Tony had offered to be a good father. But she was adamant. It wasn't quite the same. There was something about the blood. That was the only reason she was turning him down.

"Sorry, Tony, I can't explain it."

Nor could Tony.

CHAPTER SEVEN

June 1944

David Ashton had heard enough enemy aircraft to know that this open-throated roar piercing the black sky was something new. He was puzzled even more when, for apparently no reason, its single jet-engine cut out. The silence was an ominous contrast. What stupid pilot would shut down like that? Over London in the black-out? Asking to be shot down.

Suddenly the Leicester Square basement called the "Services in London Club" shook with a massive explosion; debris flew everywhere. The girl in David's arms fell screaming to the dance-floor and he dropped with her. When David helped her to her feet the four-piece band was in a heap with its smashed instruments; some dancers were extricating others from ceiling debris; the bar was awash with liquor and splintered glass.

Everyone took it that a conventional bomb had fallen, too near for comfort, but far enough away to save their lives. But this bomb hadn't been dropped from an aircraft. It was the aircraft itself.

Soon all South-East England was going about its wartime work with ears cocked for the unmistakable roar of a "doodle-bug" – dubbed typically light-heartedly by those who were its target. But it was to prove the most diabolical weapon of the war; Hitler's penultimate death-throw with which he gambled to bring the civilians of the country which had stood between him and victory to their knees.

The "doodlebug's" official name was the "V.1." Its stubby wings and jet-engine lifted it from launching ramps arranged along the occupied northern coast of France. Its speed was over 350 miles-per-hour and it arrowed straight towards London until its engine cut out. Then it fell and exploded. Its unofficial name "The Flying Bomb" described it precisely.

When it became identifiable and understood, people hoped that its engine wouldn't stop until it had passed over them. That meant they were safe. But they knew they were wishing its death-blow on to others. It was a two-pronged secret weapon; psychologically a new and different test of morale; and militarily it threatened to wreak more havoc than all the conventional bombs in the darkest days of the blitz.

David and his dance-floor partner, whose name he never knew, escaped with nothing more than powdered plaster in their hair. He took her to Charing Cross Hospital and never saw her again.

Fortunately for other big towns, the Flying Bomb's maximum range was about one hundred and fifty miles. So its strange throaty note was never heard north of Northampton.

Ian Mackenzie took Freda to his home to meet his mother. They got on splendidly although both had been sceptical prior to their meeting. Mrs. Mackenzie dearly wanted to see Ian married again; and happily this time. From what he'd told her of Freda she sounded to be right for him, except for her age. Wasn't she perhaps a little young?

"Young? Wait 'til you meet her." Ian had said.

Freda had voiced the same doubt. "Won't she think I'm a bit ... You know?"

"Wait and see what she says, Freda."

The first meeting was in the Mackenzie conservatory, where Mrs. Mackenzie nursed her plants. There were none of those awkward pauses which similar situations often cause. Ian barely got a word in. In fact, he saw he wasn't needed and left them to it. It didn't matter a bit to Freda that he'd been married. Mrs. Mackenzie reassured her that Ian hadn't been to blame; and she wasn't saying that as a doting mum. Freda could see she had more sense than to be prejudiced.

Mrs. Mackenzie warned her that he was quite a serious person, maybe she'd already found that out. "A bit overmuch at times, Freda, d'you think?" No, Freda didn't think so, she liked him just as he was.

Mrs. Mackenzie felt she was too quickly reaching the conclusion that Freda seemed right for Ian. Then Ian came back. Mrs. Mackenzie said she must not neglect her plants, and Ian took Freda into the lounge.

"Yes," Mrs. Mackenzie told herself, "she isn't as young as her age; he was right. She'd be ideal for him ... perfectly ideal."

The doodlebug incident foreshortened David's stay in London. He knew he ought to have spent his leave in Liverpool anyway. He was only putting off the evil day. He really must make one more effort, a last, last-ditch effort. And when he did, he found his key didn't fit; Sheila had had the locks changed; to keep him out.

He spent the night at the Ashtons, announcing that he was home to see a solicitor and start divorce proceedings. The next morning Edwin called to see Sheila. Not that he was trying to get her to change her mind. Just to make sure, in view of David's announcement, that she had really made up her mind. That she knew it would be the point of no return.

She had; she did know. Edwin frankly couldn't see what else she could do. Was there any way he could help make it easier for her? Sheila couldn't let him help her; David was his son.

Tony Briggs, spending sick-leave leaning on a stick, answered the door when David called at the Briggs.

Tony cut explanations short. He'd stepped on a land-mine; his own fault. To hear his version, no-one else had been involved.

When Sefton came in he greeted David and shook hands as if the wrangle over his shares had never happened. In the circumstances David was glad.

"I just wondered, Uncle, having the right sort of contacts, could you give me the name of a good solicitor?"

"Well, it depends what sort of legal advice you want."

"Divorce."

The word conveyed everything. Sefton looked grave.

"Look lad, you are sure I suppose, or you wouldn't have got as far as this. I suppose there's no point in my saying anything, is there. Go and see George Askew. Tell him I sent you. I'll give you his address. Oh, you know it don't you?"

"Thanks Uncle, I will." David did not refer to his previous visit to Askew's Chambers either.

Tony had very different thoughts. "What about Sheila?"

"She wants a divorce more than me. What about her?"

Tony wondered if she had the privilege of "mention my name" to a good solicitor; but counted it wiser not to think aloud.

Considering that they were on the same duty on the same ward day after day, or night after night, Freda and Doris worked well together. There was only one disparity. Freda was becoming in Doris's phrase a "one-man girl". Whilst Doris was, as she said other people called her, "Yank-mad". Well, what was there to be ashamed of? She had a good time; people who talked were only jealous and to hell with 'em.

Freda teased her, asking when was she going to go out with the same man twice? What did Freda mean? There'd been several she'd been out with twice. Some three or four times. "We can't all have Mister Mackenzie, you know, Freda." Doris sounded envious under the jokiness. Freda tried to advise her to be "a little more choosey".

"You know what me mam once told me dad, Freda, when he was reading the Riot Act? The great thing about advice, Joe, she said is 'you don't have to take it.'"

"Course you don't, Doris; but it's usually for your own good."

"Like nasty medicine, yes."

"All I'm saying is, you should watch it a bit. I wouldn't like to see you hurt, that's all."

"You won't, don't worry."

But Freda was worried; that's why she'd brought it up. Doris took the clean kidney-dishes back to the ward cupboard. Freda took the hint and didn't resume the subject when she came back.

Edwin Ashton was coercing David to stay one more night, so that he could come with them to the Church Garden Party at the Mackenzies'. Mrs. Mackenzie wanted the Church to benefit handsomely, so the family was supporting Freda.

But David was browned-off. In London people were still living in fear of sudden maiming or death, whilst here it was garden parties and wondering what was one going to do when the war was over. Well, his war wasn't over yet. Anyway he was thinking of staying on in the peacetime R.A.F. A commissioned officer should be a cushy number, and he might try for it.

Edwin knew there was more to his moody reaction than that and said so.

There was. A junior partner at Askew's was the cause. He'd looked at David as if he'd come from under a stone. "The Guilty Party", as he called him, treating him like some sort of criminal.

Edwin knew what was coming next. Of course David had walked out; he didn't have to stand for that, did he? What did he expect him to do? Let that self-righteous pig talk to him like that? Just sit there and take it? Not David Ashton.

Edwin despaired of him. Didn't he realise he'd got to have a solicitor; and by walking out he'd have to start all over again?

Tony was appalled to see how Sheila lived. The living room, if you could call it that, seemed a hovel compared with how the Briggs lived in the same suburb.

She hadn't realised that she had to have her own solicitor; she couldn't use the one his father had recommended to David. Tony gave her a card; it was someone he knew personally, so mention his name.

Sheila took the card gratefully. It was clear to Tony that she knew nothing about the procedure at all; and had not thought of finding out.

Tony also made a last-ditch effort to rescue the marriage. But nothing and no-one could budge Sheila's resolve to divorce David. It had built up to a pitch where she was unshakeable. And, like Edwin, Tony admitted that he didn't blame her.

"Sheila, I do wish I could do something to help you."

Sheila smiled wanly. "You can't. Tony; because you can't put yourself in my shoes. You'll find yourself some nice girl and she'll say 'Yes', and you'll live happy ever after. No problems; not even money."

Tony remembered Barbara and Stevie. "That's rose-coloured spectacles, Sheila, believe me."

"I doubt it. That's what it'll be for you, you'll see. Oh, I don't mind, I'm not jealous. In fact, come to think of it, it helps."

"Helps? How?"

"I don't know. Knowing some people settle down and bring up their kids together, see each other every day; makes it easier, when you haven't got all that. I don't know why, but it does."

Tony had a chilled feeling. He sympathised, knowing how David had played her up time after time. But the longer he stayed, the more he sensed the gap between them. She had no reasoning, or logic. Only her emotions guided her.

"There's no use talking about it, Tony. You can't understand. Honest you can't."

"I'm just trying to find some way of not being as helpless

58

as I feel." Tony was dredging for something worth saying.

Sheila indicated his solicitor friend's name. "You have been a help. I'm very grateful."

"Yes, well ... if there is anything. ... Let me know. Won't you?"

"Yes. Yes, I will. If there is. 'Bye, Tony."

Tony had thought he would come away knowing he'd done something worth while. Instead he felt uncomfortable. Why couldn't he get in contact – in simple human contact – with someone like Sheila? He didn't like to think he'd failed to. It disturbed him.

The weather was uncharacteristically splendid for a Garden Party in Liverpool. Sunny days at that Northern latitude were usually reserved, ironically, for the blackest days of the War. Outdoor events, limited as they were to very few, were usually unblessed by the climate.

The vicar raised his hands to the sun, and told Mrs. Mackenzie that their prayers had been answered. It would make all the difference to the proceeds. He visited the hoop-la, the bring-and-buy and the ring-a-watch stalls, beaming to helpers and to the guests who were supporting the cause in their wartime summer finery. Each time he heard coins drop into one of the tin-cans serving as cash receptacles he punctuated his smile with a Freudian blink.

Mrs. Mackenzie had done far more than donate the use of her garden. She had organised the operation for weeks in advance and was now moving unhurriedly among the guests, offering cucumber sandwiches.

Edwin told Helen that David had gone back to his Station the night before. For one with roots deep in the Yorkshire mining community, Edwin suffered the Garden Party tolerantly. It was so long since he was part of that different world. It was Helen who recalled the difference, not Edwin. Time was when he'd always been on about it. Was Edwin mellowing, maturing, whatever the right word was?

Doris directed her lanky U.S.A.A.F. Master Sergeant towards Ian and Freda and introduced him as if she'd known him rather longer than two days – or evenings. "This is Clark. We're at the same hospital, Freda and me."

Mrs. Mackenzie had delegated Freda and Ian to run the tombola stall. Master Sergeant flashed a fistful of money and bought more tickets than Freda had sold since the stall opened.

One ticket married up with a trussed chicken. "Stick the ticket back in the drum, babe," the American ordered. The Vicar intoned something about the generosity of friends across the sea.

Sefton pitted his aging muscles against the "Try Your Strength" machine. He couldn't understand why he used to be able to swing the hammer to send the button up the scale to clang the bell; and now he couldn't raise it half-way. The more he tried the lower it registered. And the hammer grew heavier.

Edwin smiled. "You'll do yourself an injury, Sefton."

"Aye, mebbe I will. I'm sure that bell's higher than they used to have 'em, you know. They can't leave anything as it was, these days."

Helen let him down lightly. "It only seems higher, Sefton."

Doris and her Sergeant completed a round of the stalls. By bringing him along, her contribution to church funds had been considerable. But now he led her behind the bushes and pulled her to the ground.

"No, love. Not here." Doris struggled.

"Why not? No-one can see."

"It's not right. It's Ian's house. My friend's boyfriend."

"So it's your friend's boyfriend's place. So what? Aw, come on, kid?"

"No, Clark, I don't think –" But she couldn't tell him what she thought, and return his kiss at the same time.

Mrs. Mackenzie was distributing a new consignment of sandwiches when she caught a glimpse of Doris's bright dress through the rhododendron leaves. Her cry of disapproval brought others to the spot as Doris brushed her skirt and the Sergeant dusted his trousers.

Although they both apologised to Mrs. Mackenzie, Freda really had no choice than to tell Doris it was best they should go. She accompanied them round the house to the gravel-drive.

"Look baby, we didn't mean no disrespect. Tell the lady, huh? With my compliments?"

"Yes, I'll tell her. See you in the morning, Doris, okay?"

Doris apologised again as Freda ran back to the lawn.

Freda apologised yet again to Mrs. Mackenzie. It was a

relief to find she had dismissed the incident and was helping Ian with the tombola.

When his mother had gone off with the sandwich plates, Ian said "I think she went a bit too far."

"Doris?"

"No. Mother."

"I don't. She was quite right to make a fuss. There's a time and a place for everything. Buy a ticket for the tombola, Dad? Come on."

Edwin looked at the prizes. "Anything left worth winning?" His one ticket won the chicken; without his knowing it was, in a way, second-hand. He had hardly picked it up before Sefton was offering to buy it from him.

"I can't sell it, Sefton. I won it for next to nothing."

"Course you can sell it. It's your property."

Edwin put the bird on a table beside the stall. "I'm not selling."

Sefton was adamant too. "I want to buy it, Edwin. Stop holding back for a good price."

"I'm not holding back. If you want it that badly, take it. Have it. Go on."

"You mean you're giving it me? For nothing?"

"Course I mean for nothing."

"No, that won't do. I insist on paying its value."

"I don't know its value. Take the damn –" Edwin turned to pick up the chicken and thrust it into Sefton's hands; but it had gone.

Mrs. Mackenzie's labrador wasn't interested in its price; only in putting as much lawn as possible between chicken and negotiators.

Edwin and Sefton stood with mouths open: then joined in the laughter. It was part of the fun of the fair. Moments of levity were precious in war-time.

Ian had been delegated to clear the remaining litter from the lawn; Freda had volunteered to help. From the conservatory, Mrs. Mackenzie watched them as the late sun caught their faces.

Ian lifted the sack. "That's it. I told you it was a back-breaking job; but you did insist."

"Would've been dark before you'd finished, if you'd done it on your own."

"See how mother gets out of it? She's brilliant at organising.

Next thing you know she'll be organising you, too. I can see the signs."

"Oh, I don't know, Ian. She's worked very hard, you must admit." Freda liked the idea of Ian's mother treating her as one of the family; but didn't say so.

Ian emptied the sack into the incinerator. "Thanks. For your help. For coming For...."

Mrs. Mackenzie watched Ian kiss Freda tenderly. They must know she can see them, she reasoned. Good. Was he going to ask her to marry him? Not until he was absolutely certain, beyond any possible doubt. Knowing her son.

CHAPTER EIGHT

July 1944

Ian and Freda had their private joke about the cliched doctor-and-nurse thing. So when Margaret began making little digs, Freda laughed them off. "I'm falling madly in love with the handsome doctor? Is that what you're hinting? Well, I've seen enough of marriage round here not to want to bother, thanks very much." Margaret noted the underlying seriousness. Freda hadn't seen very good examples of happy-ever-after marriages. Their father and mother; Margaret's in-laws, Harry and Celia Porter; David and Sheila. And Margaret's own marriage was hardly unscathed.

But the facts belied Freda's jokey denials. Almost every time she came home from the Hospital, Ian happened to be leaving about the same time and gave her a lift. She had no time for other boy-friends; nor girl-friends, except Doris whom she saw mostly in the ward kitchen.

Mrs. Mackenzie was watching the relationship develop with approval. They weren't rushing into anything. They were getting to know each other first. Yes, she did so approve. All was going very well. It was, until an unexpected knock at the door; and the arrival of literally the last person she expected to see. It was Mary. Mary Ramsden.

"But of course you can have a word with him." Mrs. Mackenzie explained that Ian would be home shortly. But not that he was taking Freda out to dinner that evening. She thought it wise to ring Ian to see if he couldn't come home a little earlier. Something told her it would be better if Mary was no longer there when Freda arrived.

Doris took the call on the corridor telephone and brought Mr. Mackenzie from the Ward. Then she joined Freda in the kitchen and joked. "Eh. Your boy-friend's in the corridor. On the phone."

Before Freda could reply that she didn't have to see him every moment of the day, Ian came into the kitchen. She detected concern in his voice.

"Er ... something's cropped up. I'm going off right away so I won't be able to give you a lift, sorry. See you later though. Don't be late."

"Oh. All right. I won't."

Doris watched the exchange, straining to glean a crumb of information.

As soon as he'd gone, Doris closed the door. "Looked a bit upset, didn't he? I wonder what's up?"

"I've no idea. Probably not going straight home himself, that's all."

"It was something to do with the phone call." Doris could have kicked herself. Why hadn't she asked the switchboard who was calling.

Freda refused to discuss it any more.

Mary Ramsden looked around the Mackenzie lounge. It seemed an age since she'd lived there. But it wasn't all that long. Two years, going on three.

Mrs. Mackenzie came in from the telephone in the Hall. "He'll be about ten minutes, that's all. Anything I can do Mary, is it?"

"Well ... I'd rather tell Ian first."

"Nothing wrong is there?" Margaret asked as Harry Porter slumped wearily onto the dining room settee. She could see that there was. He looked drawn, his skin was sallow, his eyes were underlined.

"No, Margaret, I've come over to ask your father's advice, that's all. You all right yourself?"

"Yes. Oh, you mean when I said I'd only just got back from the Doctor's. He's having some tests done. They inject rats or mice or something. I'll know in about a fortnight. Whether

I'm going to have your second grandchild or not."

"What's John think about that?"

"I haven't told him. You know, he'd worry about his job, hates it, wants to get something else. If this turns out to be a false alarm, it saves heartaches, doesn't it? So mum's the word."

When Edwin arrived home from the printing works, Margaret warned him in the hall that Harry didn't look too good. As they shook hands, he could see it wasn't just a question of his health; Harry was a very worried man. But he couldn't be drawn. "No, Edwin, it's not Celia this time, for a change. London's getting a pasting from these flying bombs. Casualties nearly as bad as the blitz, the paper says."

Edwin noted the change of subject. He was covering up something.

Ian and Mary kissed cheeks. Mrs. Mackenzie asked should she leave them together but only half-heartedly made for the door.

Mary reacted quickly, almost jumpily. "No, don't go. You might as well know, too. The fact is Ian ... Gilbert has left me."

Gilbert Ramsden had been the catalyst, not the root cause, of the Mackenzie divorce. It had been coming anyway. Gilbert was nowhere near so serious-minded, she'd snapped at Ian. But Mary was to find out, not long after she had married Gilbert Ramsden, that he had no mind at all. He had a talent for telling dirty stories, that was all. "Did you hear the one about this feller –" soon began to pall. She had to listen to the same embarrassing jokes every time they met someone who hadn't heard them. But worse was to come. Gilbert began to drink. Excessively.

"I don't like to say it, Ian, but he's an alcoholic. Incurable." She wouldn't bore them with the sordid details. But their parting was not as civilized as the way she and Ian had agreed to separate.

No, there was nothing Ian could do to patch it up, thanks. Gilbert had left Oldham, she'd no idea where he was. And she didn't want to know.

"Ian has to go out, Mary...." Mrs. Mackenzie checked the time.

"Oh then I musn't keep you. I'm sorry."

Mrs. Mackenzie thought a little more detail was necessary.

"She doesn't like to be kept waiting, does she, Ian?"

"She won't mind. Just a few minutes."

"Oh, it's a girl; funny, I never think of you having girl friends. Do you tell them about ... us?"

"Freda knows, yes. Well, I'll nip and change quickly and we'll see what time's left."

As soon as he had left the room Mrs. Mackenzie put the record straight. "I was afraid Freda might be too young for him. But I'm keeping my fingers crossed."

"Oh, it's ... getting serious is it? Someone ... younger than me, I suppose?"

"Oh yes. Quite a bit." Mrs. Mackenzie tried not to make it too pointed.

"I envy her. It's terrible how you have to lose something before you find ... just how precious it is."

Freda dashed straight into the kitchen from the front door. "I did say 'no tea for me', didn't I, Margaret?"

"Yes, at breakfast; three times. Harry's here. Say hello."

Freda put her head round the living room door. "Hello. Sorry I can't stop. Heavy date." And she was off to her bedroom to change.

"Wish we were that young again?" Harry had aged since Edwin last saw him.

"No, Edwin. I was in the trenches. Muck up to here, we were in."

John heard the tail-end as he came in from work. "That war took the best years of your life, dad. And this one's taken mine." He sounded very depressed.

"You have had a bad day, John." Edwin put down the evening paper as Margaret came in to lay the table.

"Every day's a bad day in that place. Adding up figures, checking the same blasted forms. It's ... soul-destroying. That Mister Temple; what a man to have over you. So bloody pernickety he doesn't hang his hat up. He positions it. At exactly the same angle. Every flaming day." Margaret thought of her pregnancy tests, hoped and prayed they would be negative.

Mary expressed approval; Ian did look smart. "Any girl would be thrilled to go out with you."

Mrs. Mackenzie was getting more anxious. "You know your trains back to Oldham, do you Mary? We have a time-table somewhere, if you don't."

65

That brought out the full story. Gilbert had got so he was selling anything and everything they owned in order to buy liquor. Mary hadn't found out the extent of the debts he'd run up, or how far the rent was behind, until after he'd left her. So she'd had to get out. "Oh dear, I'm making it sound as if I've been turned out into the driven snow. Sorry. I didn't mean to. You must go, Ian."

But how could he go? "What about your brother, Wilfred, couldn't you go there, Mary?"

"He was killed in Burma. Of course, you didn't know did you? I haven't written since then. Sorry."

Mrs. Mackenzie said something about Wilfred being the only relative she had left, just to make the situation crystal clear; to warn Ian what they were getting involved in.

Mrs. Mackenzie felt very sorry for Mary, but was more concerned for Ian. And Freda.

"Ian, dear," Mary apologised, "the last thing I want to do is impose on you. But er. . . ." She paused long enough for Mrs. Mackenzie to wonder what favour she had really come to ask. "I thought, if I could go back to my old job. Maybe you'd know of a vacancy for an almoner's secretary. Where I could live in, that would solve my problems, wouldn't it? Something at a hospital where I could get away from Oldham . . .?"

Mrs. Mackenzie was relieved. "I think that's a splendid idea, Mary. I really do. There's bound to be something somewhere . . . in the country." Again she tried not to be too pointed.

"Oh I wasn't expecting Ian to get me into his hospital. I didn't mean that."

Ian was thinking about the problem. "Everywhere I know is bursting at the seams. I'll ring the Hospital Secretary. I've got his home number. He might know of somewhere off the top of his head."

It was unlikely he would be able to put Mary's mind at ease then and there; at least it showed they were trying to help her. But his telephone call was abortive. He returned from the Hall. "He's promised to look through his records in the morning. Is the bed in the back room made up, mother?"

It wasn't, no. Mary protested she couldn't stay. But as Ian said "What else could she do?" Freda's knock ended the discussion.

Mary was anxious that he should go. "Ian. Don't bring her in, please. She may not like to see your ex-wife here." Mrs.

Mackenzie thought it best not to go into explanations, too. Ian said "Women do have funny ideas." He took Freda from the front door straight to his car.

"Where are we going?" Freda noticed he turned away from down-town Liverpool, heading into the countryside.

"I said tonight was going to be a surprise. Be patient. Wait and see."

"You sound a bit worried, Ian. Something wrong?"

"No. Well, nothing I need bother you with. I don't want to spoil our evening."

Mary had peeked through the bay-window curtains. "She is rather young for him, isn't she?"

"She's right for him, Mary. Believe me. I know her."

David had got hold of the name of another solicitor and had special leave to come home to see him. Home meant the Ashtons; he had given up thinking of the dump where Sheila was as "home".

Edwin was reading the evening paper. "Sounds as though the invasion's going well, David. From what we're told in the papers." Edwin followed the Allies advance into Northern France day by day.

"Yes, provided they find a way of intercepting these doodle-bugs before there's nothing left of London."

"I thought our Spitfires were bringing them down." John expected David would know more than they reported in the papers.

"Well, I've seen 'em leave our kites standing, that's how fast they are. To get one, a Spit has to hang about up top, get extra speed from a power dive, tilt the bug over with his wing-tip, and down it goes."

Margaret could hear through the serving hatch. "But doesn't that kill people just the same? When it hits the ground and explodes?"

"They try to get 'em in open country. Before they reach the outskirts. I was in Sevenoaks when one blew out all the shop windows. Would've been much worse in London. The only other way is to try and explode 'em in the air. Pump cannon-shell into the jet. I saw one Spit get too close and they both went up; pilot bought it, too."

"Machine against machine," John prophesied. "It's coming."

David said he'd take John for a drink; he needed bucking up. A few pints was the medicine.

John kicked a stone along the pavement in the warm light of the evening. "Remember David? When we were kids? Playing out 'til bedtime? No idea what was really going on in the world, had we? Our dads back from their war with damn-all except medals. It'll be just the same after this lot, I'll bet."

"You do need a drink, mate, you do. You're getting morbid."

Once Edwin had got Harry alone in the living room he put it to him straight. He hadn't just come visiting, had he?

"No. You're right, Edwin. To tell the truth; I'm in a bit of a mess."

It was no fault of Harry's. He'd been taken off the powder-filling job when his health began to suffer, but clerking jobs in the Ordnance Factory didn't pay as good money. Oh yes, Celia knew it was less, but she didn't know he hadn't been able to make ends meet without letting the mortgage payments slide. Now he was nearly a hundred quid in arrears, and they were pressing for it. Where could he find that sort of cash?

Edwin said he would've liked to be able to lend it him himself. Harry admitted he had wondered if he could. Edwin offered to ask Sefton for him, but not with any enthusiasm. Harry said he wouldn't let Edwin do that on any account. Edwin didn't know what else to suggest, he really didn't.

Neither knew what else to say.

Ian turned off the main road onto the cindered parking-area in front of "Bessie's Cafe." Most of the vehicles were R.A.S.C. vans, lorries, tank-transporters and 3-ton trucks. He parked in the shadow of an R.A.F. "Queen Mary", laden with the jagged fuselage and remains of the wings of a crashed Wellington.

"Bessie's" was a large unglorified wooden hut. The only decor was a drawing-pinned gallery of Government posters from "Walls Have Ears" to "Keep Food Clean, It's Precious". Bessie herself was serving two A.T.S. Transport drivers. She caught sight of Ian. "Hello, love. Take that one, there. With you in a sec."

As they sat on the bright-coloured bentwood chairs, Freda watched Bessie go back into the kitchen. "She's Mrs. Rigby. Still-born twins, just before D-day."

68

Ian nodded and smiled. "Caesarian section. Said if I came for a meal, I'd eat like a lord. Bring my best girl-friend if I liked."

Bessie was already back to take their order. "I'm right glad you've come Doctor. Eh up, wait a minute, this is nurse, too, isn't it? Nurse Ashton, course it is. You've come on the right night, too. Had our week's allocation this very afternoon. Bessie spelt out "S.T.E.A.K." as if it were code for some secret weapon.

Steak was in extremely short supply; but transport cafes had special allocations. They were staging-posts for the war effort's pack-horses: the men and women who drove the lorries and articulators which carried everything from spam to teleprinters.

Ian and Freda protested; steak was for those in uniform.

"Well, if you two weren't in uniform when I last saw you, I don't know who was." And she left for the kitchen door before they could argue.

Ian thought he would leave what he really intended to say until later. He talked about the Beveridge Report and the possibility of a National Health Service. All the doctors he knew were for it. But the top echelons of the B.M.A. were against it.

Bessie served steaks that conjured up pre-war memories. Talking gave way to tucking-in.

Edwin dashed to the serving-hatch. "Quick Margaret. A glass of water. Harry's passed out."

By the time he was coming round John and David had come in from the pub. Between them they talked poor Harry into staying the night. John and Margaret helped him upstairs.

"No, Dad," replied David, "we weren't long at the pub because John's getting to be a right comedian these days. He really is. Keeps on and on about what's going to happen when it's all over, where's the world heading? It gets on my wick."

John came down looking concerned. "His skin's an awful colour; he's come out in a rash, he was breathing like mad at the top of the stairs. I looked at him lying there. Come back a hero from his war, he did. To a land fit for blokes like him to live in, did they say? Well, where is that brave new world? He hasn't seen it, for one."

"Aye, John." Edwin consoled him . "Hitler happened, didn't he? That's part of the reason."

Bessie paid token lip-service to the Food Regulations. She was very sorry, but the steaks had put paid to their having a sweet; took them over the maximum five-bob-per-person. But as she took away the plates she added quietly: "I'll squeeze you in two coffees though."

Ian decided to ignore Mary's advice. He told Freda his ex-wife had turned up out of the blue, that her husband had walked out on her.

Freda paused, as if the news required weighing-up. "Well. It was her turn. It's only what she did to you. Isn't it? After all, she picked him; so she can't grumble. Sorry, I shouldn't have said that. Why has she come running to you?"

Ian explained that Mary was asking if he could help her get back into hospital work.

Freda bristled a little. Mrs. Mackenzie had told her how Ian had bent over backwards to make the divorce easy for Mary's sake. And now she was getting a taste of her own medicine, she didn't like it and she was asking Ian for a lump of sugar. What a cheek.

Ian couldn't understand Freda taking it like that. "What should I have done? Said, well too bad, and refused to lift a finger to help her?"

"No, I don't mean that." Freda forced a smile. "I'm glad you told me anyway. Better late. . . ." But her voice was edgy.

Ian explained that he hadn't wanted to spoil their night out. He was thinking of his original plans for this particular evening, which seemed somehow to be going awry.

Bessie brought the coffees, but neither of them noticed.

"Why should it spoil our evening?" Freda suddenly realised Ian had come straight out when she'd called for him. "She was there, wasn't she? When I came round. Why didn't you introduce us? D'you think I can't face up to your ex-wife?"

"That's quite ridiculous. You're making a lot of fuss about nothing."

"Well, if you think it's nothing after the way you've kept quiet about it, I'd like to go. Yes; please take me back, if you don't mind. Now." She pushed back the bentwood chair noisily as she stood.

Bessie could see something was wrong. But what could she do about it? They'd done so much for her. He'd saved her life in fact. It made her sad to see them go so unhappily.

Ian gripped the wheel tightly as he turned the car onto the

road from "Bessie's" car-park. "It never even occurred to me you might want to meet her."

"I didn't say I want to meet her."

"In fact it was Mary who said not to keep you waiting, wasting time introducing her."

"Oh, it was her idea, was it? I see."

"I don't think you do see. Mary and I married too young. I wanted a home, a family. She wanted ... something quite different. She thought Gilbert could give her a good time. But that doesn't make her a monster. Come and see for yourself."

"She's staying the night, I suppose?"

"Well where d'you suggest she sleeps? In the Mersey tunnel?"

The ensuing silence lasted all the way to the Nurses' Home.

Mary was urging Mrs. Mackenzie to go to bed. She could see she was tired. She didn't have to wait up for Ian, did she?

"No. He has his key. Neither of us need stay up."

"Will he bring his girl-friend in? She seemed rather nice. On second thoughts I would like to meet her."

Mrs. Mackenzie said it was most unlikely Ian would bring Freda in. They were both on early duty the following morning. "I'm really very tired myself. I'm going to call it a day." As she went upstairs she added, "I wouldn't be late either, if I were you, Mary. It must have been exacting for you, too."

Ian pulled on the hand-brake outside the Nurses' Home.

"Don't you think you're being just a little bit childish, Freda?"

She put on her jokey smile, which normally he loved. "Must be the wide gap in our ages, then."

Ian caught her arm to stop her getting out until he'd kissed her. But she turned her cheek to his lips.

"See you tomorrow?" he whispered.

Freda turned the door handle. "Course. Be doing your rounds, won't you?"

She slammed the door. They had to be slammed to make them shut properly, but not that hard. Ian gripped the wheel tightly, blew out his cheeks, and drove off.

Ian came into the lounge to find Mary alone. "Your mother

was very tired, so she went to bed, Ian. I thought someone should wait up for you. Nice evening?"

"Yes, thank you. Not quite as planned!"

"Oh, I'm sorry," Mary continued to talk as Ian turned to leave. "Strange, isn't it; you and me under the same roof again. Remember our late-night routine? I locked the front door, you locked the back."

Ian was thinking of Freda, but said, "Yes. Yes, I remember."

"Pity its taken me so long to grow up, Ian. But I have. At long last."

"Well, we'll see what can be done in the morning. When I see the Secretary."

"May I . . . bolt the front door? For old times sake?"

"I already have. When I came in. Good night Mary. Don't worry. Try to get a good night's sleep."

Ian held open the door and Mary went out into the hall.

"Yes. I'll try. Goodnight, Ian."

The telephone rang and Mary picked it up as Ian had gone to secure the back door. "Hello."

Freda was ringing from the public telephone in the Nurses' Home, a suspicion of tears lining her eyes.

"Mrs. Mackenzie, could I have a word with Ian, please?"

A strange cool voice replied. "Mrs. Mackenzie is already in bed. Just a minute, I'll get Ian for you." Then Freda heard: "Ian, love, it's for you," and Ian saying "Thank you, Mary," as she handed him the telephone.

Freda hung up angrily.

Ian turned to Mary. "Funny. Did they say who it was? Emergency, anything like that?"

"No. It was a woman's voice. Just asking for you." Mary knew full well it must be Freda. "They'll ring again if it's important, won't they? Should we wait up, in case?"

Ian wondered if it could be Freda. "No, you go on. Goodnight Mary." Reluctantly Mary went up to bed.

Ian picked up the telephone again. Should he ring the Nurses' Home.

Freda picked up the telephone again. Should she try again? Was she just being childish, as Ian had said?

Freda decided no, she jolly well wasn't; and slammed down the telephone angrily.

Ian decided it was too late to disturb the Home. If it was Freda, why on earth did she hang up on him? He slammed down the telephone angrily.

72

Doris went on and on to Freda about her latest Yank every time they were alone in the Ward kitchen. As they came off the ward she picked up where she'd left off. "I mean, three pairs and he thought he owned me. Okay, they were real silk, but only rejects. Mind you, he was a real card, one laugh after another. We had a smashing time. What's up, Freda?"

At last Doris realised that Freda had just been saying "Yes" and "Really" in the right places. "You seem a bit quiet, have been all day. Something wrong? You and Ian? I'll bet it was that phone call he had. You know; when he couldn't take you home. I knew something was worrying him the moment –"

Freda snapped, "Doris, drop it, please!" and hid her tears by dashing into the Ward corridor, where she collided with Ian as he came off the Ward. Freda mumbled "Sorry" and made to go into the Ward. Ian used his authority unfairly.

"Nurse Ashton."

Freda had to stop, but replied as coldly as she knew how. "Yes, Doctor"

"I want to speak to you a moment."

Ian took her arm and propelled her down the corridor. Staff and patients were passing in and out of earshot, so he opened the linen-room door and he pushed her inside. He snapped on the light and pushed the door shut behind him. They were hemmed in by slatted shelves of Ward linen.

Did you telephone last night? Yes, to say she was sorry if he must know. She had been a bit childish, she admitted. Why had she hung up, then? Was it because Mary answered the telephone? "Don't you trust me, Freda?"

"Yes. I do; course I do. It's just ... well, I can't explain. I'm unhappy about the whole thing, somehow."

"I'm not very good at explaining my feelings either. Maybe this is the best way."

Ian grabbed her with a strength she wouldn't have dreamed he possessed. Her back arched as his arms pulled her waist to his. He kissed her so hard that his lips forced hers apart. If she had wanted to she couldn't have done anything but submit. It was a feeling she'd never experienced before.

When he let her go, he said brusquely, "That's the only way I know to give you some idea how I feel," and he left her alone with the stock of sheets and blankets. She stood in a daze, trying to get her breath back, literally and metaphorically.

73

She tried to shake herself back into the day's routine as she returned to the kitchen. "Doris, love; I'm sorry I snapped." She heard herself apologising.

"No, it was me, Freda. I do go on a bit, I know. Sorry, love."

"No, it wasn't your fault. It was mine." She was thinking more about Ian. "It's me. It must be me. . . ."

When Edwin got home, Harry Porter was reading a bed-time story to John-George and looked much brighter.

As Margaret took his grandson from him to hoick him off to bed, Harry told Edwin he was off back to Chorley.

"Remember Jean and me saving up for a car before the war?" Edwin asked. "One of our dreams that never came to anything. A Ford Popular: £105 ex-works they were, then." Edwin took a manilla envelope from his pocket. "The money hasn't been touched; it might as well do some good instead of lying in the bank." Edwin extracted twenty copperplate-written white fivers. "Pay me back when you can."

Harry was visibly moved. He desperately needed the money but didn't want to take it. And when Edwin slapped the notes in his hand he said, "I'll never be able to repay you, Edwin. What am I saying? of course, I'll repay you; soon as I possibly can. What a thing to say."

They laughed to cover their mutual embarrassment as John came in from work. "Tell us the joke then. I could do with a good laugh after today's lot."

But Harry had put the fivers into his pocket.

John had had another bad day. Margaret came in in time to hear him say: "I was right on the brink of telling Temple just where to stick his Public Health Accounts."

Harry read her face with knowledge that neither John nor Edwin had, and followed her back into the kitchen. "Don't lay a place for me, Margaret. I'm off back now. Er. . . . Did you get the results of your tests?"

"Yes. Positive."

"You don't sound . . . excited about it."

"Not going to help John get out of that job, is it? One more mouth he has to think about. Don't you think he'd have walked out before today, if it hadn't 've been for John-George? And me?"

"Yes, I suppose so. Well, pick the right moment to tell him That's important."

74

Margaret patted her tum. "I will, Harry. Thanks for the advice. Life doesn't stop, for this rotten old war, does it?"

Mrs. Mackenzie had waited patiently for the right moment. But it didn't seem to come. Ian would be home soon, so she decided not to wait any longer. "Mary, I've been trying not to say this all day. At breakfast I could tell something was wrong with Ian. I managed to get out of him that Freda wasn't very happy last night."

"Yes, I got the impression there was something; I've no idea what it was, have you?"

"Yes; I know, Mary. I'm sorry my dear to have to say this, but it's you. Your being here."

"How d'you mean? Oh, does his girl-friend think I've come to try and get him back. She is taking him for granted, isn't she?"

"I asked Ian point-blank if he'd made it quite clear to Freda. That there wasn't the slightest possible chance of that happening. Of your getting him back, I mean."

Mrs. Mackenzie waited for her reaction. Mary's voice betrayed how keen she was to know. "And what did Ian say? When you asked him that?"

"He said he'd left Freda in no doubt about it. No doubt whatsoever. She knows there is no question of it."

Mary felt a chill in her cheeks, which stiffened her forced smile. "I'd hate him to think I'd come between him and the happiness I wasn't able to give him. I think too much of him for that. I must tell him."

"Yes, I would, if I were you, Mary. It might help."

Mary made to go up to her room, but turned at the staircase. "I would have him back, if I could. Like a shot. You know that, don't you?"

"I knew it the moment I saw you at the front door."

As Mary disappeared upstairs, Mrs. Mackenzie heaved a sigh of relief. She'd done what she set out to do. She hoped it was enough to save the day.

David was really mad, taking it out on Edwin and John as he explained bitterly. "No, this chap didn't treat me like something from under a stone, like that other legal twit. He was on the ball. Told me exactly what he wanted me to do. And what Sheila's solicitor insisted I should do, too. Passed on his orders. How about that for cheek?"

Edwin tried to pacify him; without much hope of success, he knew. "You are the guilty party, David, after all."

"I know I am. I'm prepared to admit that in Court. But will the law accept my signed confession? Will they hell. You know what they say I must do? I've got to go through the motions of staying the night with some paid bint. So the solicitors can use it as evidence of adultery. How about that for sheer bloody hypocrisy?"

Edwin was firm. "You can't expect it to be a joy-ride, David. Don't keep complaining. Get it over with, for God's sake."

"You know, Dad, I can't remember when you were on my side. Not once. From the very start. From the night I told you we were going to get married because Sheila was pregnant. It was all my fault, wasn't it. All mine. Well, I'll tell you something for nothing now."

"Oh don't keep going on, David." John escaped to the kitchen.

David was too angry to stop. "No, I will go on; because you ought to know this dad. She'd made up her mind to get me. Whatever. She knew what she was doing, that night in Sefton Park. Exactly what she was up to. I was muggins, make no mistake about that. Muggins."

Edwin picked up the paper. There was no point in answering.

Margaret asked John what that was all about, in the living room.

"Oh, you know; David sounding off again. Never mind him, luv. Give us a kiss." John's arms were round her. They kissed and laughed at the same time.

"John. Not so rough. Mind my back, I need handling gently. In my condition."

"Condition? What condition?"

John looked into her eyes. They told him she was pregnant. He pulled her to him. Was he happy about it, she asked. Of course, he was. Then he suddenly thought about his job. Could he risk giving up the security of Local Government work?

They stayed locked together; Margaret could almost feel what he was thinking.

Ian explained the difficulty he'd had to his mother. It wasn't easy to find a vacancy for an almoner's secretary where Mary could also live in. So many hospital staff were working away

76

from home these days; bomb-damage had made drastic re-
ductions in accommodation; re-building was non-existent. It
could be a week or more before the Hospital Secretary had
any good news. Ian agreed that they didn't want her staying
with them until something did come up for her; but where
could she go meanwhile?

"Ian, love, it hasn't occurred to you, has it? That she came
to get you back? All this kindness and consideration is building up false hopes for her. Don't you see? I've tried to make
it clear but it would be much better coming from you."

"If that's what she thinks, I'll spell it out."

But at that moment Freda arrived. "Could we talk, Ian
please?"

Mrs. Mackenzie left them alone in the lounge.

"Freda. Before you say anything. I'm asking Mary to go."

Freda tried to make it an insignificant piece of news. "Not
because of me. I mean, not on my account, is it?"

Before he could answer, Mary entered. Ian made the introductions; they exchanged a very friendly "Hello" but no more.

Ian began to explain the hospital accommodation problems,
but Mary interrupted him.

"It's very sweet of you, Ian, dear, but I've been thinking.
You remember my friend Pauline? Sister Roberts she was
then; it seems so long ago now. She gave up nursing when her
husband opened that private hotel in Blackpool, remember?
Maybe you don't. Unfortunately, he was badly injured on
D-day. She ran the place whilst he was away, and wrote and
told me that if ever I wanted to, she'd welcome the help. She's
full of Raff boys; they train in the Winter Gardens, she says.
Well, why don't I give that a try? It never occurred to me
until now. Might work very well, solve the problem. Should've
thought of it before, shouldn't I? Well ... we've hardly said
'hello' before it's 'goodbye', Freda."

"Goodbye, Mary. Good luck."

"Thanks. And to you, too." She steeled herself to add: "To
both of you."

As they said goodbye again at the front door, Ian added,
"If it doesn't work out, Mary, you know where I am."

"Oh, don't worry about me. It will, I hope, somehow. But
it's very sweet of you, Ian. Then you always were."

After she had gone, Ian was about to say something like
"Well, all's well that ends well," when Freda said, "You real-

77

ise what you've done? You've given her an open invitation to come back any time she liked."

"Well, she was my wife. If ever I can help her I will. Is that wrong?"

Freda didn't know what to say. Ian did.

"You might as well know why I took you to Bessie's place last night. The whole object of the exercise was ... to ask you to marry me."

Freda was off-balance. "Oh. Was it? Fancy. Sorry if I stopped you. Good job I did, I suppose, now you know me better, or worse rather. I mean look what you'd 've been stuck with. . . ."

"Freda, you're not being rational."

"That's another thing against me, then, I'm not rational."

Ian took hold of her firmly. "Look, I've just been told this afternoon that I have to go away. Tomorrow. For at least three weeks. I don't want to leave things like this."

"Well, d'you think I like it?"

Freda wrenched free and ran out of the house. Ian made to follow her but she didn't even look back. What more could he do to explain. She wasn't going to see it his way. And he couldn't see it hers.

CHAPTER NINE

August 1944

Freda kept hoping she would hear from Ian whilst he was away. But she didn't. And she had no idea where he had gone. It was the longest three weeks of her life. It was of slight comfort when she finally telephoned Mrs. Mackenzie to learn that she didn't know where he'd gone either. Nor had she heard from him.

Life without Ian would be like this? She kept telling herself there had been years when she'd never known he'd existed. But it didn't help her forget him.

Doris tried to take her out of herself, but it was no good. Why hadn't he written? Just a card would have done. Just one line on it. He didn't need to say I'm sorry, even. "What am I saying?" Freda thought. "It's me who should say sorry."

"Sorry? About what?" asked Doris from the other side of a patient's bed.

"Did I say something? Must be thinking aloud." Oh, she'd been so stupid. Why on earth shouldn't Ian have tried to help Mary? Supposing Freda had been married herself; and her ex-husband had come to her, in trouble, knowing she was the only one who could help him. Oh, Freda, you clot; no wonder he hadn't written. You must have driven him up the wall.

"Eh, look!" Doris suddenly said when she straightened up from folding in the blanket corners. "Look what the wind's blown back." Freda turned to where Doris was staring. There was Ian, on his morning rounds with Sister.

"Morning Nurse Ashton, Nurse Jackson," he smiled as he toured the beds. Freda tried hard to read something into the way he said it, but couldn't.

As soon as they got back to the kitchen, Doris said, "He doesn't look any different, any road."

Freda tried to seem off-handed as she turned on the hot-water. "Didn't really notice. What did you expect, sunburn?"

Doris gave an old-fashioned look. She thanked her lucky stars that she never went that daft over any chap she went out with. That'd be the day. No feller was worth it, she knew more of them than Freda did.

She was about to say so when she discovered that Freda had slipped back onto the ward on some pretext.

When duty ended they walked across to the Nurses' Home. Doris couldn't resist, "Don't suppose you'll be staying in to-night."

"Matter of fact I am, Doris. I may pop out for an hour, that's all."

"Not made any arrangements, then? With Ian?"

"We haven't spoken. After his rounds he went down to the Theatre. I haven't seen him since."

By the time Ian got back to the ward after a long operating session, the Night staff were on duty. He telephoned the Home and learned that Nurse Ashton had gone out. So he had a quick meal in the Doctor's dining room and drove straight to the Ashtons.

Freda wasn't there, either. He stayed for a while in case she came in, and got drawn into a debate on the fors and againsts of a National Health Service.

"I think you're getting the wrong idea about it. A lot of people are. It isn't going to be free. We'll pay for it in National Insurance – the suggestion is to include it in the weekly stamp. That means it's not charity, it's a right. We pay whilst we are able. And when we're ill or old the Service is available whether we can afford it or not. For everybody in the land."

Edwin was impressed. "In that case it'll be the first good thing to come out of this war. And you reckon ... when, Ian?"

Margaret interjected. "Doesn't look as though Freda's coming tonight at all."

Ian was glad to get off the hook. "It doesn't, does it? If you don't mind, I've had quite a hectic first day back. I'll ... get off home."

Mrs. Mackenzie had been surprised to see Freda alone. "Didn't you see him at the Hospital?"

"Just about. It's been one of those days."

"He's probably had his meal there. I haven't seen him since first thing. He said he expected cases for surgery would have piled up for him."

"You ... still didn't hear from him whilst he was away?"

"No, I didn't. Then I'm only his mother. Did you ... not?"

"No, he didn't write to me."

"Probably he didn't have time." Mrs. Mackenzie knew it was a lame excuse.

"He told you? Where he'd been? When he got back?"

"No. He didn't actually. Mind you, it was very late."

They heard the front door open. Mrs. Mackenzie told Freda to stay in the lounge. She went into the hall so that when they came face to face, they were alone.

"Hello, Freda."

"Hello ... Ian."

They should have rushed into each other's arms, but they didn't. She thought his eyes looked tired. He thought she looked more beautiful than the memory he'd carried with him for three whole weeks. But neither expressed their thoughts

"Must have had a long session in the theatre?" Freda sympathized.

"Yes. We did. I lost count. Backlog caused it."

"You weren't avoiding me, then. Good."

"Look, don't let's go over it again. Certainly not tonight. I'm too tired."

"You were too tired to write, whilst you were away?" Freda tried to ask lightheartedly, but failed.

"I'm sorry, Freda, this is not the best time to air our problems. Come to dinner tomorrow night. Let's sort it all out then. What d'you say?"

"I see." Freda walked very pointedly into the hall. Ian opened the front door.

"Honestly, Freda. It would be best. I'm out on my feet. If we talk now, I'll get irritable and perhaps we'll say things we don't mean and ... Well, I don't want to make any mistakes, do you?"

Freda hid her true feelings behind a smile. "No. No, of course I don't. Good night, Ian."

As Freda turned onto the pavement she realised he hadn't wanted to kiss her.

As Ian turned away from the front door his mother scolded him. "You might have kissed her. Just to show willing."

"I don't think she really wanted me to."

"You didn't try it to find out, did you?"

Ian sighed from sheer exhaustion. "Yes, I should have, shouldn't I?"

Sefton Briggs had telephoned John Porter to come and see him. John guessed he was on again about that job he's offered him. "He must need someone badly, mustn't he?" he'd said to Margaret.

"You might as well find out what it's about, John. You'll never know, unless you go and find out," was her advice.

John found he was right. Sefton, with his back to the empty firegrate said, "I hope you've given some serious thought to my offer, lad. As I haven't heard a blind word from you, I've taken it you're still thinking. What's the delay? I'll answer any questions or queries."

"It's just that I don't want to jump out of the frying pan, Mister Briggs. How do I know I'll be any happier working in your shop, than where I am now? I'm no more interested in printing and stationery than I am in Public Health Accounts, to be frank."

"Not in the shop, lad, not serving behind the counter. I'm planning an expansion of the retail side of our business; and what I need is a good account's clerk. That's where you'd fit in. Didn't I make that clear to you at the time?"

"I can't remember that you did. And the other thing is

81

about the regulations. The Control of Employment Regulations. Would I be allowed to make the move? If I decided I wanted to."

"Now that's one thing you don't worry your head about. I've one or two good friends in the right places and they'll ..." He paused to phrase it vaguely. "They'll get round that problem. Legitimately, of course." Sefton lit his pipe, sucked it into life. "What else worries you? Anything?"

"Well, I'm not sure I've got enough experience for an accounts job."

"That's what you're doing now, isn't it?"

"Yes, but I'm in an office with others and I work on the same section all the time. And there's always someone to refer to if I've a query."

"Gordon Temple; yes, he's a member of my club. I had a word with him. He said you ought to make a move."

"You mean, he doesn't think I do my work properly?"

"No, he didn't say that, lad. He said you do it quite well. But he can tell your heart isn't in it. So if you work there under that liability, you'd eat this. Be virtually your own boss you know. Do things your own way. Be a big fish in a little puddle, instead of t'other way round."

"I know you're trying to help me, Mister Briggs, and it's very kind of you. But you are helping yourself too, aren't you? What I mean is, with all due respect, you need someone badly for this job, don't you?"

"Course I do. I make no secret of it. But it's in our mutual interest, that's what you've got to bother about."

"How would it be if I suggested someoné else? Someone with more experience than me."

"Oh? Who's that, then?"

John's answer made Sefton raise his eyebrows.

Freda arrived at the Mackenzies' for dinner. She stopped out of sight of the house and checked the time. She was determined not to be late. But not to be early either; to seem overanxious would be even worse. She was right on the dot. Good.

But Ian wasn't. Mrs. Mackenzie explained that he'd telephoned to say he'd be late. He was still working to clear the operating theatre backlog. Freda hoped that was why she hadn't seen him all day.

"We won't wait for him to offer us a sherry. You will have one, Freda? I'm going to."

A sherry became two. And then three, as they tried to kill the time with small talk. Mrs. Mackenzie began to show some irritation. "It's a good job I planned cold cuts, isn't it?"

The wine reached Freda's tongue. She suddenly said, "I suppose he is coming; some time tonight."

Mrs. Mackenzie poured herself yet another sherry. She so wanted tonight to go right. It meant as much to her as she hoped it did to Freda; as she knew it did to Ian. It wasn't going very well as yet.

John had telephoned his father to come over. Something he wanted to talk about which he couldn't discuss on the telephone. "And don't bring mum, for God's sake."

When Harry Porter arrived he was met by Edwin. "Things any better, Harry? I hope. It's all right to talk, John isn't home yet. About his financial problem," Edwin was implying.

"Well, I er ... paid off the arrears on the mortgage. Thanks to you. But ... I'm worried, Edwin. I don't see how I can avoid getting into the same mess. I'm still not making ends meet and the payments are bound to fall behind again. I didn't think of that until I'd paid your hundred quid over. I can't see how I'm ever going to be able to pay you back."

Edwin hated hearing Harry tear his heart out. It was a lot of money but he would have gladly kissed it good-bye to get Harry out of his troubles. To learn that it didn't was distressing. But he said hopefully, "Well, Harry, something'll turn up, it's bound to. It always does, given time. The darkest hour ... and all that; you know. How are you in yourself?"

"Oh, a little better, if anything. Any idea what John wants me about? He isn't in trouble himself, is he?"

"I don't think so. He still hates the Town Hall, but he's been to see Sefton about working for him. I'm not too happy about that, unless he treats it as a stepping-stone to something better. You never know in this world, Harry, you never know, do you? So take heart."

Margaret had been watching for John's arrival by leaving the kitchen door open. She waylaid him in the hall.

"Has Dad come?"

"Yes, but I've something I want to tell you before you see him. I'm not having a baby. After all." Margaret explained that her Doctor hadn't been quite satisfied with the tests. They were only eighty per cent accurate anyway. He'd checked again and it was a false alarm.

"In fact, love, he told me a bit more. He said ... possibly due to the air-raid accident, he couldn't be sure. John-George might never have any brothers or sisters."

John took it very well. "Well ... that's life isn't it. But why did you want me to know before I see Dad?"

"Because it's a point, isn't it? To take into account, I mean. You've not got the responsibilities you thought you might have. We've only John-George to think of now."

"Only? Anyway it doesn't change anything. If we try hard enough we might prove the doctor wrong."

Margaret pushed him playfully towards the living-room. "Go on with you."

John was glad to see his Dad looked a bit brighter. He still had a yellowish-pallor but his eyes were not so dull.

"I've got good news for you, Dad. Well, I think it'll be good."

"Oh? What's that, John?"

"Mister Briggs – Margaret's Uncle Sefton – has offered me a job, as an account's clerk. Not a bad job, the pay's better than I'm getting now."

"So you're taking it John, are you?" Edwin hoped.

"No. I told him I knew just the man for it."

"Who's that?"

"You, Dad. You know more about bookkeeping than I do. I only know Public Health Accounts."

Edwin saw that Harry was moved at his son's selfless gesture.

"That's very good of you, John, but it's not your Dad he's offering the job to. What did Sefton say, when you suggested your father?"

"He said he'd like to talk to you about it. So I suggested you came over. He'll be here about seven, to discuss it."

When Ian at last arrived home he looked even more tired than he had the night before.

"What's happened?" Freda and Mrs. Mackenzie asked, almost in unison.

"A patient died. Septic womb. We fought it all the way. But ... we lost her. And the baby."

Neither Freda nor Mrs. Mackenzie knew what to say. Suddenly the sherry's effect had disappeared.

Mrs. Mackenzie broke the silence. "Well, the dinner's not spoiled so ... we'll eat, shall we?"

84

There was very little table conversation. They found they were ravenously hungry; until then, they hadn't noticed.

John's good intentions went sadly awry. Sefton Briggs took one look at Harry and decided he didn't want an invalid on his hands. But he said, "No, I've set my heart on John. I've had good reports from his present employer, Mr. Porter. I could map out his future in the Briggs family business. You do see the point, don't you?"

Harry did see it. He urged John to take the job.

Edwin knew that Sefton was, as usual, turning the situation to his own advantage. He wanted a young man with the energies to get through a lot of work. Sefton had used Harry to put the pressure on John.

But it back-fired. John dearly wanted his father to have the job and told Sefton it was that or it remained vacant. He wasn't interested in it for himself.

Sefton left in a huff. Without an account's clerk.

Mrs. Mackenzie had left Ian and Freda in the lounge. "I'll do the washing up; and on my own." Ian remarked to Freda on the significance, knowing his mother was usually the world's greatest expert in delegating domestic chores.

The sparkle came back into Freda's voice. "Why? What's she think we're going to do? Alone." Her eyes were mischievous.

"I haven't the slightest idea. Steal the silver, such as there is. Or something even more diabolical."

"Such as?"

Ian was at one end of the settee. He reached out gently and pulled Freda round so that her head rested in his lap. He repositioned a wisp of her hair which had become misplaced by the manoeuvre.

Freda probed very gently, delicately almost. "Ian. Where did you go?"

"I'm afraid I can't tell you."

The jokiness returned, low key, but lighthearted. "Oh. A military secret, is it?"

"Well, yes it is. They suddenly needed ... people like me. We were sworn to secrecy."

"Gynaecologists? You're pulling my leg."

"Don't forget that I qualified as a surgeon, first."

"You mean, the Second Front? They're bringing back more casualties than they can cope with?"

"I said nothing about casualties. Let's say there's been fierce fighting in one or two hot-spots."

Freda wanted to be proud of him. "You've been to France? Into the battle area?"

"For a short while they needed extra hands. Surgeons' hands, particularly. The crisis is over. And I haven't said a single word about it, have I?"

"You couldn't write to me? Or your Mother? Because it was top-secret, where you were?"

"Don't ask questions. If you want to know, I went off with this smashing blonde and she took up every moment of my time, day and night, and said if I wrote a single line to any of my hundreds of girl friends back here, she'd . . ."

Freda put her hand on his mouth. Ian took it in his slender fingers and kissed it. His serious face came on almost imperceptibly. He spoke as if he were thinking aloud.

"I've failed once, Freda. I want to be certain that I don't the next time. Particularly as it would be you I'd hurt this time. I must be very, very sure that the reasons why I failed no longer exist. And never will exist, for you and me."

"You know what they say? If at first . . ." Freda whispered.

"You believe in that old proverb?"

"In our case, yes. I think I do. Don't you?"

He never did say, "Will you marry me?" or anything remotely like that. One minute they were "just good friends", the next they were engaged.

More precisely they were in each other's arms so oblivious of the world's existence that, if Mrs. Mackenzie had walked in and said "The war's over", they wouldn't have heard a word.

CHAPTER TEN

September 1944

On "Freda-Day" minus-one preparations for the wedding stood life on its head at the Ashtons. Edwin spent every spare moment surreptitiously preparing a speech. "What I say will come from the heart," he told Helen in confidence. "But unless I think it out carefully and then work at it until it's exactly what I want to say, it won't, will it? That's how Churchill does it, they say. And you know what he can do with a speech."

Helen had come to offer general assistance. "Anything I can do for anybody, just shout." But preparations were in advance, so that Helen's kind contributions created anxieties where they didn't exist. "You've got gloves to go with that outfit, have you Margaret?"

"Yes. I think so. Now where did I put them?"

"Does your suit need a bit of a press, Edwin? Give it to me."

"It has been pressed, hasn't it, Margaret? I didn't notice it needed it. Yes, maybe it does."

"What about the flowers, has anyone a list of who has what?" Helen was enjoying herself. "Would you like me to take charge of them, when they arrive?"

It was all intended to see that everything went smoothly. And had the opposite effect.

On the evening-before-the-big-day Ian had brought home a tin of dried-egg and set it amongst the wedding presents displayed on the Mackenzie sideboard. "From a grateful patient on the occasion of my marriage," he explained to his mother. "Has Derek telephoned?"

Derek Turnbull had been Ian's best man when he married Mary. He had promised to ring Ian that afternoon and as he hadn't telephoned the Hospital, Ian presumed he knew only their home number. But Mrs. Mackenzie said there had been no call from him. Ian and Derek had worked at the same hospital in Blackburn, and as Ian's other eligible friends were abroad winning the war, he had asked Derek to stand again.

Mrs. Mackenzie had not liked his choice. She was in favour of a complete change from his first wedding. Everything else was: here in Liverpool; the ceremony in a registry office instead of that old church; and what a different girl. Yes, Derek Turnbull again was a mistake in her opinion. But what other choice did Ian have?

As if Helen's "helping out" were not causing enough chaos, Tony Briggs turned up; he'd managed to get leave for the wedding. Margaret prevailed on him to take Freda, Sheila and Doris for a "final-fling drink", as she put it. Tony complied with a knowing wink.

Several "Green Goddesses" later they were in a sing-song mood. "Swing on a Star", then, with special reference to

Tonys uniform, "Sailor, who are you dreaming of tonight?"
Freda snuggled up to Tony to render "Just a little fond affec-
tion." Doris threatened to tell Ian to call the wedding off and
Sheila couldn't stop giggling. It was the feminine equivalent
of "the last night out with the lads."

Sheila hadn't had such a carefree time for years. "D'you
know who they say was somewhere in the North West last
week? Singing to the Yanks – Bing Crosby. I'd loved to have
seen him, wouldn't you? To have been there listening to him."

Doris was the expert, "Just you, Sheila? With the U.S. Air
Force? You wouldn't have been safe, Bing Crosby or no Bing
Crosby. Any road, the blokes I've been out with say this new
crooner's better. Frank Sinatra his name is."

Sheila spoke for all. "Better than Bing? Can't be. Frank
who?"

They listened whilst Doris explained the impossible. This
Frank Sinatra was the sexiest singer ever; girls fainted when
he sang. His records were already selling more than Bing's in
the States. Doris's boy-friends should know.

She would have gone on about it, but Freda preferred another chorus of "Swing on a star" to a lecture on the latest
crooners. Nobody could last like Bing any way ... "Carry
moonbeams home in a jar." Freda was developing a slight
slur in her voice.

Tony told her she'd had quite enough, and not so loud.
She linked her arm through his and looked into his eyes; all
good fun the "Green Goddess" doing the talking. "Well, you'll
look after me, cousin Tony, won't you? You'll take me home?
After all, if I'm going to be married tomorrow ..."

"If, the bride says. What a thing to say!" Sheila pouted in
mock disapproval. Tony put his arm round Freda's shoulder,
as she swayed towards him.

Freda defended herself. "Well, I'm entitled to a last romantic night out, with the boy of my childhood dreams, aren't I?"

Tony searched her face to learn how much she was joking.
It was hard to tell, the alcohol made her eyes sparkle even
more than usual. Tony reflected how he'd always felt about
Freda: a super girl for some lucky man one day; that day
now so nearly here. This had better stop before it went too
far. "Come along girls. There's tomorow to think about.
You've all to look your best."

There were mock groans all round. Freda looked up at him.

"Just one for the road, Tony. Please. It's a very long road I'm setting out on, don't forget." She sounded slightly regretful. "As a special favour to me." She began singing "Auld Lang Syne" quietly, sadly.

Tony couldn't refuse her. "All right. One for the long road."

Sefton's way of showing he approved the marriage was a material gesture. He told Edwin that he intended to pay for the reception himself. He didn't offer, he took it for granted Edwin would say, "That's very nice of you, Sefton. Thanks."

Edwin did say that, but then added, "But it's my privilege. You're only her Uncle. It's me that's her father. If you don't mind."

Sefton couldn't understand. Turning down his offer? Refusing good money?

Edwin couldn't understand Sefton either. Did he really think he'd let him take away the pleasure of giving his daughter her wedding reception?

They would never understand one another.

When at last Derek Turnbull telephoned it was from London, where he'd had to go urgently. His father had been killed that morning by a flying-bomb. It had cut-out over Waterloo Bridge. A few moments later all that remained of Turnbull's offices was a vast hole in the ground.

So Ian had to apply himself to the question of a new best man. He decided to ask Tony Briggs.

Tony and the girls made their way home via Sheila's, where they dropped her off, and made sure Doris caught the last tram to the Nurses' Home. Freda was staying her last spinster-night at home. At the door she had difficulty getting her latch-key out of her bag. Tony found it for her.

"Thanks for a smashing time, Tony. Been great fun."

"Quite like the old days."

"Yes. I had a crush on you, in the old days. Don't think I ever dared tell you that before, did I?"

"No. Never. In your gymslip, you mean?"

"Well, yes. And after I'd left school. It was a real secret crush. Burning inside me." She giggled, then became serious. "I did. Honest." On impulse Freda moved closer to him.

"Now she tells me." Tony moved closer, too.

The kiss went on so long that they broke and looked surprised at each other. Freda sounded sad. "Nice to think back before the war, isn't it? Happy days."

"Yes. Down memory lane. Do we remember it better than it really was? I wonder. Probably we do."

Freda put her key in the lock at the second attempt. "Oh, I don't know. It was romantic. Very." She pushed open the door, whispered, "Good-bye to romance," and was gone.

Tony walked away thinking, "If I'd have known she had that much of a crush on me . . ." Poor Freda. Was she scared she was shutting romance out of her life for ever when she closed that door on her last unmarried night?

On "Freda-Day" the Registrar was doing a brisk trade in weddings. As Tony ushered the Ashtons, the Mackenzies, the Briggs and a few friends into the Registry Office corridor there were two weddings queuing ahead of them. But almost immediately the first party were called in.

"Next!" would be a G.I. Sergeant and his very-pregnant bride-to-be.

Sheila, one of the first to arrive, said that, unless the Registrar got a move on, he might have a birth to register at the same time.

Tony was relieved that Sheila wasn't finding Freda's day evoking memories of her own marriage.

Sheila thanked him. "I was very grateful Tony, for that solicitor. I don't know what I'd have done . . ."

"Good. If this gets a bit much, let me know, and I'll help you slip out."

"No, I'm all right. I thought it might upset me, but it isn't doing. I'm – what is it they call boxers? – punch-drunk. I can't be hurt any more."

Edwin proudly helped Freda into the hired car. "You look marvellous, love. Sight for sore eyes." He had always visualised her in white satin and having to tuck in a billowing veil, but it didn't seem to matter.

"Well, if I don't today I never will."

He got in beside her. "All your doubts gone?"

"Did I have doubts?"

"Oh no, not much. A good job Ian was persistent. Feel nervous?"

"Course I do. It's the end of part of my life."

"And the start of another, Freda. Right, driver." The car moved off.

"Oh yes, I meant that, too."

"You do love him?"

"What a time to ask. Course I do. Just because I didn't jump at him. It's such a serious step, Dad, it frightened me. If some of our family had given a bit more thought – Sorry, I wasn't meaning you and . . ." She stopped, embarrassed.

"You mean, you've learned by our mistakes. Seeing what some of us made, or didn't make, out of our marriages."

"Remember when Ian went away? Those three weeks? I know it sounds corny, but it taught me I just couldn't live without him. But it still scares me."

The car turned into the Crescent. Mrs. Mackenzie was at the bay window.

"Ian. She's here."

"I'm ready."

Mrs. Mackenzie kissed him lightly. "I haven't put any lipstick on you, have I? No. Good. That would never do. Now, I've not told you this until now because I want no argument. After the wedding I'm going back to Bournemouth."

"For a holiday?"

"To live. Oh, I'll call back for a visit sometimes. But not to take root again. It doesn't work. Mother-in-laws should be neither seen nor heard; except in small doses. I've been arranging it very quietly; it's all fixed up. Go along, there's no time to argue."

Before Ian could say a word the hired-car driver knocked on the door. Mrs. Mackenzie had timed her announcement perfectly.

Uncle Sefton's face fell as he saw the crowded Registry Office corridor. "I think I'd rathe've gone to church. Not even a vestry here. More like queuing for t' pictures." Then he saw the mother-to-be. "Aye, a church wedding's more proper, I think. Much more proper, from the look of things."

The American and his fiancee were called in to legitimize her unborn child. But before their ceremony had begun two muscle-bound "Snowdrops" – white-helmeted U.S. Military Policemen – elbowed their way down the corridor and into the Registrar's presence.

Ian and Freda arrived behind them with Edwin and Mrs. Mackenzie.

The unmarried father was escorted unceremoniously and unprotesting from the Registrar's Office to the waiting M.P. jeep. The mother-to-be wept floods of tears as she saw her loved-one driven off.

"What's happened?" Margaret asked her.

They could just make out between her sobs that Jake was under twenty-one and hadn't his parents' consent, nor his Commanding Officer's.

The Registrar's assistant opened the door again, looking rather less on top of her job than when she'd last done so. "You're next, are you? Mackenzie-Ashton? We might as well carry on. In spite of the ... altercation. It's happened before, you know. I think there's room for everyone." Wartime weddings rarely had many friends and relations as witness.

Ian and Freda were manoeuvred into a church-like position, opposite the Registrar, seated at his desk. As the ceremony began, Freda's mind stayed with the poor girl left crying outside.

"You are Ian James Mackenzie?"

The poor girl didn't seem to have anyone to console her.

"Yes."

"You are Freda Ashton?"

Perhaps someone in the party could have stayed with her. Sobbing her heart out she was. "Yes."

The Registrar's assistant, in spite of her conscious effort, failed to bring feeling into words she recited several times every working day. As she droned on, Freda looked out of the corner of her eyes at Ian. He was looking at her the same way. Did this official ritual mean any more to him than it did to her, she wondered.

As Tony was asked for the ring, Freda's mind wandered again. Would that poor girl ever marry her Yank? "... to remind you of the solemn and binding character of the vows you are about to make. Marriage, according to the laws of this country, is the union of one man with one woman. ..." Did the people who made the laws of this country believe that a soldier didn't understand it was the union of one man and one woman? Just because he was under twenty-one?

When Ian "solemnly declared" that he didn't know of any lawful impediment, Freda realised it was as old-hat as the church service she'd read in her mother's old prayer-book. Grandpa Briggs had given it to Jean on her twenty-first birthday, it said on the fly-leaf.

"Freda". Her name jerked her back to the ceremony. She "solemnly declared", but lack of concentration caused her to say that she didn't know of any "unlawful impediment". She was asked to repeat the words from the beginning. This time she didn't know of any "lawful" impediment. So they must consider the words important after all, she thought, in spite of the way they said them.

But that poor girl in the corridor; what would happen to her?

After the reception Mr. and Mrs. Mackenzie were given a confetti send-off, as they got into Ian's little saloon.

Freda threw out her bouquet, as custom demanded. Tony had to catch it to prevent its hitting him. He watched the back of the car recede, as he handed the flowers to Doris. It seemed as if Freda had aimed it in her direction.

CHAPTER ELEVEN

February 1945

The last person Sheila had expected to call was Freda. She had not seen her since her wedding and that was five months ago. She remembered her own honeymoon year when she and David had lived in a world peopled only by themselves. How things had changed.

Freda looked at Sheila's meagre rooms with dismay. They looked pokey and gloomy, in contrast with the Edwardian grandeur of the Mackenzie residence.

"Yes, thank you Sheila, we had a lovely honeymoon. Short, mind you. Ian could only take two days off."

Where was it they went? Well, Scarborough was as good as anywhere. As far as one could go in that direction in wartime.

Freda realised that Sheila wasn't trying to tidy the place because she had called. She was packing: children's toys in an old linen-basket, clothes in a large cardboard box.... "Are you packing, Sheila?"

"Doing my level best to. I can't stand this place much longer. Look at it. The Council would condemn it, if there wasn't a war on."

Sheila admitted that she had nowhere definite to move to.

It looked as if she thought the act of beginning to pack would cause some available place to materialise, where she would like to start a new home. Just like that. It was so pathetic that it disturbed Freda.

"Sheila love. It's not much use packing 'till you've found somewhere to go, is it?"

"No. But it's a start. I've got to get out of here, Freda, or ... I dunno what I'll do." Sheila seemed so on edge, her nerve-endings so close to the surface, that Freda felt something had to be done about it. There and then.

"Tell you what; I've an idea. Come and stay with us for a few days. It's no further for you to get to work. Make a bit of a change for you."

"No, Freda. Three's a crowd; Ian wouldn't want me around the place, would he?"

"He's not a bit like that. Anyway, why shouldn't I invite a friend? More than a friend; my brother's wife, for heaven's sake."

"Not for long I shan't be, now."

"Oh, it is going through then, the divorce? No last minute change-of-heart?"

"No, none whatever. My solicitor's getting in touch with that girl, you know the one who had David's baby. But it does take time."

"Well then, what d'you say? I'd like you to come, Sheila, honest I would."

"You are sure Ian won't mind?"

"I told you; he won't mind a bit."

"All right then. Thanks." Sheila stopped packing.

But Ian didn't take to the idea readily. "I'm not quite clear, Freda, what you're saying. You're going to ask Sheila Ashton to come and stay with us? If it's all right with me? Or you have already invited her? And she's coming."

"Yes."

"Yes, you have? And she is?"

"Yes. You've no objection, surely."

"No, I've no objection. Except I don't find her easy to talk to. I always get the feeling she's going to burst into hysterics any minute. . . ."

"Is that surprising? The way my brother's treated her?"

"No. But it makes conversation a little . . . difficult."

"Leave the conversational chat to me, then. She's really

94

down, Sheila is. Hit rock-bottom, she has. If I can chirp her up a bit. .... It's the least I can do. I'm surprised you don't see that."

"I do. I said. I've no objection."

"Doesn't sound it." A row loomed on the horizon.

"I just happen to think you've gone about it the wrong way round, that's all." Ian tried to prevent the situation degenerating.

"How d'you mean? Do we have a right and a wrong way of inviting people?"

"I mean the wrong way for us. Didn't it occur to you to ask if I minded first? Before you invited Sheila?"

"No, it didn't, frankly."

"Why not?"

"Because I never dreamed for a minute that you'd object."

"I don't object; how many more times? But I'd've liked you to ask me first."

"If you don't object what was the point of asking you? If it had been someone I knew you'd object to, I would've asked you first, of course."

Ian began to realise he wasn't going to get anywhere. "I see. Fine. Let's leave it at that." He made to leave the lounge.

"If you really don't want her here, just say. And I'll put her off."

"That's the very point I'm trying to make. Don't you see it's too late, now you've asked her. You can't put her off without hurting her."

"You really don't want her to come, do you? To be honest." Ian took her shoulders as if to shake some sense into her.

"I don't mind. I really don't mind. .... Oh, let's drop it."

As the door closed behind him, Freda tried to understand why he'd gone on so. And could think of no other reason than that he really didn't want her to come, but he wouldn't admit it. Why not, for heaven's sake? Anyway Sheila was coming, and that was that.

The Solicitor's clerk found Sheila's front door barred. His knock was answered by Sheila calling to him that it didn't open and would he go four doors to the left, turn down the back-entry and round to the backyard.

An old wireless-set was distorting Alvar Liddell's six o'clock news-voice so much that it jarred on her nerves. "Eight hundred planes of Bomber Command have carried out a massive raid on Dresden. Extensive damage was inflicted on military installations."

It flashed momentarily across Sheila's mind that David was probably involved, as she switched-off and let in the Solicitor's clerk. She had been doing more wishful-thinking packing.

"Are you changing your address, Mrs. Ashton? You will advise us when you do, won't you? We must keep our records up-to-date. You can imagine what a job it is in war-time. People moving about all the time, and it's all extra work you know, creates all sorts of problems. Now, I'll come straight to the point, if I may, because it all takes time, doesn't it? Mister Osgood – the partner you saw – asked me to call on my way home. It isn't out of my way, well, not more than about a minute-and-a-half. Where was I? Oh yes. Mister Osgood was wondering, as he's had no reply to his letter to Mrs. Gartside – the er ... other woman – nor to the follow-up: we do that automatically you see, it comes up in my diary if there's no reply. We enclose a copy of the original letter, asking whether it had been received. D'you follow, Mrs. Ashton?"

She didn't entirely, but it didn't seem to matter. "Yes, I follow."

"So as we haven't had a reply, Mister Osgood was wondering whether perhaps she's written to you direct. Mrs. Gartside that is. Has she? Written to you, I mean?"

"No, I haven't heard from her. I'm not sure she has my address anyway. What would she write to me about?"

"Oh, you never know, some people hate writing to solicitors. She may have preferred to tell you. That she is prepared to make a statement for your divorce proceedings. On the other hand she may have written you a vitriolic letter saying how dare you put your solicitors on to her. You never know with people."

"I don't suppose her husband likes the idea of her admitting anything."

"Well, if she does write – whatever she says, or doesn't say as the case may be – Mister Osgood would be grateful if you'd let him know immediately. Bringing the relevant document with you, of course."

Sheila tried not to smile as she listened to him talking like a solicitor's letter. "Of course. I will."

"Well, I'll be going then. I mustn't take up any more of your valuable time."

"Sorry you had to come round the back. I've had to bung up the front door because it gets the North winds. It really needs a man on the job and my husband ... well, you know, don't you."

"I understand, yes. Well, goodnight Mrs. Ashton. Don't hesitate to refer to us if we can be of the slightest assistance. Goodnight."

As soon as he had gone, Sheila began to wonder. She went to the front door and dragged away the chest of drawers which helped keep out the draught. Behind it there were three letters which must have slipped down from the letter box.

The top one was from Mrs. Thomas. Peter and Janet were so enjoying the snow. The second was a note from the Council; some form or circular she didn't understand or want to bother about. The last was from someone whose writing she didn't recognise. At the bottom of the second page it was signed "Peggy Gartside (Mrs.)."

She ran out into the backyard; but the little man in the black coat and striped trousers had gone. She started to read the letter, as she walked slowly back into the scullery.

> Wildhill Farm,
> Nr. Greenfield,
> Oldham, Lancs.
> 19.2.45.

Dear Mrs. Ashton,

I hope you will forgive me for replying to you instead of your solicitors. I was able to find your address in an old diary. I remembered making a note of it when I knew David. He said it was in case anything happened to him. I don't know what he meant, really, because, if something had, I could not have very well written to you, could I? He said that you did not know about me but that you would not be surprised if you did.

Well, now, with reference to your solicitor's request re your divorce. I am very sorry for all that you must be going through. And I sincerely hope that everything will work out for you all right, in the end. It always does, you know. At least that is what Tom, my husband, and I have found out. Please take comfort from that in your hour of need.

My little girl June was a bit of a problem, but we finally
sorted it out and we now have a new life, the three of us,
at this little farm. (See above address). Do you know this
part of the country? It is pretty bleak in winter. But any
time you are this way we would be pleased to see you.
That is if you wanted to come, of course.

My husband Tom, and my little darling June are the
most important thing in the world. I would like to help
you, of course, but I am sure you will understand that I
cannot do anything to destroy what we have saved from
the mess I was in. And I am sure you would not want me
to. So I am afraid there is nothing I can add.

Peggy Gartside (Mrs.).
Yours sincerely,
Hoping this finds you well,

Sheila didn't expect her knock on the Ashtons' door to be
answered by Tony Briggs. He was home on short leave again,
making his usual call.

"Hello, Sheila. They've got a visitor; Marjorie, that school-
teacher friend of Margaret's. Who did you want to see?"

"Oh, hello Tony; no-one particular. Just ... after a bit of
advice, that's all."

"Would I do? Come in the kitchen. I volunteered to wash
up. They're getting too deep into politics for my liking."

Marjorie had taken the floor and was in full spate. "We
intend to fight this election on all counts. We stand for freedom to do what is right, and by that we don't mean Right with
a capital 'R'. We want the reforms that are crying out to be
made; irrespective of party, creed or religion or anything. The
trouble is the rank apathy. Getting people to work for the
cause."

Margaret was pragmatic. "They haven't all got your enthusiasm, Marjorie, that's the trouble."

Edwin was practical. "You should get some new volunteers
now that the Home Guard's been disbanded. Several of them'll
find time on their hands, and want to join something else; if
only to get away from their wives for an evening or two."

John was sceptical. "That's not the sort of recruit you want,
though, is it? What a reflection, that people don't feel strongly
enough. There's so much wrong with things the way they are.
Can't they see it?"

Marjorie wasn't slow to seize the opportunity. "Then what about you, John? We need a new Treasurer. That would be a very useful contribution."

Margaret encouraged him. "Why not, John? You know about accounts."

Edwin supported her. "Give you an interest, John. Something to stretch your mind more than that job you're always grumbling about."

John resisted. "That's no reason to take up a cause. You have to believe in it. Passionately. I've discovered I do. We must come back to something better than my father did after the last war. And that's worth working for."

Marjorie applauded. "We could do with a few speeches as heartfelt as that at our meetings. The Treasurer doesn't just keep the books, you know. He's an executive of the committee, too."

Margaret wanted John to be sure. "D'you think you'd stick at it, John?"

"Why not? I don't change my mind as easily as that. Anyway, I've been thinking about this a lot. I've had time to. Look at Uncle Sefton. Never gone without a thing, has he? Always knows someone who knows someone who can get a bit of extra on the side. In other words, more than his share. I don't suppose he's ever had to make do with his fair ration of anything."

Margaret reminded John that Sefton sometimes brought them little extras. John had not refused the bacon that morning. Or even questioned where it came from.

"I didn't know, did I? If you'd 've told me I'd 've gone without. I would. I bloody would."

Politics at the Ashtons ranged from the general to the particular. As the subject should.

The washing-up was finished almost neck-and-neck with Sheila's story. "So I took the letter to Mister Osgood and he said he needed her to admit that her child was David's. But she hadn't done that in the letter. And she didn't intend to."

Tony was thinking hard, his hand poised to close the crockery-cupboard door. "Well, Sheila, the great thing about listening to advice is that you don't have to take it. Mine is that there's only one thing to do. You need her admission and if she's as sorry for you as you say she sounds in her letter, you might just be able to convince her. I mean if you

99

went and talked to her. Of course, it means you'd have to . .. maybe see David's child. And that might be a bit tough to take. But. . . . Yes, I think so. Even if it is. I'd take her up on her invitation."

"Oh, I don't think she meant to talk about it."

"Well, you have her address? I'd do my damnedest to talk her into making a statement that's going to get you that divorce."

"Yes, I see what you mean. But I don't fancy it, you know, meeting her face to face. Talking to her. And David's kid there, too."

"It depends how badly you really want a divorce. It's a good test for you, isn't it?"

"Yes. It is. It's the only way of sorting it out, I see that."

Tony closed the cupboard door. "I can't see what else you can do that would help."

"Yes, you're right Tony. Thanks." Sheila had made up her mind. She did want her divorce that badly.

Freda took Sheila's cheap attache-case from her and set it down in the hall. "We'll go up to your room in a minute. We're in here."

Ian put down the evening paper to say "Hello". But as Freda did most of the chatting, telling Sheila how his mother was getting on in Bournemouth, hospital news and, inevitably, Doris's latest G.I. boy-friend, he went back to reading the latest news of the war.

But he noted how Sheila looked around the room; how its size seemed to dwarf her. He tried to put her at her ease. "This is big for two. Make a better nursing home really."

Freda was quick to counter. "Not whilst we're living in it, Ian. And I don't want to move out."

Sheila was still impressed with the size. "I'll bet it takes some cleaning though, Freda."

"It's a bit bigger than you're used to, that's all." Freda passed it off lightly and left for the kitchen.

"Your place is smaller I take it, Sheila?"

"Oh yes. Much." Sheila put her hands between her knees and looked around the room yet again.

"You're very wise. I'd be happier in something like that myself."

Sheila realised he had no idea what her "place" was like. She couldn't resist replying: "Well, I'm moving out, soon as

I find something else; so it's coming vacant if you want it. I'll give you the address if you're interested."

"Oh well, yes, I would like to have a look."

Freda returned and Sheila winked at her. "My place, Freda. Suit you two perfectly, wouldn't it?"

Freda played along with the joke. "Oh. Yes. It would. Absolutely down to the ground."

When Ian had gone to get ready for duty – the Mackenzies were, unfortunately, on different duty-periods – the girls roared with laughter.

"You'll have to tell him I was pulling his leg, Freda. I daren't, now."

"I'm not going to tell him. I'd like him to see how some people have to live. Do him good."

David had been trying the back door when Mrs. Duffy, next door, looked over the backyard fence.

"Mrs. Ashton's gone away, don't ask me where, she never tells me nothing. Oh, it's you, is it? Well, don't make no difference. I still don't know nothing." She wiped her nose on her apron.

"Hasn't she left the key with you, Mrs. Duffy?"

"Well, yes, she has that. But she didn't say nothing about you coming, or giving it to you if you did."

"I'd like to get in, just the same, thanks."

She got the key and made to open the door for him. But David took it. "Thanks. I'll put it through your letter-box when I go. If she's not back."

First thing David saw was the signs of packing. Naturally he wondered. Then he saw the letter from Mrs. Gartside behind an ornament on the mantelpiece. He had no qualms about reading it.

He smiled; what a nice letter. Not surprising; super kid, Peggy. He was glad she was happy. She deserved to be. She was quite a girl. Especially in bed.

David had just copied out Peggy's address and pocketed the paper when Ian arrived. He stopped dead as he realised he'd had his leg pulled. He explained to David and invited him back with him. It was hard to believe that Sheila was still living in a place like this. Or that David allowed her to, in spite of their differences. But Ian knew better than to interfere between man and wife.

101

Sheila had to take the train to Manchester, change for Oldham then get a bus. The conductress pointed across the fields to the old drystone farmhouse. Sheila trudged down the unmade farm road and through the slush of the farmyard. She came face to face with Peggy as she came out to feed the chickens. Somehow, although they'd never met, they knew each other.

"Peggy Gartside?"

Peggy smiled, welcoming but wary. She was pretty even in rough working clothes. "You're Sheila, aren't you?"

"Yes. Different world this, from Liverpool; all these lovely fields. Reminds me of when I visited Peter and Janet. They're my two. Evacuated; North Wales."

Peggy took her into the flag-stoned kitchen. Yes, she knew about her children. It seemed David had told her everything; about Freda too. But that was when her baby was on the way. Before that, she hadn't known he was married, even. Sheila believed her: that was David all right.

No, Peggy wasn't bitter. She was so lucky now, it no longer mattered. "He did ask me to marry him, Sheila. He said you'd be all right, because someone wanted to marry you. Isn't that why you want your divorce now? Well, I'm sorry...." Peggy wiped her hands on her hopsack apron.

"No. There's no other man. David thought there was but there never has been. I just want ... to get away from him. He's worn me out. I've no feelings left for him at all. So there's no point in staying married."

Peggy could tell Sheila felt strongly and was sympathetic. "I would help if I could, really I would. It's...." She pointed through the small leaded window to a man repairing a stone wall on the brow of the field. "Tom says he's not going to have it dragged out in public. You see, June is his girl now, completely; he is her father, her Dad. He doesn't want anyone to know any different. For her sake. If it came out in the Liverpool papers, he says, someone round here would get hold of it. Bound to do."

"I understand that. I see his side of it." There was no animosity between them.

"Am I the only girl David's told you about? Couldn't he help you, by giving you evidence of ... someone else?"

"Oh, I know there've been others. But you know David. He never keeps to the same story twice running. He says he'll provide evidence but then nothing happens. Then he says he won't. The solicitors don't know where they are with his chopping and changing."

A child toddled in from the farmyard in tiny gumboots. "Daddy. Daddy."

Peggy picked her up and pointed through the window. "There's Daddy, Junie. Look. And this is Auntie Sheila. Say hello. She's come on a puff-puff, just to see you."

Junie smiled and held out a wavering hand. Sheila put out her finger but the child playfully hit at it, instead of gripping it.

Sheila steeled herself. "Hello, Junie." She winced to see David's eyes smiling mischievously. "She's ... She's a lovely kid. Looks like you Peggy, doesn't she."

"Yes, quite a bit. Tom jokes, swears she's more like him – Tom, I mean. More like Daddy than Mummy, aren't you? Look, Daddy's coming in for his tea. Go and fetch him, good girl."

David's child toddled out into the farmyard.

"Peggy, I just thought I'd come and ask. I'm sorry you can't help, because it would help. You know, really help me."

Peggy looked at Tom, picking up Junie as he came towards the farmyard. "Well, I'll try and talk to him. I can't really hold out any hope. But I will try. I promise."

"Well, thanks for that anyway."

"You going to stop and meet Tom?" It was clear from the way Peggy spoke that she didn't want the embarrassment of their meeting. Tom would not receive Sheila as sympathetically as Peggy had, that was obvious.

"No, no. I'd rather leave it to you. I'll get on my way back, if you don't mind."

Sheila crossed the yard to the farm lane as Tom reached the gate from the fields, opening and closing it to amuse Junie. Her laughter carried to Sheila but she didn't look round. She pulled her thin coat around her and trudged towards the bus stop.

Ian had shown David the Mackenzie ground floor rooms. "So you can see the joke; suggesting we might move to your place."

"Sheila always had a weird sense of humour. Still, it is a fair size, this; wouldn't mind something as grand meself, if I could afford it. And provided I had my family, you know, all in one piece. Your mother not with you now then?"

"She's gone to live on the South Coast. Always had a hankering after the warmer climes, as she used to put it."

"Freda not in?"

"No. We're in different hospitals now and our duties don't often coincide. I was overdue for a move anyway. I'm at the Nightingale."

"That's right across the other side of the City, isn't it?"

"I get a petrol allowance."

"Oh yes, doctor, I was forgetting."

David didn't ask where Sheila was. Ian was glad not to have to tell him.

When Freda came in she was surprised to find David there. "Haven't you told him, Ian? That Sheila's staying with us."

"Yes, I mentioned it."

"And where she's gone?"

"No."

"Where has she gone?" David was puzzled by Freda's intonation.

"I'll leave her to tell you herself."

"Tell me. Ian, where's she gone?"

"No, Ian. It's up to Sheila."

David was angry. "Look, are you my sister, or aren't you? You're on her side more than mine."

"Well, if you must know, she's gone to see a friend of yours. Knowing how many women you've left in your trail, who could that be?" Now Freda was angry, too.

"It's Peggy, isn't it?" Sheila's letter told him that. "I know her solicitor's been trying to get a statement from her."

"I'll leave the sordid details to Sheila when she gets back. I presume you're here for more than five minutes."

"He is. I've invited him to stay the night."

David smiled cruelly. "Not in the same bedroom, of course."

"No reason why he should stay in that place on his own, is there?" Ian could see she was objecting.

"Sheila's had to, hasn't she." Freda was angry with them both.

"You might have asked me first, Ian." She'd said it before she realised it was boot-on-the-other-foot. She said she'd prepare something to eat and got out of the room as fast as she could.

"Women," said David, shaking his head.

"Men," said Freda to herself in the kitchen as she sliced murderously at an innocent loaf.

John was looking through the accounts in the church hall rooms the Party used as headquarters.

Marjorie watched for his reaction. "You can see, John, they haven't been kept very well."

"Well, you don't have to be a financial genius to enter funds collected on one side and the expenses on the other. This is quite adequate, I'd say; you don't really need me, you know."

John seemed to have had second thoughts about being Treasurer and he closed the ledger as an indication. But he didn't actually say so.

Marjorie was puzzled. "You don't seem as keen as you did that night in your house. You were going to help us put the world to rights, then."

"I said it needed putting to rights, something like that. I still say it does."

"But you're not prepared to put yourself out a bit to help the process."

"What bit can I do?"

Marjorie clenched her fists in anguish. "Oh, God preserve us from people who say 'What can I do?' If everybody takes that attitude, how do we beat the Tories? With Churchill as their leader. With his war record. They've got a head start."

"Yes, well, I've been asking myself that. How do we? With his popularity, he'll walk it. And the Tories with him."

"No, he won't. If we make a big enough shout about it. That's what we can do, John. Shout. Make sure everybody knows it won't be Churchill they'll be voting for. It'll be for the old order, for a return to pre-war days: two million without jobs, without the right to work, or to earn a decent basic living. . . ."

John opened the account book again, almost involuntarily. "Well . . . there are one or two ways we can improve the way the figures are kept. For example, so we can always see the financial situation at a glance."

Marjorie noticed he'd said "we". The Party now had a Treasurer, who knew his bookkeeping and which way he wanted his world to go.

Sheila had called in to see Edwin on her way back to the Mackenzies from the station. She'd convinced herself that it was just to say she had decided she must get somewhere better to live; and ask if he knew of anywhere. But it proved more than that.

She found herself telling him about Peggy; and the little girl with David's eyes. And the man who had become her father. Not her natural father; better than him, worth two of him.

Edwin made it easier for her. "What you're saying, Sheila love, is that in spite of hanging on and hoping – and all the times you've told me you still loved him and you thought he still loved you, deep down – in spite of all that, it's finally all over. Between you and David. Isn't it?"

"Yes. I even blame him for losing me Colin. If I could've seen that little girl's eyes on the day Colin asked me to get a divorce and marry him – pleaded with me, he did – I would've done. I came so near, and now Colin's married someone else."

Edwin took her hand, held it tight. His grip told her everything he felt.

Ian made his peace with Freda by keeping up the joke she and Sheila had played on him. "Oh by the way, I'm thinking of making the landlord an offer for Sheila's place. Just what we're looking for."

"Making an offer to pull it down, you mean." Freda's comment was within the context of the joke but incisive.

David took the point. "I'm glad she's getting out of it, anyway. I've been on at her long enough."

"Oh have you? What've you fixed up for her? A suite at the Adelphi Hotel?" When Freda was sarcastic she hit hard.

"Well, she must have somewhere in mind, Freda. She's getting packed, isn't she, Ian?"

Freda snapped back, "Tell me something I don't know," and went to answer the knock at the door. She told Sheila that David was in the lounge.

"I don't want to see him. Where can I go, while you get rid of him?"

Ian came into the hall. "David wants to talk to you, Sheila."

"I've got nothing to say to him."

"If she doesn't want to, Ian, she doesn't."

"What harm can they do by talking? If there's the slightest chance some good comes of it. Please, Sheila, see what he has to say."

Ian led Freda into the dining room. Sheila thought for a moment; then heaved a sigh and went reluctantly into the lounge.

David smiled an embarrassed greeting. "Sheila, I want to talk to you. You know, without blowing our tops."

106

"What about?"

David didn't know where to begin. "You didn't tell me you were getting out of that hole."

"Any reason why I should? How did you know anyway?"

"I couldn't help seeing, could I?"

"How did you get in?"

"The key from Mrs. Duffy."

"Then I'll give her strict instructions for next time."

"There were things of mine still there. I went in to get them, that's all."

"You could have written to me for permission."

"Permission? Who d'you think you are, talking to me from a great height. I'll give you 'permission'. Going to see Peggy. Stirring it up for her, too."

"Me stirring it? After the bloody-awful way you treated her? You don't care about her kid any more than you care about ours. She's lucky. She's got a damn good father for Junie. What have I got for Janet and Peter? A great big nothing. All I want from you, David, is my divorce. I just want to get shot of you. Well and truly shot. Once and for all. All right, there's another reason. I want to be rid, so that if the chance comes – if I meet someone who'll be as good to my kids as Tom is to Peggy's, I can grab him for them. Like Colin would've been."

Sheila turned angrily to the door but David moved quickly to block her way.

"Listen to me, Sheila. Listen to me, please!"

"Listen? I've done nothing else for years. Let you talk me round. Explanations. Excuses. All charm and sweet-talk, just to get your own way. Well, I'm listening no more. I mean it, this time."

Sheila tried to move past him but he grabbed her arm. She tried to wrestle free but he held her fast, his temper augmenting his strength.

"Listen to me, blast you!"

"No! Let me go!"

Ian and Freda could hear the raised voices through two closed doors. They looked at each other helplessly.

Sheila gave a sudden twist in angry desperation, and escaped his grip so unexpected that she overbalanced and fell heavily.

David dropped to her side. "Sheila, I didn't mean to hurt –"

His sentence was cut off as she hit his face viciously. As his cheek turned blood-red he realised it really was all over.

Irreparably. Irrevocably. He helped her to her feet. Then he spoke as if making a legal statement.

"All right. You'll get your divorce. I'll tell my solicitors to make it as easy as possible. That's what you want, isn't it?"

Sheila said nothing.

"Okay; that's it, then. It's all over. I give up."

Sheila still said nothing. So he walked out of the room and out of the house.

CHAPTER TWELVE

March 1945

As they dropped from the tailboard of the truck which had ferried them to their aircraft, David told Peter Bryant that the cheque wouldn't bounce. And thanks for the loan.

Peter smiled knowingly. "Never imagined for a minute it would, old boy. Worst crime an officer and a gentleman can commit, write a dud cheque. Very few of us are gentlemen, but we have to go through the motions." Under his banter, Peter was relieved. Grace had told him how tight for cash David usually was on the weekends he stayed with her. Now Peter could risk banking it without danger to David's service character.

They split as they made for their respective Lancaster bombers. Flying Officer Derek Robbins caught up David and they walked in step. Robbie's plane was parked on the far side of David's. "Well, how's it feel, Dave? To be lining up for your last op of this tour?"

"No different from any other. Not as yet; maybe when we're heading back, I'll feel something. How many have you to go? Not a lot now, is it?"

"Seven. Not many if you say it quick."

"They'll soon pass, Robbie."

"Won't, you know. They clock up slower and slower. I suppose it's having Jill and the kids here. Every time I get back I cross one more off, like days-to-go to the end of term. No matter how flaked out I feel when I get back, I never get into bed 'till I've tiptoed into Michael and Judith; just to look at 'em, miles-away in never-never land. You probably think I'm an old fuddy-duddy."

"No, I don't. That's why I never brought my family near the Station. Too close to what it's all about." David suddenly realised what he was saying. "On the other hand, if Sheila and the kids had been here, maybe things wouldn't be so dicey now."

"Pretty rough is it, David?"

"It's all over." David peeled off to the underbelly of his Lancaster and reached up to hoist himself inside.

Robbie walked on: "Don't forget you're eating with us tonight. Last thing Jill said was to remind you."

David looked from Robbie to Jill Robbins, at either end of the table. There was a lull in the conversation during the main course. Okay, David was telling himself, it's only a rented house, but they've got it nice, least Jill has; it's her doing, must be. And it's ... well, it's a home, a real home. I mean, would Sheila keep a place like this? Like a home should be. Mind you, Robbie's way of going-on would drive you up the wall. Never hangs around in the Mess, does he? Looks at his watch. We can all set ours to the minute when he says "Well, the little woman'll be waiting." And he's off. Not even one for the road. And here she is, waiting; predictable as he is. Nice. But how bloody dull it must get, day-in, day-out. Is that what life's about?

"Meal all right, David? Best I could do I'm afraid." Jill was genuinely concerned, but had no reason to be.

"Great. Lovely. Look, one night why don't we all go out to that place down the road; what's the pub called, 'The Millers'. The food's not half-bad there, they say, considering. I mean, it's the only way I can return all this. Help out your rations to say the least."

"Jilly doesn't do too badly, do you darling?"

"Well, it's nice of you David; the difficulty is getting someone to come and look after the children. Mother's very good when I want to go into town, but we can't overdo it. And we couldn't leave them."

Derek got up to clear the plates. David noticed Jill made no protest. "In the oven, darling. The custard's on the side. And put the coffee on, there's a dear."

Derek acknowledged the orders breezily. "Wilco."

David thought she waited purposely until the kitchen door had swung to behind Derek before she spoke. "Nice of you to come, David. It's pretty lonely here, you know, miles from anywhere except the aerodrome."

"You? Lonely? With Derek around."

"Oh I know I'm lucky compared with most. But.... Well, apart from Derek, I've only the kids to talk to. It can get you ... a bit screaming sometimes."

"Screaming? Come off it, Jill. Not you."

"Derek says there's no chance of your patching things up. With ... Sheila, isn't it? I'm sorry. Very sorry." Her eyes showed she felt for him.

"Oh, I'm used to it, now. Seems to have been breaking up longer than it was okay."

"And it's your last op tonight, isn't it?"

"Last on this tour, anyway. Jack Ridley says he's arranging for the war to go on long enough for me to clock up another thirty. You know, Jack, don't you? Great skipper."

"Yes, he's been here. Is it tonight, the next raid? I know I shouldn't ask."

"Rumour is it's a daylight. I wish they'd get it over with; night or day, I couldn't care less."

Derek came in and served the pudding. "Coffee's operational."

"Thank you, darling."

Yes, thought David as they ate, imagine Sheila in a set-up like this. You can't, can you?

"Penny for 'em, Dave." Robbie broke into his thoughts.

"Oh, I was just thinking.... What about the people you rent this from? Where are they?"

"He's Royal Signals. Major, isn't he now, darling? She went back to mother in Guildford when he was posted Far East, didn't she, darling?"

"Yes. Thousands of miles away, dreaming of the day he's back here. And her the same, probably. We should count our blessings." She sighed. "But we never do, do we?"

Robbie suddenly said "Sh". They listened for an air-raid warning or the alarm siren from Station Control.

"That's Judith, isn't it?" The dutiful father had heard her whimpering. "I said she hadn't gone straight off. All right, darling, I'll go."

Robbie was striding up the stairs two at once before Jill had risen from the table.

David was noting the extent of Derek's domestic involvement. "Jill. D'you like your man ... to be ... er..."

She knew what he found difficult to put into words. "Fussing around so much, you mean?"

"Well, being so swept-up in the chores. The kitchen. The kids."

"You weren't, I suppose?"

"Well ... not ... as much as Robbie is."

"Yes, I like a man to be a man, David. If that's what you're asking me."

David searched Jill's eyes and she looked away; to his empty plate. "More, David?"

"Er ... just a small piece. Thanks."

Jill concentrated on the pudding. "One can't have everything in a marriage, I suppose. I'm sure you've found that out." David waited for her to look at him, but she didn't.

Robbie came downstairs. "She was chuntering in her sleep, that's all."

Jack Ridley was watching two scratch teams of air-crew playing rugby with an old flying-boot that would never see another tour of ops. He lit his bent pipe and sucked until it drew well. He had the urge to join in, but was deterred by the extra ten years most of them could give him.

As David Ashton came out of the Flight Office he saw Jack standing on his own.

"Not in the thick of it, Skip? Not like you."

"Anno domini, Dave. It'll catch up with you."

"What's our chances today? Weather reports are okay, they say."

"Want to get the last one over with? That it?"

"Be nice to notch up the round thirty, yes. Bet they're laying on something pretty rough for me." He assumed the "wizard-prang" accent. "Now look here, chaps, this fellow Ashton's not getting away with an easy one! What can we dream up for him, eh?" David pretended to groom the handlebars moustache made famous by the R.A.F. "few". "Had dinner with Robbie last night, Skip. Very nice."

Jack Ridley seemed suddenly to take more active interest in the game. "Forward pass, Jumbo. Forward." He didn't take his eyes off the play. "Oh, did you? How are they? Jill and the youngsters."

"Fine. You've two yourself, haven't you?"

Their eyes never left the boot, flying from hand to hand.

"Yes. Two boys. You've two as well, haven't you?"

"One of each. Yes."

"Oh well taken Parky, you're through." Jack clapped the well-taken try.

"I'm ... getting a divorce, Jack. I was hoping I'd ride the storm out, but I suppose I don't deserve to. I've given her a bit of a tough time. Not just her; other blokes' girls, too, come to that."

Jack looked at David for the first time since he'd mentioned the Robbins. "Doesn't make it go away though, Dave; talking about it, does it?"

There was a call for Jack Ridley from the Flight Office. David went with him. Could this be it? He hoped so. But on the contrary, the news was that there would be no op that day. As the weather wasn't the reason, no-one had the slightest idea what was.

Jill had telephoned her mother to say that Derek would be Duty Officer until six o'clock, and her friend in London had a day off. Mrs. Crawford always made a great effort to come over to let Jill go, because she could tell how she looked forward to a trip to town.

"It would get me down I think, too, dear; stuck out here."

"Well. . . ." Jill decided to deny it. "No, it isn't that actually. I rather like the open country."

"Is it Derek, then?"

Jill alerted, but tried not to show it. "Derek?"

"All this flying. You say he's done how many trips over there, now?"

"Twenty-two ... no, twenty-three I think, I'm not sure. Well yes, of course that worries me, naturally. Does it show that much?"

Mrs. Crawford was tactful. "Come along then, let's make sure you catch that next train, or you'll keep her waiting."

It wasn't in David's make-up to hang around playing rugby, or to kick his heels to kill time. The unexpected free day meant the chance to go where the Bright Lights used to be. And as he crossed the footbridge to the London platform, he saw Jill Robbins waiting for the same train.

They shared a compartment with an Intelligence Corps Major and two Wren Officers. The five-handed conversation was continuous, but boring. He would rather have had Jill on her own.

At the London terminus she began looking anxiously for her friend as soon as they were walking down the platform. David sensed Jill didn't want him to meet her, and wondered why. His reputation wasn't that bad, surely.

"Well, it was nice to travel with you, David. Quite a pleasant surprise, I suppose you're off meeting one of your girl-friends, are you?"

"Not particularly. Where are you meeting yours?"

"Oh me? Er . . . here. At the barrier. Can't see her yet. She's not usually punctual, I'm afraid."

"I'll hang on with you, then." They handed in their tickets.

"No. No, don't do that. Don't spoil your day. Really. I'd rather . . . wait alone."

"I see. Bit of a smasher, is she?"

"Well, er . . . put it this way. She's . . . not available David, I'm sorry. She's . . . very happily married."

David joked. "I can take a hint when I'm not wanted."

To his surprise she took him seriously, and apologised to excess. It dawned on him she may not be meeting a girl at all.

"Please David." She knew what he was thinking.

David smiled, nodded, said, "See you, Jill," and walked off.

As he reached the main entrance something made him stop and turn round. Was it a bloke? And, if so, what type makes a girl like Jill Robbins come all this way? He must have something. . . .

Jill was still alone. Behind her Jack Ridley came through the barrier, the last passenger off their train. She turned as he touched her shoulder. They smiled and walked off into the station concourse together.

David said under his breath: "Skip. You crafty old whatsit."

Mrs. Crawford was suspecting even more that all was not as rosy as Jill cracked it up to be. "Everything is all right, isn't it? You look as if you've had a tiring day in town."

"I'm fine. Oh you've got the meal ready."

"Well, I thought I'd better. Derek will be home soon won't he? He is all right, isn't he?"

"Not too bad. He doesn't sleep as well as he did. Particularly after an op. He's absolutely all in, just lies there, awake. Lives through it again."

"Oh, dear," said Mrs. Crawford, as they heard Derek arrive. Jill escaped from the kitchen to greet him.

"Look who I've brought and look what he's brought. A present for Michael's birthday. Been up to town today specially to get it."

David handed her the parcel. "Well, not specially, Jill. Not much you can get for kids round here though is there?" His face betrayed nothing.

"That's kind of you, David. I'll hide it. It's not until to-morrow." Jill put the package in a cupboard.

"Where's your mum, darling? In the kitchen? I'll tell her we're one more."

"No, I'm not staying again," David's protest was ignored as Robbie went to tell Mrs. Crawford.

Jill spoke almost in a whisper. "I wish you hadn't come."

"I used the present as an excuse. . . . Because I've been worried ever since. What's this doing to Robbie? Have you thought about that?"

"You haven't told him?" Jill feared the worst.

"Not yet I haven't. Maybe I won't. Provided you finish with Jack."

"David Ashton of all people, saying that? I'd 've thought you at least would understand."

"I understand what it will do to Robbie, if he –" David had to stop.

Robbie came in. "Well, let's have a drink."

Jill almost snapped. "Drink of what? I told you we were out."

Robbie kissed her on the temple. "Well, don't worry, darling. It isn't the end of the world. I'll nip down to the 'Turk's Head' and talk George into selling us a little something. Coming. Dave?"

David looked at Jill and smiled. She couldn't tell whether it meant, don't worry he wasn't going to tell. Or that he was going to. She tried to ask him not to. "Yes, David, you go. We've plenty of time to talk when you get back."

Mine Host at the "Turk's Head" refused to serve Jack Ridley. He'd already had more than enough. He'd been at the bar since opening time, downing neat whisky as if it were water.

When Peter Bryant brought Chrissie in, Jack didn't even

114

see them. And when Peter saw Jack he steered the leggy W.A.A.F. to a table out of his line-of-sight. Mine Host George got the point and went quietly to Peter to serve them.

"Had a few, hasn't he, George? For this early?" Peter whispered.

"More than he can handle. I've told him enough's enough, and now he's sitting there moping."

"Bad news, you reckon?"

"I asked him that. He said mind my own business."

Chrissie watched the landlord go back behind the bar, then changed the conversation brightly. "Well, I never expected to be here tonight."

Peter had taken a shine to Chrissie since before poor Frankie started taking her out. Then they got engaged and Frankie had bought it over Essen, or somewhere like that; you try to forget the really dicey ones. Peter couldn't very well move in straight after that. Now she seemed to have got over it. She never mentioned Frankie. And Peter had been too chary to ask what she felt about the pilot who'd been the only one to come out of their prang alive. It wasn't his fault his crew had all bought it; but what would someone as simple-minded as Chrissie think?

George set down their drinks; Peter paid him quietly. He didn't want Jack Ridley joining them, particularly in that state.

"Cheers, Peter." Chrissie sipped her brown ale. "You know something? You're the first officer I've ever been out with?"

Peter had almost forgotten Frankie was a Sergeant. "We're no different, underneath the blue serge." Chrissie giggled. "So I hear. Some of the W.A.A.F.'s have been out with both, I mean. We're allowed to talk, you know, whilst we're packing 'chutes."

"Chrissie. You know it wasn't my fault, don't you? That my kite pranged."

"Course I do. Who's said it was? It was a marvel you got it down in one piece. Is that why you asked me out?" Chrissie sounded very disappointed that it wasn't for herself.

"No. No, of course it isn't." He looked at her crossed legs, smashing even in regulation lisle stockings and brogue shoes, "I just wanted to know that – Hold it!"

Jack Ridley, white-faced and drawn, had slipped off his stool and was staggering at speed through the "Gentlemen" door.

"I hope he's going to be very sick."

"Why, Peter?"

"Because we're on call in the morning and the sooner he gets rid of that lot, the less risk for everyone flying with him."

Almost as if on cue, David and Robbie came in. David ordered two pints; and Robbie took George aside as Peter came to the bar.

"Your skipper's in the bog, Dave. Heaving his heart out, I shouldn't be surprised, after what he's put away."

David was in the toilet almost before Peter had finished explaining. Jack Ridley was desperately trying to vomit, but without success.

David was concerned. "Look, mate, if we go flying tomorrow, I want to get back in one piece, right?"

"Oh," moaned Jack, "David bloody Ashton. Never mind tomorrow. What about today? You saw us today. Didn't you?"

David wondered whether it was going to help anyone to admit it. Or to deny it for that matter.

"You saw me. With Jill. I saw you too late. You bastard."

Before David could answer, Robbie came in holding a carrier-bag which concealed a bottle of Scotch and one of gin from "under the counter". "You're in a fine pickle, Jack. Come on Dave, let's get him home."

"Okay," David pulled one of Jack's arms round his shoulders. Robbie took the other. They helped him through the bar. Peter had rejoined Chrissie. George was drying glasses, impassively.

In the fresh air Jack became more helpless.

"Come on, Skip," David encouraged him. "It's a fair old walk back to the Station."

Robbie hadn't meant that "home". "He'll never make it. Get him home to my place."

Twice they stopped in the winding roadway when Jack warned, "I'm going to be sick." Each time he wasn't, in spite of their encouragement.

Mrs. Crawford said she knew how to make him bring it up. With Robbie's assistance, she took him into the downstairs lavatory. She made Jack put his hand in his mouth; then she pushed firmly on his elbow so that his fingers stuck down his throat.

David sat with Jill, who was staring into space. "Poor Jack. He never said he'd seen you. All afternoon."

David asked, "You reckon that's why he's drunk himself

silly? Because he'd been rumbled? And thought maybe you wouldn't see him again?"

"Poor Jack," was all she could say.

"Not poor Robbie?"

"We only walked and talked, David. We hadn't booked into some sleazy hotel room or whatever it is they do. That's not what we were looking for. I don't suppose you believe that. All I needed is someone for ... company. I can't think of a better word; and Jack's good company. Marvellous to talk to. Don't think I haven't thought about Derek? Knowing I was going behind his back?"

David knew what she meant. How well he knew; and sympathised. She was so near to tears that might give her away when Robbie came back that he put his hand on hers. "I do understand, Jill, love; honestly I do –"

Robbie came in from the downstairs place, and David instinctively withdrew his hand.

"Okay, Dave, he seems to have got rid of most of it. Let's get him back, shall we?"

"Right."

Jack was able to walk very gingerly. He said goodnight and apologies to Jill, to her mother; and to Jill again. The three men set out for the Station, arm in arm.

Robbie was about to get into bed. "I've just remembered. The Scotch. I could do with one, after all that, couldn't you, darling?"

Jill had been in bed some time but she hadn't been able to sleep. "No, thanks. Not now."

Derek got into bed again wearily. "Jill?"

"Yes."

"Dave Ashton's quite a boy. You know, don't you?"

"Girls all over the place, they say."

"Not just girls. He does a nice line in ... married women, too. Peter Bryant's sister, to name one."

"I've heard that, as well."

"Has he ... tried anything with you?"

"He might have; if I'd given him the slightest encouragement. Why?"

"You haven't, have you?"

Jill turned over to face him. "What d'you think I am?"

He remembered seeing Dave's hand on hers. "Sorry. I shouldn't have even thought it."

117

Jill wondered why he had. She turned over again and tried to sleep. Without success.

The next morning – young Michael Robbins' birthday-morning – the air-crews assembled. It was a daylight job; a big show. Fighter cover all the way. For a change. High-level bombing, too; so with a bit of luck they might miss most of the flak.

Jack Ridley was last into the locker room. Not all the colour had returned to his cheeks; his eyes were bloodshot and underlined. But his voice was crisp. "Thanks for last night, chaps. Apologies all round."

"Why, what happened?" said David. And that wrote it off for the few who knew. And for those who didn't.

The station trucks carted them off to the Lancasters dispersed in various parts of the airfield. As they climbed into their aircraft, Jack reopened the subject. "There's nothing between us, Dave. Don't get any dirty ideas about her."

"Did I say I had?"

"So long as we've got that straight. I'm not coming between them. It's not going to happen again, now there's a chance Robbie may find out."

"Find out from me?"

"I don't mean Lord Haw-Haw."

"You got sozzled because it's all over? That it?"

"Ask me something I know the answer to. – Okay, Flight are we?"

"All okay, sir." The Flight Sergeant closed the trapdoor, sealing them in the fuselage.

Jill was dusting the sideboard. She stopped, looked at her mother. The first plane was taking off.

"You seem to hear them before they're in the air, Jill. I can't. Oh yes, I can now."

"Sh! Count them."

The object of the exercise was to check with the number they counted when the planes returned. A simple subtraction which Michael and Judith often did, too. The difference told them how many hadn't come back.

The Lancasters joined up with other squadrons and droned towards their ill-fated target. The German town, half-

118

industry, half people's homes, was dead ahead, inexorably moving under them as if by death-wish.

As they flew deeper into Germany, the flak intensified, sometimes bursting so close that Jack Ridley had to reset course from being blasted off his bomb-run line. His voice was distorted by the intercom. "Target should be dead ahead, Dave. How d'you read it?"

David pinpointed their position and waited one, two, three seconds. "Yes, Skip, spot on. You're not bad for a young 'un."

Jack was very calm, almost off-hand. "Okay, chaps. Let's get it over and get out of here."

David concentrated on his instruments, as if nothing were going on around him. "Steer two-seven-eight. Two. Seven. Eight."

One of the gunners said, "Plenty of flak today, Skip."

Jack came straight back. "What d'you expect? We're not on top of a bus in Piccadill –"

A shell burst dead ahead and just below. The Lancaster leaped like a salmon. Then its nose fell sharply, the plane swinging and twisting as if out-of-control.

David heard Jack say, "I've been hit."

The Flight Engineer grabbed the unmanned controls, as Jack keeled over into a bundle of flying-kit, held only by his seat-strap. His helmet receded almost inside his fur-lined collar, his neck no longer able to support it.

As the Lancaster was forced back onto even keel, David clambered forward, released Jack from his strap, and laid him on the deck.

"Drop the lot. Anywhere. And head back," he shouted.

Jack looked up at David sadly. A jagged piece of shrapnel was embedded in a gash in his flying-suit. Hopeless for David to try and get it out. It was rapidly becoming covered in blood.

Jack knew he hadn't very long.

So did David. "I'll get the morphia, Jack. Hang on."

Jack clutched his arm weakly. "Glover can get you back. Don't worry about me."

"Chin up, mate. We'll all make it, if we try."

Glover got the plane back and down. But Jack didn't make it. He bought it.

David hared along the lane on an R.A.F. Norton 500 c.c. he'd borrowed. He must be the first to tell her. Not that bloody official telephone call, anything's better than that. He wanted to be able to.... He didn't know what, just let her grab his hand, or cry on his shoulder or tell him to go away. Anything, so long as he was there for her to take it out of. Or ... whatever she needed.

He'd had two or three stiff whiskies to help get him through the coming ordeal. And the more he thought about it, the more he twisted the throttle open. And it was a long time since he'd been on a motor-bike and these Service jobs were more powerful than he knew.

On the last bend before the Robbins' house the Norton's rear wheel slid from under him, as he took the curve too fast.

The motorbike was a write-off. David was slightly more fortunate.

CHAPTER THIRTEEN

April 1945

Margaret was surprised at Sheila's reaction. David was injured and in hospital but Sheila didn't want to visit him; as far as she was concerned, it was as if they were already divorced. His father had gone to see him immediately, so he had someone to listen to his usual excuses. The accident wouldn't have been David's fault, you could bet on that. It was just his bad luck; it always was.

Margaret realised for the first time how determined Sheila was. She didn't even ask how badly he was hurt. Margaret volunteered that he was in a hospital near the airfield and suffering from concussion. Sheila didn't even want to know the Hospital's telephone number. But then did David deserve any better?

"Well, I promised Dad I'd come round and tell you what he'd phoned to say."

Sheila held the back door as Margaret was leaving. "You see Margaret, David feels the same. About me."

"How d'you know that? I mean, for certain?"

"He didn't ask them to let me know, did he? They sent for his dad. I'm not even his next-of-kin, as David sees it. And that's the way I see it, too."

Jill's mother had stayed on but was unable to console her

or to prevent her keep repeating in abject despair: "It's all my fault. It's a punishment. He'd be home. Here. Now. If I...." And then she would stop.

Even when better news came, that Derek's plane had crash-landed in Holland, Jill couldn't be consoled. She was sure he was badly injured, killed even. They were hiding it from her, trying to break it to her gently. Nobody could convince her that neither of the two air-crew killed was the pilot.

When Derek was brought home he showed little sign of recognising the place, or his wife, or Mrs. Crawford, who began to wonder if her daughter had had some premonition.

Marjorie had come to the Ashtons to talk to John. There was fire in her eyes; wasn't the news great? The Russians advancing so deep into Germany; it must be all over soon. Comes the General Election, and the Party must be ready for it. They must start a big recruiting drive. Now. They must work out ways of raising funds. No time to lose. A meeting of the Management Committee was called for that very evening, and in view of the financial ramifications the Treasurer must be there.

"Yes," John agreed. "Course I'll be there."

Margaret had heard snatches of Marjorie's tract of "musts". whilst she served John's meal. "Tell me, Marge. Aren't our lads fighting their way towards Berlin from the west, as well as the Russkies are from the east?"

Peter Bryant saw Derek Robbins coming towards him across the tarmac, apparently none the worse for his crash. But he walked past him without recognition. "Robbie. Hey. How's it going?"

Robbie stopped, turned, looked at Peter and furrowed his brow. "Fine. Fine, thanks ... er Peter. Forgot your name for a minute ... Peter. Yes. Just hanging about at present. Waiting for my replacement kite 'til it's been tested"

Was that a kind way of telling Robbie he was grounded, Peter wondered.

Robbie seemed to have difficulty translating thoughts into words. "Yes. I've still got, er, how many ... six to go you know. Six ops, yes, it's six, isn't it? Yes, six; I was right first time. They'll have it on my records anyway. You can't get away with not doing your full ... er stint with this mob."

Peter was surprised. "The M.O. says you're okay for flying,

does he? I mean, soon as your new kite's operational? You've got replacement crew, have you?"

"Just on my way to meet 'em. My new rear-gunner's a chap called ... er ... and my sparks is.... Huh, I was given their names minute ago. Anyway, you'll be meeting 'em."

"Robbie You have told the M.O. you're still a bit dicky, haven't you? You need a break; I mean, until you get your bearings."

"If you think I'm going sick to get out of half-a-dozen ops, Peter, you can forget it."

"You mean, you haven't reported sick?"

"Course not. I'm okay. Not a scratch. Dead lucky, but there it is."

"Robbie. If you don't ask the Doc. for a few days stand-down, I'll bloody-well ask him for you."

Derek Robbins snapped anxiously. "You'll do no such thing. I'm not having any fingers pointing at me. I'm finishing this tour if it kills me." He meant it metaphorically. "If you breath a word to the Quack, or anyone else for that matter.... Well, just don't, that's all."

Robbie walked off to meet his new crew members. Peter knew what worried him. To report sick and be taken off operational flying duties for anything less than being physically incapable smacked of cowardice. It was a fate worse than death.

Margaret arrived at the Hospital, half-expecting to see David pale and prone. But he was sitting up and taking notice, particularly of the nurses as they passed his bed. But she soon detected he was depressed about his chances of flying again.

He'd overheard a whispered consultation at the foot of his bed: a hairline fracture of the skull, his balance might be upset, something to do with the inner ear. That would kill it stone-dead for an R.A.F. career in peacetime, wouldn't it? He was very down about it.

Margaret told him frankly, that it was just about the best thing that could happen. If it kept him on the ground until the end of the war, it was one less to wonder about back home, every time the phone rang. It left Philip the only one still on active service. The Ashtons had already made more than their contribution to this war, in her opinion. "Think a minute, David; Dad, Mum, the five of us; before it all started. And look at us now."

David preferred to recall his hanging round the dock-gates, hoping for a day's pay for a day's work. But usually ending up in line for dole money. The Air Force was the life for him, even in peacetime. He pointed to the wing on the tunic hanging by his bed. "But I've got to finish the war flying, Margaret. I've got to, if I'm going to make a go of it afterwards."

Then suddenly David switched to asking her about Sheila. Was she all right? Would she tell her he'd like to see her.

Margaret said she would; she didn't add that she knew exactly what Sheila's reaction would be.

When Peter Bryant visited David the conversation was R.A.F.-banter: jokey, superficial.

"Come on, Ashton; stop malingering; up out of that chariot and into your flying-kit; there's damn-all wrong with you."

"Tell that to these bloody quacks, mate, and I'll be at five-thousand feet before you've got your Mae-West on."

They talked about anything except David's injury. Was Robbie back on ops? No, he was still waiting for his new kite. Well, that's the official reason: his crew's dreading the day he takes them up. If he ever gets aloft again.

David felt strongly. "He really should go sick; somebody should tell him, Peter. He came to see me with Jill and he's very dicky."

"D'you think I haven't told him? He gets uppity, old boy, soon as you broach the subject."

"Then you've got to tell the M.O. He can't know he's not spot-on upstairs, can he? Unless somebody tips him the wink to have a good look at Robbie."

"I can't do it, not behind his back; you know I can't."

"Who's to know, Pete. He won't have a clue who it is. Just put a word in the Doc's ear, that's all. Robbie'll never admit he's scared of going up again. One of us has to do it for him. As a favour. And I'm holed up here, so it's yours Pete. All yours.

Sheila read the letter through once; then again. Then a third time. Then she went straight to see Margaret, and asked her to read it.

123

"Dear Mrs. Ashton,

You won't know me but my husband is a pilot in the same Squadron as your husband. Derek brought David home once or twice before his accident and today we have been to see him in Hospital.

He is all right, so do not worry on that score, but he is terribly depressed because he thinks that his R.A.F. service may be terminated due to something to do with his ears and his balance. You've probably been told more about it than David told us.

Anyway, I am writing to ask whether it is difficult for you to get to this part of the country? David did say there was not much chance of your coming and seemed rather sad about it. You see, we have a furnished house near the airfield and not far from the Hospital. So if you think it would help, you would be very welcome to stay here for a few days whilst you visit David.

I know he would love to see you. He as good as said so in fact.

Yours very sincerely,
Jill Robbins.

PS. Derek and I know, to some extent from David, that your marriage is going through a difficult period. I hope you don't think I'm interfering when I say it seems almost fate that this accident gives you the chance to come and see David. But if I am presuming, please ignore this letter and forgive my intrusion. J.R."

Margaret handed the letter back. "What a kind thought. Are you taking her up on it?"

"Well, I don't know. What would you do, Margaret? He could be up to his old tricks. Getting at me now through a pal's wife. I know him; I know just how he works. I'll bet he really laid it on with a trowel, how I want to come and see him and would she write and offer to put me up. Then I can't refuse, can I? He's so crafty, you've no idea; you can't have any idea."

"Sheila. I've been to see him. Since I last saw you."

"Why didn't you tell me?"

"There wasn't much point was there? After what you said when I suggested you should go."

"Yes, well. Yes. That's right. There wasn't."

124

"He did say he wanted to see you. To me, I mean. There was no craftiness about it. He's very down; honest, love, I've never seen him so down."

"You mean ... ill?"

Margaret sensed something remained. "No, not ill in that way, but I really think there's only one thing that'll buck him up. And that's seeing you."

"Oh. I see," Sheila thought hard. "So you think this letter's ... genuine?"

"She wouldn't have written to a complete stranger, now would she? Not a letter like that. Unless she felt strongly that you should go."

Sheila felt herself weakening. She was about to give David another chance. Yet again.

The hospital radio was relaying the news. The Russians were nearing the outskirts of Berlin. Italian partisans were searching the mountains for Mussolini and his mistress, fleeing towards the Swiss border.

David took the headphones off as Sheila approached his bed, some magazines under her arm.

There was more embarrassment in their greeting than emotion. She gave him the journals, recent issues of "Picture Post".

"Thanks. I can't read for long at a stretch but.... Thanks anyway."

The silence was brief, but they both noticed it. Sheila smiled, the wan smile he knew so well; it was uniquely Sheila's smile.

David put the magazine aside. "Have you been to see the kids recently?"

"No. I've had a letter from Peter. He's started playing rugby." She dug into her handbag. "Oh, I must have left it. It was such a rush, once I'd made up my mind. Jill Robbins' letter did it; I must admit. Nice of her to write?"

"She wrote to you?" David sounded surprised.

She recounted the letter almost verbatim, she'd read it so often. She was relieved that David really didn't know about it. She could tell when he was genuine. The David she'd married, the old David, was genuine.

"Damn nice of Robbie and Jill to put you up. Good types, aren't they?"

"Yes, except that.... Well, he is pretty edgy, isn't he? I've only been there for one meal, since I arrived. He snaps about the place all the time."

"Yes, well, that's not him really. He's got good cause. After all the ops he's done."

"You've done a lot of ops too, David?"

"A few more than Robbie, in fact. It comes out in us differently. He's got edgy. I've got. . . . What have I got Sheila? You tell me. No, don't. Let's not get onto that subject. So you're not having the kids home, yet?"

"No, not yet. And I don't know how I'm going to break it to Mrs. Thomas when the time comes. It's going to be a problem."

"You're not having them home until you find a new father for them, eh?" David couldn't keep off the subject, with all his good intentions.

"No, David. Not until I've found a decent place for them to come back to. Until I can afford to keep them as they should be."

"I'll do what I can, Sheila, I promise. Once I'm operational again, we'll find a place, honest."

"No, David. It won't work. It had to come; for thirteen years we've been coming to this."

"In spite of the fact that I love you? And you love me?"

"Who says?" Sheila was denying it.

David became impassioned and banged the bedclothes with his fist. "Well don't you? You're here, aren't you? You've not come all this way just to tell me there's no chance —"

David fell back, breathing heavily, pressing his finger-tips against his forehead, and screwing up his eyes with the pain.

"You all right, David?"

"Yes, it'll go. Don't worry."

She nearly said, "You're not playing up. Are you?" and was glad she didn't.

A nurse came up and said he must rest now and she should go.

"Goodbye, David."

"Don't go."

"I must." She looked at him from the door. The unique wan smile just wouldn't come.

Jill had heard the planes climbing into the sky. She counted, even though she knew Derek's was unlikely to be with them.

The habit was ingrained. As the last engine-roar died away towards the east she heard the front door slam.

It was Derek. "I've been grounded. The M.O. sent for me. How did he know? I'll tell you how he knew. Bloody Peter Bryant. Sneaked it to him. Must have. The bastard." He saw her glass. "You drinking? This time of day?"

It wasn't the first one, but Jill kept it secret. "Yes, why not? Join me?"

Jill poured his gin. "I'm not sorry. Not a bit sorry. I don't care what you feel about finishing your tour. I'm glad you're grounded. I'm going to celebrate it."

She expected him to argue, but he didn't.

He pointed at the gin, "Make it a double."

Jill saw a tear fall down his cheek. "Go on, Jill. I'll celebrate with you." Derek started to laugh hysterically.

Jill brought the large gin to him. He spilt it, he was to shaking with laughter.

She realised it had all been bravado. He'd been secretly hoping for this. He'd never have gone to the M.O. himself, he threatened Peter for suggesting he should, he'd called him a bastard now that he had. But the tears, the laughter, the relief. They told the truth.

They stood drinking and crying. Then Derek stopped suddenly. "What are we crying for? I've come through. My war's over. I'll be back to teaching, and coming home every evening, with the pay-cheque in the bank, and you and the kids provided for. That's what you wanted, isn't it?"

Jill sank to the settee sobbing, buried her face in a cushion. "Come on, Jill, stop it. We've won. We've won our war." He gripped her shoulder and turned her onto her back. Her eyes were red, her face wet.

"I'm not crying about that." She tried to wipe away her tears with her fingers.

"Then why, for God's sake?"

The gin freed her tongue. "I'm thinking of Jack. Jack Ridley. He hasn't won his war, has he? He's dead. Jack's dead."

Derek looked as if he was about to hit her. But he lunged down on her, pinning her with his body as he tore at her clothes with the fury of a rapist.

She didn't struggle; nor did she co-operate.

Sheila let herself into the Robbins house with the key

they'd lent her. Jill lay on the settee, naked, dishevelled, red-eyed.

"Don't worry, it was only Derek. We hit the bottle; celebrating. That's the only way it happens these days, when we've laced ourselves. I can't stand him touching me otherwise. Is that how it's got with you?"

"Celebrating?" Sheila ignored the intimate question.

"Yes. He's finished flying. Like your David. Oh, sorry, how did you find him?" Jill gathered her scattered clothes and began dressing.

Sheila was more concerned about the Robbins. "He's not too bad. You mean, you've just made love and as soon as it's over, it . . . doesn't mean anything?"

"The man it would have meant something with is dead. Gone. Before he'd even. . . ." Jill shook her head slowly.

"Didn't you love Derek? When you married?"

"I thought I did. I didn't realise that wasn't love until I met Jack. Isn't it like that with you?"

"No. It's not. David's the only man I've ever loved."

Jill caught sight of herself in the looking-glass. "My God, look at me."

"I can't honestly say David's changed in that way. I mean, when I saw him today . . . just for a minute, he was his old self."

"Oh, the war's had a terrible effect on Derek. On me too. Don't you blame the war?"

"Sometimes. But I don't really know. Would it have been different if David and I had been . . . together? All the time?"

"Course it would, Sheila. Look what it's done to me. I'm trapped."

Sheila wasn't convinced it was the war. She couldn't see it Jill's way. And Jill couldn't see it hers. They were married to very different men.

She thanked Jill and caught the next train.

CHAPTER FOURTEEN

May 1945

Edwin began to suspect Sefton was up to his tricks again. Even though he had not mentioned a word about selling the printing business ever since he'd failed to get a majority in favour.

Since Sefton's defeat, General Eisenhower had led Allied Forces into France and they were now nearing their intended goal. The obscene reign of Adolf Hitler and his fascist henchmen was nearly over. Mussolini had been caught before he reached the Italian border; shot and hung upside-down for his countrymen to see.

During those eventful months Sefton hardly bothered to visit the works. Paper was still in short supply and rationed, licences to print were still difficult to get, replacement parts for the machinery were almost unobtainable. But Sefton left the problems to Edwin.

It was now certain that the financial year just ended would not show a profit; Briggs and Son may just break even. Sefton should have been going round with a sore head, complaining and grumbling to Edwin. But he didn't say a word. Something was going on in that devious mind.

Edwin asked Helen if she knew what Sefton was up to. Funny, she was going to ring and ask Edwin the same question. Sefton had told her there would be one extra for dinner that evening and he didn't act the grand host without an ulterior motive.

They agreed to keep in touch, exchange information, if and when. Edwin would keep his ear cocked during business hours; Helen her ear to the ground in the lion's den. What more could they do but wait?

The R.A.F. medical specialists had been very definite. There was no question of David's staying on for the remainder of the war, let alone take a Regular Commission in peacetime. His plans for a career in the R.A.F. were shattered by their recommendation that "Flying Officer Ashton D. be invalided out as soon as practicable".

He came on leave pending discharge. Sheila took him in, not without apprehension. But the turn of events had shaken him; he set about looking for a job, day after day, with a doggedness she wouldn't have believed he possessed.

"I'm going to rope in the sort of money that'll get you out of that N.A.A.F.I. canteen, love; get us a decent house to live in; and those kids back with Mum and Dad, where they belong."

It didn't sound like David. But he wasn't just talking. He really was trying hard to make his words come true. Even when he came home after a long day of traipsing from one side of the city to the other, his head aching and playing him up, he never complained. Could this be a new David? The David she married? Sheila's questions were unspoken prayers.

No-one had seen Doris Jackson for months. Without any warning, or the slightest hint to Freda, her only close friend, she had walked out of the Nurses' Home one night, and literally disappeared. Not even her parents knew where she had gone. The Police had been advised by the Hospital authorities. All that Freda had been able to tell them was that she had said she was going out that evening with her current boyfriend. Whoever he was; American, probably. But there were so many missing persons in wartime, they were unable to trace her.

Freda knew that one day Doris would turn up. Which she did. But not at the Hospital, as she imagined. She arrived out of the blue at the Mackenzies, pale and worried and reticent. The old bounce and chatter had gone.

"Why didn't you write or something?" Freda couldn't understand her friend's behaviour.

Doris didn't offer any explanations as to where she'd been or why. "Dunno. Not much good at letters really."

It was clear to Freda and Ian that this wasn't the reason. They sat down to dinner but Doris neither ate nor spoke. So they did not press her. The chances were that if they had, she would have run out of the house and disappeared again.

Sefton's dinner guest was Trevor Howells, a local businessman noted for the diversity of his interests. He seemed to have a finger in many pies – too many, some people said. He laughed at war-time difficulties and scarcities; he always knew somebody who knew somebody who could get round the regulations or could put a hand on whatever was in short supply. At a price, of course. And, when rumour was rampant, he always knew somebody who knew somebody who could confirm or deny.

"Give your Aunt Helen a hand with the washing-up, Tony, will you?" Sefton made it clear that he wanted to talk privately to Howells. Tony made it clear he knew it, as he left the room.

Sefton produced brandy and cigars. Howells accepted both without asking about the source of either. "Next on the cards, Sefton, is getting shot of this damned Coalition Government. Necessary-evil, that's all it's been. All these wartime controls; they've overdone it, you know."

"Couldn't agree more. Paper quota's crippling the printing works. Crippling it."

"Take heart. Pal o' mine's got a relation who works in White-hall. Drives one of the big-wigs cars, I believe. And she had it from the horse's own mouth practically, that soon as we've knocked out Hitler, Churchill's going to resign and have a proper election."

"With political parties contesting it? He'll walk it, will Winnie. Be a landslide for him. Then they'll take all controls off; and abolish rationing, not a day before time, I say. Free healthy competition, that's what we need quickest, Trevor. That's how to start recovery after the war."

"Right. Now. What's the homes-for-heroes situation? No houses built for six years, right? And plenty destroyed or un-inhabitable by bomb-damage, right? Not to mention slums no longer fit to live in. I don't mind telling you, if I didn't have so much capital tied up in other projects, I wouldn't be inviting anyone to join me in this venture. Not even you, Sefton."

Sefton boxed equally cleverly. "Aye well, you see that's where we'd make good partners. 'Cos I'm in the exact op-posite situation. Very shortly I'm going to have spare capital on my hands. Because I've made up my mind to get rid of the printing works. With controls about to come off, it'll bring a fair price. And I intend to reinvest the cash from my shares in a project where it'll make the most profit."

Howells drew on his cigar confidently. "Well, I challenge you to find a better way of turning money into more money, Sefton. You won't, I'll tell you. Get sufficient votes in favour of selling Briggs and Son, can you? I did hear you'd already had a stab at it?"

"I didn't push it hard enough, that's all. It'll go through. The way I've got it planned. Don't worry about that."

131

Sefton might not have been so cocksure if he'd known what Tony Briggs was up to. He'd told Helen he was quietly slipping-out to tell Uncle Edwin that his father was almost certainly talking about selling the works to this chap Howells. But his first call from the telephone box was to ask for "Trunks operator, please." It was only after that call that he rang the Ashtons' number.

Edwin was very concerned at the news. "It can only mean one thing, Tony. Somebody else must have agreed to sell their shares. Your father wouldn't be taking it this far, unless he was sure of over fifty per cent of the votes."

Throughout the meal, Freda and Ian had exchanged glances as Doris toyed with her food, eating almost nothing. Ian deduced there was little chance of her saying what trouble she was in whilst he was in the room. He made the excuse that he had some reports to read and took his coffee into the study.

Freda didn't beat about the bush. "Doris, it's a man. Isn't it?"

Doris shook her head, but without conviction.

Freda suggested she might feel better if she talked about it. She hated seeing Doris like this. What could she do to help? "You know about the hospital, do you? They sent your dad a letter saying your training was ... what was the word they used? Terminated."

"I haven't been home. Doesn't matter. Nothing does." Then it began to come out. "We were going to be married. Soon as he was demobbed."

It was almost exactly as Freda feared. Doris had gone to live with him near the U.S.A.F. base at Warrington. Now he'd been posted back to the States, and she'd learned he'd got a wife and three kids. But she loved him, couldn't get him out of her mind. "Don't look at me like that, Freda. He was different. He didn't see other girls."

"Oh, Doris." What was the point of telling her how blind stupid she'd been.

"Go on then, say it. I know. You told me a thousand times. I was Yank mad."

But Freda didn't tell her. What was the point, now?

Whilst David had been out job-hunting, Sheila had hit on what seemed a good idea. She carefully chose the moment to

132

put it to him. Gentle massage of the nape of his neck helped to relieve his headaches; she suggested a session after their evening meal.

"Mm. That's doing it good, Sheila. I can feel the pain shifting. Bit lower love now. There, yes. Ooh."

Sheila complied. "David. Didn't your Uncle Sefton say he might have a job for you?"

"Well, he must know I'm looking. I'm not crawling to him."

"But even if he's nothing himself, he's got business contacts. He may know of something; or somebody who does."

"I tell you I'm not going on my hands and knees. And that's the end of it."

Sheila resolved that it wouldn't be.

Both Sefton and Howells had been referring to papers from their brief-cases and were scribbling calculations. Howells produced a surveyor's map from his case, and unfolded it with the air of a conjuror at the finale of a trick. "Where's a suitable piece of land, you ask, Sefton? I was coming to that." He spread the large-scale map over the dining room table. "There's a piece here. Between this road, and this one. There are country bus-stops here, and here; and one here. All on direct routes to the City Centre, too. Couldn't be better. Just the job for our purpose."

Sefton scrutinised the map. Then pronounced his approval obliquely. "Aye. But is it for sale? And if so, at what price?"

"Well now, I told you I've had this idea buzzing round my head for some time. That land came on the market over a year ago. So I snapped it up."

"How much for?"

"Never mind how much. The point is, I'm prepared to sell it to the company you and I are going to set up; and at the going market-price. A price which you and I agree on. In other words, quite reasonable."

Sefton would have done the same in his shoes, and said so. "Fair enough; 'cos we'll make a damn sight more profit developing it than you do selling it to us."

"When controls come off, Sefton, we'll be able to build about two hundred houses on that site."

Sefton surveyed the area. "More, if we really squeeze 'em in."

When Tony came in, Trevor Howells folded the map calmly but making sure it couldn't be identified; and Sefton switched the conversation deftly. "Well, my theory's different Trevor. I don't believe Hitler is dead at all. I think he's got clean away. Escaped to South America or somewhere. Pop round my office in the morning then. I'll see if I've got any more news."

Howells knew exactly what he meant. Tony knew his father meant something quite different from what he was saying.

Whilst Sefton Briggs was seeing Howells out of the front door, Tony couldn't resist looking at the sheets of figures sticking half out of his father's briefcase. There were several copies of Briggs Printing Works new Balance Sheet. He slipped one in his inside pocket as Helen came in, nearly catching him.

Almost immediately Sefton returned, announcing he was now going round to the Ashtons. As he pushed the papers back into his briefcase he announced it was about business and as they were both involved, they'd better come too. "I don't intend to go through the whole rigmarole twice, so come on."

Clearly this was the direct outcome of his talk with Howells. Helen said she would go; but surprisingly, Tony refused, adamantly. As Sefton and Helen went out, Tony heard him say "You can't talk to his generation. They know nothing." The front door banged in anger.

Tony picked up the telephone. "Trunks operator, please." And as he waited to be put through he took the Balance Sheet from his pocket, ready to read vital figures from it to the person he was calling.

Sefton handed out cyclostyled copies of "Briggs and Son Ltd. – Balance Sheet as at 31st March 1945" to the shareholders present at the Ashtons. "There's one each. Helen. I'll post your Jo's. And your Philip's, Edwin. Margaret, that's yours. And one for your Freda. That leaves one for me and one for Tony – Wait a minute, I'm one short. I told that blasted accountant's secretary I wanted one for each shareholder.

Margaret said she'd share Freda's: she didn't need one herself, much as Uncle Sefton impressed on her she was entitled to one. Even in the Ashtons' living-room he made it sound like the Managing Director's speech at a Company's Annual Meeting.

"Well, fellow shareholders, there it is. Now you know the worst. You can see the sad story for yourselves. First time Briggs and Son have made a loss since my father bought a

134

hand-printer and put it in his back room. And that's going back a bit."

When Edwin protested that they'd done damn well to keep the loss down to two-hundred-and-three pounds, Sefton agreed that it was "the economics of war". But the point was that none of them would get a dividend paid on their shares this year, not a ha'penny piece. "Anybody against selling the works after these poor figures needs putting in Whittingham Asylum. 'Cos if we don't sell before long, there'll be no capital left to sell. Just four walls and a load of machinery that's not worth shifting, except for scrap."

So Sefton was on the sell-out rampage again. He wouldn't fail for the same reason he did last time. He will have thought of that, Edwin was sure.

Sheila looked at the oak-panelling and wall-lights in Sefton's City Office. Very nice, too. She'd always imagined he had a room at the printing works, but when she'd looked up his business address, she'd found it was near the Liver Building.

"Sounds to me, Sheila, from what you say, that David doesn't know you've come to see me."

"Well, no. He doesn't, as a matter of fact."

Sefton hadn't forgotten he'd offered David a job. "I will have something for him in due course. The wheels are beginning to turn, though not as fast as I'd like." Sheila could have no idea he was thinking of his plans with Trevor Howells coming to fruition once a General Election had been won. Sheila explained that David needed something now; it was urgent.

"I can't pull a job out of a hat for him, Sheila." He flicked his buzzing intercom. "Yes, what is it?" His secretary announced that Mr. Howells had arrived for his appointment.

Sheila stood to leave. She didn't want to interfere with business. But Sefton said "No, stay where you are a minute," brought Howells in and introduced them.

Howells had lecherous eyes and they scanned Sheila from top to toe as if she were naked.

"Mrs. Ashton, Trevor. My nephew's wife. Don't know anyone who could use a likely ex-R.A.F. officer, do you? He'd do well, properly handled."

Howells considered, never taking his eyes off Sheila. She knew he fancied her, and her eyes betrayed it. He played it paternally.

"Might be able to find him something myself. He'd have to learn quick, but we'd show him how. It's a fairly new venture, going to need young men on the ball. Tell him to come and see me."

Sefton explained that David knew nothing about Sheila's visit. Howells wrote something on the back of his visiting card, asked Sefton for an envelope, sealed the card in it, asked for David's name, wrote it on the envelope, and handed it to Sheila with a smile. "Say this was put through your door. That stops him finding out, doesn't it?"

Howells tried to exploit her appreciative thanks. "I should explain, Mrs. Ashton, if he gets this job, it will take him away from home, oh, a fair bit. Does that bother you? It does some wives, doesn't it?"

"Well, he's been away in the Air Force." Sheila's answer didn't indicate whether she'd got his implied message.

Howells elaborated. "If you find he has to be away more than ... more than is good for you, just come and see me. My number's on that card, so keep it handy; phone me any time you like."

Sheila now realised what he had in mind. She looked to Sefton, but she might have known his thoughts ran on business tram-lines.

"Well, you can't say fairer than that, Trevor."

"Yes, Mister Howells. That's very kind of you." Sheila was thinking, "You dirty old man, you'll never get a phone call from me." But she mumbled more gratitude as Sefton's secretary showed her out.

"Well, Trevor, to our muttons. 'The Times' says the official announcement of Victory in Europe is only a formality now. Might even be today."

"We're only waiting for one thing, Sefton. The sale of your works. Have you pushed it through?"

"Forty-eight hours; at most. It'll be all cut and dried, I promise you."

Doris had spent a fitful night at the Mackenzies'. She didn't want anyone else to know she was back in the district. They thought it best to let her take her time. When Freda came home from the hospital, Doris was still uncommunicative; like a lost soul. Freda explained what a difficult duty she'd had. She was dying to tell the old gang that Doris was okay.

136

If only to reassure them that nothing terrible had happened.

Doris was trying to write a letter. She screwed it into a ball and held it in her fist as she tried to stem the tears.

Freda apologised. "I didn't mean it's nothing terrible, Doris. I mean they're worried in case it was something quite serious, you know what I mean. I'm sorry I made you do that; look, copy it out again."

Freda gently took the screwed-up paper and smoothed it out on the table. Doris made to stop her but then didn't; almost as though she wanted Freda to read what she'd written. Freda couldn't help but read it.

"You can't send this, Doris. You mustn't."

"It's nothing to do with you what I write."

Freda read it aloud to let Doris know what it sounded like. "My darling Ricky, If you do not get a divorce and come back and marry me I will do something drastic and you will be to blame. Because it is your baby."

It only confirmed that the root-trouble was as Freda suspected, even though the pregnancy did not show yet.

"Doris. D'you know what this would do to him?"

"I don't care if she does read it. And leaves him for good. And takes the kids."

"That's what you want, isn't it? But I'm not talking about his wife. Look, love, if he wants you, badly enough, he'll come back. Without you trying to force him. But if he doesn't, this won't make him. It'll only make him hate you; and forget you ever existed."

Doris broke down completely, heaving sighs as Freda put her arm around her. "Doris, love, you're not going to do anything drastic."

"I don't mean to. I made it up. To make him think I would."

Freda got a box of matches. "Promise me you won't write anything like that again. And I promise you we'll get something done. Come on. Burn it. Right now."

Freda was determined to speak to Ian about it, as she handed a match to Doris and held the letter for her to light it.

Doris hesitated, then struck the match and put the flame under one corner of the crumpled paper.

Sefton had been having another go at Helen. The support of her thirty per cent shareholding would see him to a clear majority. Breaking down her resistance would be the easiest way of all. But Helen was still very concerned about Edwin's job. Sefton's reassurances that it would not be in jeopardy did nothing to sway her.

"I'm sorry you can't see it my way, Helen. Because I've had a Mister Fraser on the phone today. Must be a pretty bright chap because somehow he's got wind of this sale, before we've even put any feelers out – All right, before we've officially decided to sell. Probably through Trevor Howells, now I come to think of it. The point is Fraser tells me he owns interests in publishing; magazines, that sort of line, going back pre-war. So he's got licences for printing, see? And in future he wants to produce on his own presses. So this could be the last chance we have, the very last chance, of getting a decent price. Now think on that."

Sefton thought he'd leave her to "think on" what she'd be losing if she didn't get some sense of the situation. She'd find that having principles could cost a lot of money. It would be a different kettle of fish when that dawned on her.

David flopped into a chair tiredly, stating God-knows-how-many miles he'd covered that day. But his head hadn't played up at all. It seemed to be improving. Sheila brought him an envelope, "I found it stuck through the letterbox."

David looked at it wearily. "No stamp?" He slit it open.

Sheila was so anxious she nearly gave herself away. "There's some writing. On the other side. Er . . . I can see it, from here."

Before he flipped the card over, David read "Trevor W. Howells, Esquire, Third Floor, Mersey House . . ." Then he sat up, his tiredness gone, reading excitedly: " 'Mr. Briggs tells me you could be the man I'm looking for. Come and see me. T.W.H.' How about that? He doesn't wait for me to come to him. He sends for me. Special delivery." David already had the job. "We'll be out of this dump, before you can say V.E. Day."

Helen thought she should have a talk with Edwin after Sefton's "go" at her. But neither of them could see how he could possibly achieve majority voting-power. Except that Helen felt Tony was acting a little strangely, although nothing she could put into words.

Edwin took a newly-opened air-mail letter from behind the clock. "This was stamped 'Delayed by Enemy Action', Helen. Goodness knows where it's been on the way."

"From your Philip?"
"No, it's from your Jo."

Sefton was delighted to answer Tony's questions. "What's the printing works worth, lad? You mean sale-value as a going-concern, I presume?"

"I mean what would the family receive in terms of actual money, if we agreed to sell?"

"Well, if we were offered twenty thousand, we should grab it. It's a good price Tony, and I can't see us getting that sort of value out of it any other way than by selling. I've been in business a long time, lad: I know what I'm talking about." He nearly went on to suggest that Tony took his advice without question, but checked himself in time. "Look at it for yourself Tony. Very carefully. Make a sound assessment. Don't let me influence you."

Tony's reply surprised and delighted Sefton. "You haven't; I've been giving it more thought than you realise, father. If you get a buyer offering more than twenty thousand pounds, then I'll support you."

Sefton was about to say how sound a decision that was when they were interrupted by Helen's return. Edwin was with her.

Sefton was quick to commit his new ally. "Tony was just this minute talking about selling. Weren't you, lad?"

Tony confirmed in front of Edwin with some embarrassment. "Well, I . . . Put it this way. If this Mister Fraser puts up a good offer, it might be the last chance we have, the way things are."

Sefton wasn't letting go now. "You are voting for selling, aren't you Tony? You did say so, a minute ago."

"Er . . . Provided the price is over twenty thousand pounds." Tony knew Edwin's stare was angry but didn't meet it.

"I'll get that price. I know I will."

"But you won't get the votes." Edwin was angry.

"I've got 'em, haven't I. My thirty-five. Tony's ten. And Jo's ten. That's fifty-five per cent. Which is more than half, any schoolboy knows that. Come on, admit defeat, Edwin. No hard feelings. Lets have a drink on it."

Edwin stood firm. "I wrote to Jo, Sefton, after you tried it on last time. When she didn't reply, I thought she'd disagreed with every word I said. Her reply's only just got through. She says you didn't explain a thing to her."

139

"There was no point going into a lot of figures she wouldn't understand."

"She understands the way some of us feel about it now. And she's changed her mind. She votes against selling." Edwin held out her letter as proof. Sefton did not need to read it. He knew Edwin must be telling him what it said.

Sheila was so used to David's going out job-hunting immediately after breakfast that she hadn't bothered to get dressed. Suddenly, as she stood at the stove making herself a cup of coffee, two arms snaked round her slip. She spun round; was grabbed and kissed before she could see who it was. But she recognised the lips. David's.

"You made me jump out of my skin. I didn't hear you come in."

"Could have been a burglar or anybody." David returned to the shelf by the door, where he'd left a bunch of tulips. "Special delivery for Mrs. Ashton," he joked.

Sheila hadn't smiled so broadly for years. "You've got the job? With Mister Howells." David's grin confirmed without his saying a word. "What is it doing? Tell me, don't just stand there."

"It's a new selling technique. They've bought up this consignment of pre-war radios. Been lying in an old cotton-mill. They're reconditioning them, of course."

"But you don't know much about wireless-sets, do you?"

"Only what I learned in the R.A.F. My job's to sell 'em, Sheila. They're going to be advertised; with a coupon for people to write in. I call and switch 'em on to buying the more pricey model. Simple."

"Selling door-to-door?" Sheila didn't like the sound of it. There was a sort of spiv-thing about it, she thought; but didn't say.

"Only at first. They're not going to make me manager next Monday, when I start. Give 'em a chance." He took her hand. "Come on, I've something to show you."

"What, like this?"

"Well, get dressed. Quick."

What was the tearing hurry, Sheila wondered.

In the privacy of their bedroom Freda told Ian that Doris was pregnant. What could he do to help? The answer was not what she expected from a gynaecologist. "We'll do all we can, Freda. Would you like her to stay on here, so you could help her through when her time comes?"

"And then what?"

"Well, that's up to Doris isn't it? If she wants to have the baby adopted I can probably –"

"I don't think she wants to have it at all."

"Well, there's nothing we can do about that, is there?"

"I'd 've thought maybe there is."

Ian became alarmed. "Freda, you haven't promised her I could do something, professionally?"

"I didn't actually say that, no."

"Then what did you promise her?"

"That . . . we'd do what we can. You are a doctor, after all. She can't face her friends, her parents. It's something not quite nice, isn't it, an illegitimate baby? Don't you think she came running to us because you are a doctor? Because you could do something . . . positive?"

"And you haven't discouraged her from thinking that?"

"You mean you won't help her?"

"I won't procure an abortion, if that's what you mean."

"Don't make it sound so sordid. I mean get rid of Doris's unwanted baby."

"Look Freda. Darling. I'll do anything else I humanly can. But –"

"Oh, don't be so daft. What else is there anyone can do?"

Sheila stood in the untended front garden looking at the house incredulously. Then she read the sign: "This desirable three-bedroomed residence FOR SALE. Apply Cook and Cook, Quay Street, Liverpool."

David took her arm and propelled her towards the front door. "It's a bargain. Only seven-hundred-and-ninety-five."

"That's nearly eight-hundred pounds, David. How d'you know the price, anyway?"

David took the latch-key from his pocket. It was strung to a label printed "Cook and Cook".

Sheila was aghast. "You haven't even started your job yet."

"Give me something to work for, won't it? What are you scared of?"

"I don't know. It terrifies me. But compared with the old place, it's a dream, I'll admit that."

"Yes, well, it's about time some of our dreams came true."

David unlocked the door. "Come on, I'll carry you over the threshold."

"No. I'm not going in. I mean, how much will you have to earn to afford this?"

"Come on in. It won't bite."

Sheila walked gingerly into the empty hall, looked at the bare floors and staircase. "We'll need carpets, and curtains. And you still haven't told me what your pay will be."

"How can I tell you that until I know what commission I'm earning. Could be ... anything; the sky's the limit."

"I'm not talking about the commission. I mean your wages – salary. What we're sure of every week."

"There isn't a salary. The commission's so good, very high. We can't have it both ways, Sheila."

"So if you don't sell anything, you don't get any pay? Is that it?"

"Who said anything about not selling anything? I'm going to make a bomb. It'll roll in, just wait and see."

In panic Sheila turned to run. But David slammed the front door. The sound reverberating through the empty house, made Sheila jump.

"Take it calm. Have a look round; there's no harm in that, is there?"

Sheila knew he was sweet-talking again, but she couldn't resist.

"Well ... we're just looking, David, that's all. Nothing more."

Ian was still trying to convince Freda that he couldn't help Doris however much he wanted to. He had to conform to the law.

Freda was intractable. "Oh, doctors who do abortions get arrested, do they?"

"A doctor terminates a pregnancy if the mother's life is in danger. Or might be if she has the baby. Or if she'd be mentally disturbed as a result of having it. That's the law and you can't get round it."

"So all we can do is hide her away from people who'll point nasty accusing fingers?"

"Freda. Darling. Please try to understand. It's a criminal offence to procure a miscarriage. The maximum penalty is imprisonment for life. That's how seriously the law views it.

Whether we agree with it or not. Offences Against the Persons Act of 1868, if you want chapter and verse."

"Oh. Is it. Thanks very much; it helps my argument. 1868: what's that, nearly eighty years ago? The Dark Ages. Disraeli and Gladstone, if I remember my history. Well, when are we going to start thinking about 1945 girls, like Doris. War casualties, they are. Like the wounded from the Second Front."

Ian raised his voice for the first time since their wedding. "Well, don't take it out on me. I don't make the laws!"

The door opened. Doris stood there, worried and desperate. "Sorry. I couldn't help hearing. I don't want to make any trouble. The fact is ... I'm not having a baby. I made that up, too, Freda. Just to get Ricky back. I told you, when you made me burn that letter."

Nothing they could say would dissuade Doris from going. Where, they'd no idea. But she left immediately. As soon as she'd gone Ian tried to console Freda. "We've got to let her sort it out her way. There's no choice."

But Freda was already wondering whether Doris had said she wasn't going to have the baby just to stop them falling out. Doris would, if she thought it would help. She ached to help her. She'd never felt so helpless, nor for such a need of Ian. He held her tightly, as if he knew.

The next day was officially designated "Victory-in-Europe Day". Bonfires appeared on bombed-sites ready for lighting after dark. Some enterprising kids made an effigy of Adolf Hitler and stuck him atop a pile of rubbish collected from the debris of houses his bombs had wrecked on that very site.

Freda got ready to go to a meeting Sefton had called at his home. "Something to do with the shares, Margaret says. I don't really want to go. Unless you come with me."

"I don't hold any Briggs and Son shares so I'm not entitled to be there. But you must go to look after your interests."

"Yes, I suppose so."

They listened to Churchill's speech to the Nation at three o'clock.

It ended: "... We must now devote all our strength and resources to the completion of our task, both at home and abroad. Advance Britannia. Long live the cause of freedom. God Save the King." As the bugle-fanfare began to vibrate the loud-speaker fretwork, Ian switched off.

143

Sefton turned off his wireless. "Well, now, in view of what Mister Churchill has said, it's all the more reason we should examine our own affairs. Who still isn't here?"

"Only Freda," said Margaret without apology.

"Well, I'll wait just a few minutes. Sit down everybody."

Sefton had set out chairs in his lounge to give the psychological impression of an audience facing the directors in a General Meeting. As Managing Director he would preside from a position of vantage, and keep everyone on a tight rein.

"Bit formal, isn't it?" Edwin observed.

"It's a company meeting, legally speaking. We can still be one big happy family."

Edwin doubted it, but said, "Where's Askew, then?"

"Can't we take a vote without having a solicitor?" Sefton purposely misunderstood the question.

Helen didn't; George Askew was the only safeguard that Sefton wouldn't overstep the mark. "He is the only other director besides you, Sefton."

"Aye, but only nominally. He's got a big company meeting in the City, so he can't come. We don't need him; it's all right." Sefton looked at his watch, gave Freda two more minutes.

Tony spoke privately to Edwin. "I'm sure it'll work out, Uncle. I wouldn't agree to sell otherwise."

Edwin showed his displeasure. "My guess is as good as yours about that."

"I'm not guessing, Uncle."

But before Edwin could ask what Tony meant, Freda breezed in, apologising for being late and sitting all in one flurry.

Sefton accepted her apology with a glare. "Right. This Extraordinary General Meeting is now in session. The only item on the agenda is my proposal that we sell the works. Seconded by Tony Briggs. In proposing this motion, I have an announcement to make. I've been approached by a Mister Eric Fraser and we have agreed a price. A very attractive price. All we need is a majority agreement in favour of accepting it. We've had a bad year, as you know too well; so it's now or never."

Edwin interjected. "What d'you call an attractive price?"

"I asked twenty-five thousand pounds."

"That doesn't answer Edwin's question, Sefton." Helen reminded him.

"Fraser countered with an offer of nineteen thousand."

"I don't call that an attractive price," said Edwin.

144

"But after some very hard bargaining we agreed at ..." Sefton paused to create maximum effect. "Twenty-two thousand pounds!"

The effect was created. There were gasps. Even Edwin admitted to himself that it was a good price indeed.

Tony stood up. "We should take it. We must take it. I'm sorry that it means the business goes out of the family. But we've got to look at the situation squarely."

Edwin kept fighting. "It's a good price, yes; and we might not get a better, I admit. But that's not the whole story. I was offered a better job, more pay. But I didn't take it, remember?"

"You didn't like Pringle, that's why." Sefton fought back.

"I preferred to stay where I am; that's why. I saw how a bigger works is run by a man like Pringle. That was enough for me. And what happens to our workers when your smart-suited Fraser and his cut-glass accent give the orders?"

Edwin had met Fraser when Sefton had taken him round the works, "Surveying the place from a great height" he'd told Margaret, "as if he already owned it."

Edwin got to his feet. "What will he care that Joe has to watch his bad back. That Fred's likely to fly off the handle a bit. That Nora lost her Jim at Alamein. And the place run by someone pushing buttons in London."

Sefton played his trump card. "Mister Fraser has already agreed to keep you on. As manager."

"Oh. Twist his arm did you?"

"I specified he must; as part of the deal. In writing."

Margaret thought she was helping. "Well, it seems to me that if they're forced to keep Dad on, at least his job'll be safe if we sell."

In her anxiety to contribute, Freda compounded the error. "It does mean Dad can't be fired, doesn't it uncle?"

"Of course it does. It'll be written into the contract of sale, I told you."

Edwin was burning with anger. "Whether I suit Frazer or not, he's stuck with me, isn't he? Well, it won't work. A man gets on with his boss by doing his job properly. If not he gets out. And that's the only way I can work. I say we keep the works. Not get into a panic by one bad year. And make it pay!"

Sefton paid Edwin a compliment. "Nobody's tried to do more than you have, Edwin. I acknowledge that." But it was intended as proof that they couldn't make it pay.

Freda tried again. She could see her father was losing the battle. "Do we have to decide today? Aren't we rushing it a bit?"

Sefton had an immediate reply. "Fraser wants printing facilities quickly. If we dilly-dally he'll go somewhere else. That's for certain."

Tony elaborated. "And we may never get another chance."

"Oh. I see" Freda subsided.

Sefton thought he saw a chink in the Ashtons' armour. "Does that mean you vote to sell, Freda?"

Freda wondered, looked at her father, saw defeat in his eyes, and knew how badly he was taking it. "Er ... No, it doesn't. No, I'm still against selling."

Margaret didn't wait to be asked. "So am I. Dead against."

But Sefton didn't allow the mood to pass. "Helen, you haven't said anything yet. Your share of the sale would be five-thousand five-hundred, you know that?"

Helen was annoyed that Sefton should still hope that the money might sway her and said so. Then she added. "But I wish Edwin would give Mister Fraser a try. He could be a very good boss, for all we know."

"He is." Tony quickly qualified his hurriedly-added comment. "I er ... I made a few enquiries. He's just demobbed from the Navy. I asked one or two chaps who've served under his command. And they liked him." His explanation was accepted, and Tony heaved a silent sigh of relief.

Edwin made a final plea. "Can't you see I want the chance to do it myself? To bring the works back to what it was before the war?"

"There's too much at stake, Edwin. We haven't a chance, without the resources Fraser has!"

Edwin sat down slowly. "What you mean is I'm too old now. Past doing it."

Sefton didn't reply. It was a sad silent moment. "Right. Everybody's had their say. Now we count the votes. Those in favour of selling, hands up."

Sefton raised his own hand. Tony raised his. Lips moved silently as everyone mentally counted. Forty-five per cent in favour. Then Helen slowly raised her hand. "I'm sorry, Edwin. But I think it's the right decision."

Sefton tried not to smile. "That's seventy per cent in favour. Over two-thirds. A thumping majority. The works will be sold. The meeting is closed." Church bells could be heard, but

Sefton continued as if it were all part and parcel. "Listen, everybody. V.E. Day celebrations starting. And we also celebrate the decision taken today to –"

Sefton stopped. The others followed his gaze. Edwin was at the door, leaving.

Margaret and Freda called after him. "Dad, don't go," and "Dad, wait a minute."

Edwin seemed not to hear. The door closed behind him.

The flames leapt high into the darkness, beginning to lick Hitler's Liverpool-made uniform. The swastika band on his arm had already caught alight. Children sang and danced round the searing heat. Church bells, hooters and ships' sirens punctuated their war-time songs.

Edwin was walking aimlessly, and the flames reflected the sadness in his eyes. He stopped at the fire, watched, and then turned away.

A clutch of youngsters ran after him. "Eh, mister, don't go." "No, the fun's just starting." "Come on, mister. Buck up. Hitler's dead." "Aye, the war's over. We've won."

When they realised he hadn't heard a word, they scampered back to the bonfire. Someone lit a rocket – a distress-signal type "borrowed" for the event.

As its fiery tail illuminated the scene, Edwin lifted his head to watch it rise and explode. Suddenly it was spent; and his face was dark again.

CHAPTER FIFTEEN

July 1945

John Porter, Treasurer of the Party, became heavily committed to getting their candidate in at the coming General Election. As the political D-day grew nearer, demands on John's time increased until he was going directly to the Committee Rooms from his day's chores under Temple's eye. Margaret saw less and less of him. When he did come home, she found him obsessed with politics, talking to her as if he was on a soap-box.

Edwin was worrying about what happened when Fraser actually took over the works, and hardly consoled her with edgy remarks; "Well, you wanted him to have an interest.

You put your friend Marjorie up to it. You good as pushed him into it."

"I did no such thing."

"Well, you hardly discouraged her from wooing him."

"Wooing him? What's that supposed to mean?" Margaret frowned.

"Wooing him into taking an active part in all this politics hoo-hah." Edwin threw down the latest consignment of election pamphlets to be pushed through the door. He looked at Margaret over his spectacles, as if to say "Why, what other sort of wooing did you think I meant?"

Margaret changed the subject. "No news about Frazer and the Works yet? You haven't said."

"I wish there were some news. It's over a month now since that ridiculous decision to sell."

"Have you asked Uncle Sefton what's happening?"

"I wouldn't give him the pleasure of knowing I'm anxious."

"Have you asked Tony?"

"I've not seen him since the meeting. And that isn't accidental, I suspect, either."

In the street, a loudspeaker blared from the horns atop a Labour-postered car. "Vote Labour. Vote Labour. Now is the time to build on Labour for Peace. Vote Labour." The slogans penetrated the Ashtons' closed windows.

Edwin was annoyed at the intrusion. "You know, I'd willingly give my vote to any party that made no obnoxious noises. If there was one."

Sheila never would have believed it, but here they were, in that very house they looked at. David had offered seven-hundred-and-fifty pounds and it was accepted. He'd organised a mortgage, and a van to move what little furniture they had, which meant the kitchen and one bedroom were furnished after a fashion. The other rooms, in Sheila's phrase, were "full of emptiness." David didn't worry about problems like rationing dockets, or the wherewithal to buy utility furniture. Sheila did; but she had to admit they were in the house, it was light, and it didn't have any peculiar smell about it. And there was room to swing a cat, it had a front door which you could use, and a back door.

That there was a patch of garden, front and back, didn't worry David either. He pushed his chair back from the break-

148

fast table – their only table, as David had refused to bring the old Morrison shelter which had served at the other place – and kissed her good-bye. He looked sharp in civilian clothes, raring to go and "sell to the-world-and-his-wife" as he put it. "Don't worry, love. We'll make this place really something; and get Peter and Janet home; and it'll all go like a bomb for us. Must fly, every minute lost is less time to earn commission."

When he had gone Sheila went into what she hoped would be their lounge one day. No use worrying that it was as bare as the day David had borrowed the key from the agents. But telling herself not to didn't make any difference. Sheila was a born worrier. A knock at the door shook her out of her moon-reaching. Helen told her that she had talked Sefton into parting with a few bits of furniture he no longer needed in that big house. They were on their way; but, if she didn't want any of them, not to worry. I knew you couldn't furnish these rooms with what you had. And it will help you make do, until you can buy exactly what you want. That's the van, just pulled up.

Sheila looked out of the front window as two men lowered the tailboard of a removal lorry. She turned and hugged Helen with tears in her eyes.

Margaret plonked down the large tin on the table. John peered over his coffee-cup at the label.

"Distemper? For breakfast? No thanks, I've finished."

"Don't pretend you can't take a hint," Margaret smiled.

"Hint? What hint?" John's mind was full of electioneering.

"It's Saturday, remember? You have the afternoon off, don't you?" John finished his coffee, rose from the table.

"Oh, you mean the attic. Yes, well, not this Saturday, Margaret."

"You promised. You made a bargain. You said if I got the distemper, you'd put it on."

"I've got to go to Party H.Q. this afternoon. I must."

"Must? Conscripted now, are you? I see."

"Obviously you don't see. We've got an Election coming up, in case you hadn't noticed. It's vital to the future of the country. Vital to us; you, me, John-George."

"Am I allowed to heckle the speaker on the platform?"

"Look, I haven't time to argue, I'll be late for work. You know what Temple is about being on time."

"No time to discuss the major issues with your wife. If it were Marjorie you'd start an intellectual discussion that would go on for hours, wouldn't you?"

"Marjorie? What's it got to do with her?"

"Well, isn't it her you've promised to work with this afternoon? Instead of keeping your promise to distemper the attic."

"My God, are you jealous of Marjorie?"

"What's so surprising about that? The time you spend with her these days. I see her at school every day, don't forget, and she's no longer the frumpy teacher she was before all this election business started. She's smartened up a lot. Both intelligent and attractive to men, isn't she?"

John tried to turn the accusation. "Don't you think I'm the one with cause to be jealous?"

John had never before thrown the Michael Armstrong affair at her. Without mentioning his name he'd silenced her as if she'd been struck dumb. He stormed out without another word, opened the front door, but then stopped and called back. "See you tonight, then." There was no answer, so he banged the door behind him.

Edwin came downstairs. "I wish John wouldn't slam that door. It shakes the whole house."

Margaret spoke as she went into the kitchen. "He doesn't, usually, does he?"

One house that David determined to call on wasn't going to make him any commission. He found only Margaret in and not in a very good mood. He told her she was about the only one of the family he could talk to nowadays, anyway.

Margaret was unsympathetic in spite of the compliment. "Does that include Sheila?"

"Oh, Sheila. Yes, there are subjects you keep off with Sheila, unless you want a big row. My job for instance. Now if I complained it wasn't what I wanted, she'd say it was me, see? Not the job. So I'm making out it's great."

"But isn't it any good? Sheila was telling me what prospects there are. So you said."

"Yes, well, you see, Mags, I've discovered, now I'm getting into it, that there's only one way to make a living selling junk. And that's by conning people. I mean, Howell's never says that, not in so many words. But that's what I've got to do to

150

be successful. If the mug doesn't suffer, then I do. What worries me is that if I try not to think about what I'm doing to the people I call on ... I find I'm good at it; at shooting a line, sales patter, you know. And we need the money. Okay, thanks to the shares Mum left and the Building Society, I've bought the house. But we've still got to live, you know. I want the kids back; but Sheila says not until the house is decent and we've got all the things she says we need for 'em. And don't forget, it was a hellova graft to get a job, I mean we're so hand-to-mouth that one week out of work, just one week with nothing coming in, and we're in cash trouble. Dead trouble."

"But Sheila doesn't know any of this?"

"Course she doesn't. She'd just say it was all me, as usual, and dig up the past to prove it. Oh, I know I was a bit of a ... Yes, all right, let's say I was good at conning her, too when it suited me. But those days are over, Mags, they really are. I wonder if I wouldn't be better off in some nine-to-five same-every-day job. There's a lot to be said for it."

"Ask John. He wouldn't agree with you. But I see what you mean." Margaret knew that way of life had its problems, too. No help to David to go into it, though. The grass is always greener ... whichever side of the street you're on.

After David had gone, Margaret took a telephone call from John's boss. Edwin came in as she put the telephone down and noticed her frown.

"Who was that, Margaret?"

"Mister Temple. Why isn't John in this morning, is he sick?"

"But he went in, didn't he?"

"That's what you thought and that's what I thought."

"Oh. I see."

"Yes. His work comes a poor second when it comes to the vitally important things in life. And so do I."

Edwin thought it best to give her something else to think about. "I wish the Japanese would surrender, then we could say it's really over."

"What's that to do with it?"

"Well, it's dragging on too long. Since V.E. Day people have changed somehow. There's no longer any urgency. The fighting's now so far away; and everyone knows we're going to win sooner or later. But we're not doing much to prepare for peace-time. Oh, I know all these loud-mouthed politicians are saying we are but nobody seems to be actually doing anything. You know what I mean?"

151

"John apparently thinks he's doing something." She wondered what he and Marjorie were doing at that moment.

There was something else in Edwin's mind. "And if it was really over, we'd have Philip back home from Germany; wouldn't we?"

Margaret agreed. "Yes, that would be nice, wouldn't it?"

Helen had stayed long enough to help Sheila arrange the "new" furniture as she wanted it. Long after both van and Helen had gone, Sheila was still changing her mind, moving, polishing, dusting; striving to make a maximum impact on David when he arrived home.

The effect was not what she expected. She met him at the front door. Had he had a good morning?

"Yes. Not bad at all," he lied. Going to the Ashtons had taken him out of his itinerary so he'd made only three calls. Each time the husband was home, which made a sale more difficult. He could sweet-charm the housewife, alone or with kids round her knees. Husbands were more likely to snap "No thanks, not today," before he could say more than "Good morning". Or they might despatch him with "Sorry, mate, she filled in the coupon by mistake." Or, if he actually got in to demonstrate the cheap model, with "Well, we'll think about it," which was the same as the instantaneous "No thanks, not today," except that it took up more of his time. His calls that morning had been one of each. Resultant sales nil, commission ditto.

"Yes. Quite a good morning, actually. What the hell's all this?" He saw the furniture. "Where d'you get this load of junk?"

His reaction was so antagonistic that Sheila found herself explaining and excusing. "I couldn't very well refuse, could I? It was so good of your Uncle Sefton, really."

"We don't want his throw-outs. Rubbish he doesn't want to give house-room any more."

"I'm sure they were both trying to be kind."

"Kind? Charity, more like. And that's one thing I won't have; from anyone."

"Some of it's all right, David. Look at this chair. Better than nothing, surely. Until we can afford to buy what we want ourselves?"

Sheila was abjectly disappointed. She didn't know what else

she could say. She ran into the kitchen, but David followed her.

"Tell you what, Sheila. You can keep it if you agree to have the kids back. Right now."

"No, David. Not yet, I said."

"You said we haven't a proper home for them to come back to. Well, if this stuff will do for the time being for us, it will do for them. Right? ... Won't it? Okay then, Peter and Janet come home."

"No. No, it isn't just that, David, is it?" Sheila pleaded. "We've got to be sure. That it's going to work. You and me, I mean. Let's not rush into getting them back, until we know it's for good. We've got to make it work. For keeps David, haven't we?"

David sighed, shook his head, went out into the dining room and flopped into Sefton's old armchair. To his surprise, it was very comfortable. He put his head back. He realised he could no longer talk Sheila into anything she didn't want to do. Those days were over.

John didn't find house-to-house salesmanship any more attractive than David did. Even though, in his case, it was "a Labour of love," as Marjorie said, "if you'll forgive the pun."

It so happened that the last street on their canvassing sheet was round the corner from Marjorie's flat. John remembered that she had allocated the streets to pairs of canvassers to leapfrog from door to door. He knew she'd chosen him as partner, but only now that she'd organised their route to terminate near her home.

She invited him in for a drink. "One for the road, quite literally."

Her flat was a bit arty, very bachelor-girl with Marx and Engels featured between the bookends.

Marjorie produced a whisky bottle. "American bourbon all right?"

"Easy to see where you get your liquor."

"An American political friend," Marjorie explained, pouring generous doubles.

"Didn't know serving U.S. Forces were allowed to have politics."

"This one has. He's gone back now."

"Didn't propose taking you with him?"

"Didn't propose anything. Who'd have me, John, anyway? When there's plenty of younger talent available."

"Talent? Huh. Have you talked to girls of today? Talent's the last thing they have. Be damn lucky to get you, some bloke would."

"Who, for instance?"

If Marjorie secretly hoped he might reply, "Me, for instance," she was disappointed.

"Lots of chaps, I'll bet." He surveyed the room. "I thought I'd like a place like this, once. I think I'd 've left home if I'd found one."

"You mean after you'd married Margaret?"

"No. Before. Bachelor flat. You know. Just one of my many dreams."

"You missed nothing. It can be very lonely." Marjorie sat beside him on the settee, as closely as she could without making it obvious. "You had a bad spell of loneliness yourself. Margaret told me."

"Yes. But that was in a cellar. Fraction of this size."

"And back here they thought you were missing."

"Yes. I was given up for dead. For months."

"And Margaret met ... Did she say his name was Michael?"

Margaret had told her about Michael? Not the whole story, he was relieved to discover. She hadn't mentioned the baby. But it surprised him she'd talked about Michael at all. Perhaps in an unguarded moment, as a conversation drifts, and you find yourself saying something you didn't really intend. He was relieved that Marjorie didn't know about the baby. He couldn't think why that mattered so much, but it did.

"No, I never met him, Marjorie; well, not knowing who he was. I did see him once actually. Quite a nice bloke, I believe."

"Have you never had the urge ... to get level with Margaret? Even-Stephen?" Her eyes told him exactly what she meant.

"No. To be honest, I haven't. I don't see there's anything to get even about."

John kicked himself for a fool. He should have seen this coming. The canvas-pairing, the street where they finished, the invitation for a drink. It had just not occurred to him that his wife's friend would ... well, she ought to consider Margaret more. He refused the offer of another Bourbon. Sorry,

154

he must get home, to Margaret. He'd promised to distemper the attic.

It had been an excuse to extricate himself from the situation. He knew he'd be too tired to start a job like that when he got home. As soon as he saw Margaret he confessed that he hadn't been to work.

Margaret was about to throw at him that Temple had telephoned; and still did.

"What excuse did you give him?"

"That you were sick and I'd kept you in bed. I lied for you." Margaret resisted the temptation to add that she was lying so he could be with Marjorie.

"Well, you knew where I'd be."

"Didn't take much guesswork, did it? But you might have let me into the secret. So that I'd had the excuse ready."

"I didn't know; when I left for work. I just thought on the way there; it was much more important that we win the election. It gave us a whole day canvassing. Instead of half."

"That's important?"

"Well of course it is. D'you realise what we're up against? With the Tories shouting Churchill won the war for us, now let him win the peace."

"Well, he did, didn't he? Most people believe he's done more than his share to prevent us being oppressed by Nazis. Or don't you believe that?"

"He led the people, yes. But that doesn't make him the right man to carry out reforms the war's held up for six long years. We all believe that in our Party, don't we?"

"I've never said I support your Party, John."

"You don't support . . .? I took it for granted."

"You never discuss politics with me. Not like with Marjorie. You took it for granted that your Party is automatically my Party."

"You're not going to vote Tory, Margaret? Don't tell me that."

"I'm not going to tell you anything. Dad asked me how I'm going to vote this morning, and I wouldn't tell him either. It's between me and the ballot-box."

"You won't even tell your husband? That's ridiculous."

"Well, you don't tell your wife everything you do."

"What don't I tell you?"

"Oh don't pretend to be the little innocent. It won't wash."

John couldn't understand why she flounced out of the room in such a temper. He really couldn't. But something stopped him from going after her and demanding to know why.

CHAPTER SIXTEEN

August 1945

Rumour-lovers who had forecast that a secret-weapon that would "bring the enemy to their knees" were now sagely nodding, "I told you so". The obscene wastes of lifeless Hiroshima and Nagasaki proved them right. Japan surrendered quickly, unconditionally, under the shock-wave of the atom bomb.

The official "V.J. Day" marked the end of hostilities in World War Two. It was the moment people all over the world had prayed for and looked towards for seven long years. Yet it was an anti-climax compared to the wild celebrations of "V.E. Day", three months earlier.

In Britain the event was overshadowed by the aftermath of the first General Election to be held since before the long years of war. Churchill's victorious leadership did not win him the people's mandate. Attlee's Socialist Government was given the task of making the land fit for heroes to live in, of sweeping away the injustices preserved by the war-effort's priorities.

David and Sheila had catalystic news on a domestic level. Mrs. Thomas, so kind to their children, loving and caring for them as her own, died very suddenly from a heart attack. Sudden sadness precipitated their unarguable agreement to bring them home. To their new home.

Sefton applauded Helen's support for the sale of Briggs and Son Printing Works. He praised her judgement in coming to the conclusion that it was the right decision.

But Tony worried him. Why had he changed his mind? Sefton had the feeling that there was more to it. Had Tony supported the sale for a reason that he'd kept quiet about? If so Sefton couldn't put his finger on it.

Tony had learned one trick from his father: when to play

his cards close to his chest. Even now, whilst he sat with Eric Fraser waiting for the news that the Briggs Printing Works sale was legally in effect, nobody but ex-Commander Fraser R.N. knew of his role in the events that had led up to this final act.

Fraser set out a decanter and two small tumblers. "It's rather like waiting for the signal to engage. Lying-off and shadowing, remember?"

"Funny: I was thinking of that night off Sicily. On your bridge. You killed the time talking about 'after the war'. What you were going to do. What was I going to do."

"That was when you first mentioned your father had a printing works. I remember the moment, literally seconds before we came under fire. I'd like to say this, Tony; I'm grateful to you for keeping me informed. It meant I offered the right price; and at exactly the right moment in time."

"I did it in the family's interest; quite selfishly, as I told you. I could see it was inevitable that the Works had to be sold. And that meant Pringle and a rock-bottom price. And he would only have bought to close it down to kill the competition. The end of Briggs and Son before the third generation had a chance to –"

The telephone rang. Tony grabbed it, handed it to Fraser. "Your solicitors. Askew's just left them."

Fraser took the telephone. Tony could see the outcome on his face before he replaced the telephone and said, "They've exchanged contracts. The sale's gone through without hitch." He poured the whiskies and they raised their glasses to each other. Tony felt a glow, even before the Scotch went down.

David reported to Howells' premises, after a day of mediocre response to his calls, to ask for the next day off to take his wife to Roslyn to pick up their children.

"Ah, come in the office a minute, David; I want to see you anyway."

From behind his black-and-chrome desk Trevor Howells held out a hand and smiled encouragingly. "Let's have a look at your books, David."

David produced his sale's record. "Not gone too well the past few days, I'm afraid, Mister Howells. Very little spare cash about. People are waiting to see which way the cat's going to jump, now we've got a Labour Government –"

"Past few days? Past few weeks, you mean, looking at your

157

sale's record. And don't try to blame the Government. Even a Socialist one."

"Well, I'm doing my best, I can't do more, Mister Howells."

Howells was still looking at his sales figures. "Well, if that's what this is, it's not good enough. You'll get your commission on the outstanding items, such as they are, sent by post." Howells put David's book on the desk and slapped his hand on it. "Good-bye David."

"What d'you –? You're saying I'm fired?"

"No. I suggest you resign. Looks better if someone asks me for a reference."

"But ... You can't ... We've just taken on a new house ..."

"That's your concern I can't carry passengers just because they over-reach themselves."

"I've built up a lot of contacts that might turn into future sales, Mister Howells. It takes time. You can't chuck me out now."

"Possibles don't bring in any money. Now let's not have a scene. Part good friends; just say it hasn't worked out."

"Suppose ... I take less commission. You see, we're bringing home our two kids, well, I mean, my wife is, tomorrow –"

"The chap taking over your job has five."

David glowered across the desk as if about to take Howells by the throat. "You lousy –"

Howells smiled, held up a hand indicating David should stop. "Careful. Careful what you say. One day soon you may be glad of a reference from your last employer. You won't live off your war-service all that long, you know. People have short memories in this world. I remember them coming back from the first lot."

David left shattered. His head pained him; the first time he'd felt it for weeks. What was he going to tell Sheila?

On a visit to the Ashtons', Ian grabbed an opportunity to talk to Margaret alone. Freda was in the other room talking to her father.

Frankly, Ian confessed, it worried him the way Freda continued to blame herself over Doris. Could Margaret suggest anything he could say or do? To stop Freda feeling guilty, that she should have done something positive to help Doris. And that he should have, too.

Margaret gathered that it was straining the Mackenzies' relationship. "What could anyone have done, Ian? Doris is in

158

the situation I was in. With Michael Armstrong. Whilst John was 'missing, believed killed', as they baldly put it. You knew, didn't you?"

Yes, Ian knew, but that wasn't the reason he'd asked Margaret's advice. "The ridiculous thing is that for all we know Doris might now be resigned to having the baby; perhaps even looking forward to it. We don't know. And Freda is still worrying herself silly about her; and taking it out on me, too. I don't think she realises how much."

Margaret was most concerned. "Why doesn't she go and see Doris's mother? Maybe she knows where she is. We've still got a few of her things upstiars, from when she was staying with us. She could take them back, as an excuse to call. Should I suggest it to Freda?"

"Would you, Margaret?"

Margaret reassured him. "Leave it to me."

The four stiff drinks David knocked back before confronting Sheila did not help him decide what he was going to say.

It wasn't made easier when he discovered she couldn't think about anything that wasn't connected with Peter's and Janet's homecoming. At last, things were going to be better; David's regular job and money coming in. He'd never known her so optimistic. All he could bring himself to tell her was that he was free to take her the next day to Roslyn. It was true, but not in the way Sheila believed.

Margaret asked Freda to help her parcel up the skirt, blouse and odd silk-stockings that Doris had left behind. "I've been meaning to take them to her parent's, Freda. I've got their address but there never seems to be enough time."

Freda volunteered without any coercion. "Don't worry, I'll take them."

"I had in mind that, when I did, I'd ask them. You know, if they'd got any news. Where she is, how she's making out."

Freda didn't hold out much hope. "Her mother might; if I can get a word with her alone. Doris said that if her father found out about her being pregnant on the wrong side of the altar, he'd never allow her in the house again. So she won't be at their place, because by now the baby'll be plain for all to see."

"Still, Freda, no harm asking. There's nothing for the dumb." Margaret thought she'd worked it very well.

159

A hard breeze was blowing off the river bank when Freda got off the bus. The conductress pointed towards a narrow street of aging flat-faced houses. Number 4 was far from being the best kept of them. Mrs. Jackson answered Freda's knock and said sullenly "Yes? What is it?"

When Freda explained she was Doris's friend and had brought a few of her things back, she was made no more welcome. Joe Jackson had lived by his muscles in the docks and was now too old, fat and short of breath to do much more than sit and grumble. He didn't even say "Hello" from his threadbare armchair. Freda didn't know whether they knew their daughter was pregnant, but she soon found out.

Joe Jackson cleared his throat of phlegm. "You knew this bloody-Yank? The one who put her in the bloody-family-way?"

"No. I never met him." So Doris was pregnant in spite of her denying it.

"If ever I set bloody-eyes on him I'll bloody-throttle him. With me bare bloody-hands. Slowly." His huge hands trembled as he extended his bent fingers round an imaginary throat.

"I'd like to help her. If you could tell me where she is."

"Help her?" Mrs. Jackson's voice was riddled with disgust. "Help that one? She doesn't deserve any help."

"Bloody little cow, she is, nothing bloody-more."

But suddenly, there was Doris standing at the bottom of the steep staircase.

"What're you doing in this dump, Freda? Wasting your breath talking tc them, I'll tell you that for nothing." Deeply-embedded antagonism against her parents made Doris sound cold and unfriendly. What could Freda say in return? "Hello Doris. How's it going?"

"Oh, marvellous, great. The Nursing Home's booked and I'm convalescing after in the south of France."

Her bitterness cut Freda to the heart. She turned to the Jacksons. "What's done is done. We're not helping by blaming Doris. After all it's going to be your grandchild."

Jackson tried to stand but settled for pointing angrily with his dirty-brown pipe. "Don't you come here trying to tell us what's what. She's having a bloody bastard. That's what she's having. No grandchild of ours. Get that bloody-straight before you leave this bloody-house." As he slumped back, Freda saw one foot was twisted on its ankle, wrenched out of joint irreparably. It was the result of an accident on the docks.

Freda wasn't to be daunted. "Haven't seen you for ages, Doris. I've got to get a spot of lunch somewhere. Is there a cafe we could go to?"

Doris ignored her father's angry grunt and smiled weakly, "Well, it's not up to much, I warn you."

Freda dared Jackson to say Doris couldn't come. "Right, then, come on. It's a nice day; breath of air'll do you good."

Jackson had to say something. "You're not going out like that. Put a bloody-comb through that bloody-hair."

It was the first thing he'd said that Freda could agree with. Doris had let herself go terribly.

Now that the sale of the Works was a fait accompli, and there was nothing his father nor Edwin could do about it, Tony showed his hand. He went into the Works Office next morning and Edwin listened grave-faced as he learned Tony would be Fraser's partner in the new management set-up.

Tony concluded. "I knew Dad was bound to get majority support sooner or later. And this was the only way to make sure that the buyer would be someone we'd approve of."

"So better the devil you know? As you'd served with Fraser in the Navy. Why didn't you tell me what you were up to?"

"I didn't dare, Uncle. You could have taken it the wrong way, couldn't you? Either: suspected I was doing it purely for my own sake. Or: objected to it as some sort of charity on my part. And you might well have blown the whole gaff to Father."

"You're probably right. Fraser may have been a good Naval type; but I got the impression he's ... Well, not the sort of boss I want, anyway. No offence, Tony; it's probably me. You see, I've come to the conclusion that I've had enough of taking orders, now; in my life. From anyone."

"So what does that mean, Uncle? That I've failed after all?"

"No. You spurred me into quicker action, that's all."

Edwin showed Tony a letter addressed to Fraser. It was his resignation.

The local cafe lunch was not working out as Freda had planned. She wanted to get round to suggesting that Doris came back with her. But the more they talked the more the gulf between them became apparent. Doris kept asking Freda about her marriage, and staring at her wedding ring. "Perhaps you understand better, now you've seen where I come from; why I never asked you home, all that time I stayed with you, before we lived in at the hospital."

"Doris, love, what does that matter? I'm only interested in helping you; that's all."

"You thrashed that out with your husband, didn't you? I mean, he's the expert. You asked his advice and you got his answer. There's nothing you can do. Or I can. 'Cept grin and bear it." She gave a silly laugh at the unintended pun "Bear it. Ha Ha. That's funny that is. I've got to bear it, that's for certain; nobody else can do that, can they."

Freda enquired about the long line of old boy-friends. Had she not seen any of them since . . .?

Doris laughed again, "What, with me this size? They don't want to know when it's their own doing, never mind take on somebody else's little bundle."

Freda began to suggest coming back to stay with them, but Doris cut her short. Her desperation showed in the way she attacked Freda. "Look, I don't want your help. Coming here, talking like some Father Confessor. You think I haven't thought about it? There's nothing I can do. Nothing. Don't keep on about it. I'm fed up with thinking about the bloody baby. Look, if you want it, I'll give it you! Will that do?"

The cafe was quiet, and the four other lunchers stopped eating to stare as Doris ran crying into the street. Then they all looked at Freda, who tried to pretend nothing had happened. "May I have the bill please, Miss? My friend's . . . not very well. I must . . . go after her."

Edwin had said "Goodnight's" to the staff, adding their first names involuntarily. He knew them all so well. Fraser, who had spent the day asking questions, looking, and listening, watched him return to his office and then knocked on his open door.

"You don't have to knock, Mister Fraser. You own the place."

Fraser came in. Edwin could imagine him in his Naval uniform, hands thrust in jacket pockets with thumbs cocked forward, chin jutting forward.

"Tony tells me you've a letter for me." Fraser came straight to the point.

Edwin presented his written resignation. "I know the contract says you can't fire me, but it doesn't say I can't resign, does it?" Fraser read the three sentences unemotionally. "I see you offer to give a month's notice. Is that long enough for you? Don't rush it on my account."

Edwin thought Fraser was taking it coolly. Trying to make it easier for himself, but suggesting it was for Edwin's sake. It could take him easily a month to find another manager who knew the trade. They weren't waiting on every street corner.

"No, a month's fine, thank you. In all the years I've worked here I've never had a personal contract of service; but if a month's all right with you, there's no point dragging it out."

"That's agreed then, Edwin; don't mind first names, do you? I don't like to pull rank now we're out of the straitjacket of Service discipline: you know my name. Well, you're setting me a problem by resigning, but you probably know that."

"You mean my replacement?"

"Yes. D'you happen to know of anyone? You see I intend to remain based in London, looking after the publishing side of my interests. But I intend to use Briggs Printing for more than printing my existing magazines. I'm planning to bring out a range of self-instruction booklets. Many people have found new skills and talents whilst in the Forces; things they never dreamed they had any talent for. And that there's satisfaction in creating something yourself, however modestly. And now that workday life is becoming so mass-productive and tedious, people are going to find new interest in the old crafts and old skills."

"I know what a job it is keeping this work interesting for the lads." Edwin had experience of the trend.

"I've noticed your efforts in that direction; very commendable, Edwin. I hope your successor has the same attitude. It's something I happen to feel very strongly about. And I believe you do, too; am I right?"

"Yes. You certainly are. I do." People with cut-glass accents didn't usually think on these lines, Edwin thought; not in his experience.

"You see, as soon as Tony has learned this side of the business – printing. I want him to liaise between whoever runs the works here, and London. That means your successor will be given his head to run his own show. I don't want a manager I have to watch all the time; or give orders to. That's not my way at all."

"Is that the job I've just resigned from? I must be mad." Edwin had hoped for something as satisfying as this for years and was kicking himself.

"Just a shade premature, Edwin, maybe?"

"Hasty would be a better word."

Fraser smiled and handed back his resignation letter. Edwin hesitated; then took it, and tore it up.

Later, upon reflection, he realised he had been wrong about Eric Fraser. And Tony had been right.

Peter and Janet Ashton were nearly asleep on their feet by the time they reached their new home. Their parents were dead-beat, too.

There had been tears when the moment came to leave the cottage in Roslyn, in spite of their knowing Mrs. Thomas was no longer there. The children had been fractious in the train; and they weren't very thrilled with their new home. It was too big. It wasn't old, like the Welsh cottage; it hadn't got those lovely places to hide. And no fields, no woods, no hills to climb, no bridge, no bubbling stream.

After they had been fed, they were too tired to go to bed. Peter was irritable, Janet cried. Daddy had to speak strongly before they settled and let him take Mummy downstairs again.

Sheila slumped in a chair, all in. "David. What was that you were saying to Peter?"

"What about?"

"In the cottage, when you were packing his clothes. He was asking about cars. Did you say you were going to buy-and-sell second-hands cars?"

"Yes. Something like that."

"You weren't serious?"

"I might. There's a future in it. Shortage of new ones; lot of old Service-vehicles around. And American throw-outs too; jeeps; they don't cart 'em back to the States, you know."

"But you haven't given this job a chance yet. You were full of it when you started; going to be a manager in no time. What's happened to that? Doesn't take long for you to go off the boil, does it?"

David had no choice but tell her. He tried to reassure her. "Look love, it's not the end of the world, now is it? I got that job; I'll get another. Better one."

Sheila put him straight. He hadn't got that job. She'd gone to see Uncle Sefton; Howells had done it as a favour to him. She didn't tell him about the leer on Howells' face, expecting something from her in return. Or that she could probably get him the job back tomorrow, if she was "nice" to Howells.

164

Too late she remembered that David had said the last thing he would do was go on his knees to Sefton, or anyone. He hit the ceiling; his voice went through it, and woke up the children who had just got off to sleep. Janet cried and Peter shouted for Mummy to come up, but David continued castigating Sheila until she collapsed in tears.

"No use coming the old waterworks trick. That's it, Sheila; that's definitely it. I've had just about enough. Right up to here. I'm going."

David started to pack his suitcase.

"You can't. Listen to your kids."

"Sod the kids. I'm going to London."

He slammed the front door so hard the house vibrated. Sheila rushed upstairs to console the children. She needed consolation more than they did.

CHAPTER SEVENTEEN

October 1945

The telephone rang just as John and Margaret Porter were dashing out to catch a train to Chorley to visit his parents. Margaret couldn't resist picking it up, but before she could say, "Hello," John took it from her. "Let your Dad answer it. Or we'll be late."

John held out the telephone for Edwin as he came from the dining room. The Porters left to visit the Porters.

The caller was the last person Edwin expected. "Michael Armstrong? Oh, Michael, yes; sorry, I thought you were overseas."

Michael sounded apprehensive. "I'd like to have a chat, Mister Ashton, if it could be arranged; you know, without ... er, I mean, I don't want to disturb Margaret. Is there somewhere we could meet? I'm just off the boat; we docked in Liverpool this morning."

"You mean you want to talk without her knowing?"

"Well, yes. It's something I want to talk to you about. It's ... important."

"As a matter of fact she's just gone out this minute. Off to Chorley for the day." Further relevant information was worth adding, for the record. "With her husband, John. To see his parents. His Mother's not too well. They'll be gone for the day. So you could come round here, if you like."

"Oh. All right. I'll be there, then."

Edwin put the telephone down wondering what on earth Michael could want to see him about.

Margaret and John missed the train they meant to catch. An inquest was held whilst they had coffee and a sandwich in the station buffet to kill time until the next one.

Why had Margaret taken so long to get ready? Ages, she was; then answering the phone when they were already pushed.

Margaret countered that they would still have caught it with minutes to spare, if they hadn't bumped into Marjorie, of all people. How she could talk; not a bit of use saying you were catching a train.

John explained. "Well that's why I walked on, I know what she is. If I'd stopped with you, she'd 've run down all the Government Ministers and what they should be doing and God knows what else before we'd got away."

John said he would telephone his folks to say they'd be late. Margaret snapped that it wasn't necessary; they hadn't said what train they'd be on. John said his Dad always knew what train he'd be on. A row gathered steam from this petty detail. Underlying it was the real reason for their bristling at each other.

"Be honest, Margaret. Go on. You know what all this is about, don't you. You don't want to go, do you?"

"I'm surprised that you do. After what she tried to do to you."

"Look, she is my mother and she's not well. If you can't put yourself out a bit, to come with me; just this once. My God, how often do I ask you?"

"I didn't say I won't put myself out. But I don't have to pretend I want to come."

"Oh, well then, now we know, don't we? Don't come. Don't make any sacrifices for my side of the family. Don't bloody-well come, if you don't want to."

"All right, then. I won't."

John had just bought two more coffees and Margaret still hadn't eaten her sandwich, or she would have gone back home there and then.

Edwin had been trying to anticipate Michael's arrival.

Surely nothing could have happened to Philip. The war was over. They were only occupying a defeated Germany, that was all. And if there's been an accident, Edwin would have heard officially, as next-of-kin. Maybe Michael had a message from Philip. That could be it. They were in the same part of Germany, he believed. Philip wrote that he'd met Michael. Maybe they'd met up again just before Michael had sailed.

But would Philip have asked him to get in touch? Knowing what had happened between Michael and Margaret, and that John would be here? He continued to speculate until Michael arrived in his Red Cross uniform.

"Seen Philip, have you recently? In your travels?"

"Yes, once or twice. We had the odd night-out together; snatched between duties. Your soul isn't your own in a military occupation. Nobody escapes the dictates of victory or defeat."

"Is it Philip you've come about, then?"

"Well, in a way, yes. It's something ... he and I talked about. Makes you think, you know, Mister Ashton, when you see what war has done over there. What we've done to them. Their homes. Their lives. They're people, after all; like us."

"But it was them or us, Michael. You weren't here to see what the V.1s and the V.2s did to London. We captured their launching-sites in the nick of time, you know."

"Even so, it's still devastating when you actually see it over there. Devastation's the right word. Towns, whole places ... piles and piles of rubble. Laid waste."

"We had it here too, lad. Even before the blitz. Devastation of people's minds, through hunger and intimidation. Happened to me and my kind in the coalfield. It was called the General Strike."

"At least people were alive, and could fight against that. There isn't anyone over there who hasn't lost someone, in the Forces and civilians; old people, children. Bombs don't single out those directly involved, do they? The rest, many of them, are living like beasts."

"Didn't you realise that before you went there?"

"It's not like actually seeing it. Your imagination doesn't have a fraction of the impact. And that's what's happening to your Philip."

"What's happened to him? I had a letter only a week ago.

—"

"I don't suppose he mentioned anything? That's why I waited to see you."

"Mention what?"

"I knew he wouldn't. He told me he daren't tell you, knowing how much you're looking forward to having him back."

"Are you saying he's not coming? Why?"

"He's decided not to. Well, not for some time. Not until the people out there. . . . Not until he's done everything he can do to help them."

"You mean, until he's demobbed?"

"Mister Ashton, you don't seem to grasp what I'm trying to say. No wonder Philip said he couldn't bring himself to tell you."

"Don't you talk to me like that." Edwin's anger was generated more by the news of Philip than Michael's attitude. He didn't want to accept that Philip wasn't coming home. By his own choice.

As John and Margaret left the buffet they exchanged simple apologies, and the flare-up subsided. John had telephoned his father to say how sorry they were they couldn't come after all, but he didn't go into details. His mother was, fortunately, much better.

Margaret decided she would pop round to Freda's on the way home. She'd have the results of her exams, she said, today; be nice to congratulate her.

"Yes, if she's got through."

"Pessimist. Well, if she hasn't, she'll need someone to sympathise."

"Okay. I'll get straight home then."

Unknowingly, John was heading to meet the father of Margaret's stillborn child.

But there was a complication. Freda had gone round to the Ashtons with good news. She had qualified; she was now a State Registered Nurse, and couldn't wait to tell them.

But as she burst in with "Tadah! I passed!", she stopped in her tracks as she saw Michael. Apart from his uniform, he looked the same as when. . . . As when she used to wish he'd look at her the way he looked at Margaret.

Michael stood up, shook hands formally. "Hello, Freda. How are you?" Then the telephone rang. Uncle Sefton wanted to speak to her father. She was left alone with Michael.

Freda forced a relaxed-looking smile. "Long time no see." For heaven's sake, why should she sound so nervous.

"It's all right, Freda. I feel a bit embarrassed too. You're married, I see." Michael pointed towards her ring. Had she put her hand to her cheek so that he would see it, she wondered?

She tried to sound casual. "Oh yes, some time now. Well, months anyway." Why on earth was she acting like a school-girl, she asked herself. There was nothing casual about her marriage.

"Very happy, are you?"

"Oh yes; fine thanks. You haven't come to see Margaret, have you?"

"Well, no. Actually. She's ... out for the day ... fortunately."

"You; not attached or anything?"

"Well, yes and no. In a way."

Edwin returned from the telephone, and Freda said she ought to be going. She only came to give the good news.

"Well done. How's that for a good daughter, Michael?"

The insinuation was unintentional but Michael took the inference. "Yes, you are lucky with your daughters. Congratulations, Freda."

Freda left after the formal handshake had been repeated. His grip was as if it were at her throat and she swallowed hard as she walked to the gate. Whatever for, she asked herself? Heavens, he was a teenage crush, you twit. Anyway; thank God Margaret's well out of it in Chorley.

Margaret was delighted when Ian told her that Freda had qualified for her S.R.N. She was about to leave the Macken zies' for home when Freda came in. The sight of Margaret made her jaw drop.

"Well done, Freda. Be thrippence to talk to you now."

"Margaret! Why aren't you in Chorley?"

"We changed our minds. Why? Does it matter?"

"John hasn't gone either. Where is he? Now?"

"He went straight home. Why?"

"Then he'll see Michael. He's with Dad. At home."

Margaret felt icy-cold.

There was nothing Edwin could do but make the introductions. Michael knew who John was. And took the best way out.

"Well, I'll be getting on my way, Mr. Ashton. Nice to have met you . . . John. Sorry I can't stay."

But somehow John sensed who Michael was.

"You've met Margaret, haven't you? My wife?"

"Er . . . yes. I have. Yes, I've met her."

From the way Michael answered, rather than what he said, John knew he was right. "I remember now. We have met before, haven't we? In this very house. Only I was so ill then, you thought I wouldn't remember. Both of you."

Edwin was quick to explain. "Michael's only come to tell me about. . . . To give me a message from Philip."

Michael added: "Nothing else, whatever you're thinking."

"I want to talk to Michael alone."

Edwin was apprehensive. It would do no good. "John, Michael has to go; haven't you?"

"If John wants to talk, he's every right to."

Edwin looked at them like a referee warning two boxers before the fight, shook his head and went into the front room.

John spoke first. "Are you trying to tell me that you've not come here to see her? D'you expect me to believe that?"

"That's right. I rang your father-in-law and he told me Margaret wouldn't be here. Nor you, for that matter."

"So it's all innocent-like, is it? You've not come to let her see you, sort of accidentally, hoping to pick up where you left off. Work on her again until you get her back."

Michael was riled by John's disbelief.

"It wasn't like that! Look, if you want to know, it wasn't me who made the running. She did. When we first met, she came up to me. Not the other way round. And she made the running all the way, and that's the tru –"

At the beginning of the word "truth" John swung his fist, and its contact with Michael's mouth stopped him finishing it.

Margaret ran all the way home and was met at the door by her father.

"Michael's here. Freda told me."

"Oh. Did she? No, he's just gone."

"Has John seen him?"

"He wanted to talk to him alone."

"And?" Margaret was apprehensive.

"Ask John that love. He's in there."

John sat in the dining room, one hand nursing the aching knuckles of the other. He saw her, but made no move to speak.

"You met Michael?"

"Yes. I met him."

Margaret waited but John said no more.

"Aren't you going to tell me what he said?"

"Oh sure. I took it down in shorthand. So you'd be able to hang on every flipping word. I can see now what you saw in him. What made you set your cap at him?"

"What made me what?"

"Set your cap at him. I mean you, a poor weeping widow, and there was this feller, ripe for plucking. And you went all out after him, didn't –."

Now John was on the receiving end. Margaret slapped him so hard it slewed his head round. John turned back to face her as if nothing had happened.

"Well, that's what he said. So I hit him." John showed her his red-knuckled fist.

Edwin heard John's words as he came in and immediately put the record straight. "John. It was Michael you answered the phone to. Just as you left. He wanted me to meet him somewhere. As you'd both gone to Chorley, I told him he could come here. If you hit him because you thought he was trying to see Margaret, you were wrong–."

"No, I hit him ... because. . . ." He looked at Margaret. "What did it solve, hitting him? Whatever he'd done. We never learn, do we? We never learn."

CHAPTER EIGHTEEN

November 1945

Officially and legally the war was over. All the necessary pieces of paper had been signed, the capitulation ceremonies were over, the Armistice dates were there for history to remember. But it was not over for everyone. The victorious armies were occupying the vanquished countries. Or, put another way, the aftermath, the legacies had begun.

Some families lost loved-ones after the war was over. The Ashtons was one of them.

The Military Inquiry into the death of Philip Ashton had been held immediately and his shattered body was committed to a soldier's grave in the newly-designated British Zone of

Western Germany. The officiating party was small: his Commanding Officer, Major Harkness, Sergeants Jago and Hardcastle and Corporal Cobb, of the same Intelligence Corps unit. An Army Chaplain had driven from H.Q. to intone the ritual laid down for military funerals.

The vanquished were repressed by three civilians. A man whose lined face was nearly as grey as his hair, and a teenage slip of a girl, in a dark dress made from hessian. Slightly apart stood a girl whose red-rimmed eyes never left the plain coffin until it disappeared below ground. As soon as the brief ceremony was over, she left slightly hurriedly, as if she ought not to have been witness. The man and his daughter took the path in the opposite direction.

Corporal Ashton's next-of-kin was informed; by a similar telegram to the one Edwin had received when Robert had been lost at sea. That "hostilities had now ceased", in the official phrase, did not seem to have changed the bald procedure. Edwin kicked up a fuss at not being given details of the funeral or having been asked whether he would like Philips's body brought home, and eventually, with the help of Liverpool's ex-service organisations, he received an invitation to visit the grave in a British Military Cemetery. It was marked, like all the others, with a temporary wooden cross, and on it he read Philip's number, rank and name. It had the impact of reality where the telegram had only numbed his senses.

Major Harkness, impersonally sympathetic, handed Edwin a photograph; the official memento he was entitled to by the Regulations.

Edwin looked at it. "Not much of an exchange, is it? His life for a picture of two pieces of wood nailed together."

Harkness knew there was no reply he could make. In any case, as Town Major, he had more work than he could cope with. Getting involved in the bereavement of one of his men's next-of-kin would only add to it.

Officially Edwin should have left there and then. Harkness urged him to go. There was no point in his staying. It would only exacerbate his grief.

But Edwin wanted to take back something more than a photograph; something more of Philip. He tried to explain. "My son had ... so much ... to come back to. I always felt Philip might do the things I'd missed doing. Things I now
172

know that I'd wanted to do myself. And never did. He might
. . . if he'd lived."

Harkness signed some rationing forms. "I'm sorry, I'm very
sorry. But there's nothing more here. Oh, his effects have already been sent to your address."

"I didn't mean that. I want to know more of how he died."

The official account was sketchy, to say the least. Philip
had been spending all his off duty periods working with some
Germans. Harkness wasn't quite clear what it was all in aid
of, "some sort of so-called social work", as far as he knew.
This partly-bombed house, they were trying to make it habit-
able, it seemed. There was no official information, it was
purely voluntary. "He was interested in that sort of activity,
wasn't he?" Harkness implied it was an odd trait to have.
"But to be admired of course. I understand the idea was to
turn the premises into some sort of reception-centre for
orphaned children. Frankly, I doubt if you'll find out any
more than that. Of any significance, I mean."

"It doesn't have to be significant. I just want to know. What
happened? Where? How?"

"We don't know. I'm sorry." Reluctantly Major Harkness
gave orders for a sergeant's bunk to be allocated to Edwin so
that he could stay overnight. Why couldn't people accept the
official line. That way they took up little of his time and, inci-
dentally, of their own time. Better for all concerned, surely.

The only unofficial information Harkness was able to give
Edwin was the name and address of the German woman
Philip was working with. She was organising the clearing of
this place where the explosion occurred.

Edwin climbed over the debris of destroyed homes as he
worked his way down the street. The Allied bombers had done
their job well. The few people he saw were pallid-faced, grim
and hollow-eyed. Edwin had been told to look for "a house
that's hardly standing". Most of them were not standing at all,
so it should not be difficult to locate.

He found Frau Regler in a celler under four roofless walls
which served as a merciful brake from the November winds.
The mildew and the rats were thriving better than the occu-
pant. She half-sat, half-lay on the remains of a camp-bed,
wrapped in a rag-bag of clothes in an attempt to keep warm.

Frau Regler understood little English, but the mention of
Philip's name, and that Edwin was his father, brought a brave

smile to her wrinkled face. A light sparkled in her watery eyes, and then died behind a drawn and haunted face. She did not move from the bed, as she indicated the remains of a wooden box where Edwin might sit.

Her face saddened even more as she recalled for him what had happened. Frau Regler had just left the house to try to look for some drinking water for Philip and the children helping him when there was an explosion. She turned to see the building collapsing. Only one or two of the children were dug out still alive.

Edwin asked what caused the explosion, but she did not know. It just ... happened. For no reason. The authorities had interrogated her. They asked many questions. But she knew nothing. It happened, that is all she could tell him.

Herr Regler came down the cellar steps, a stiff-backed man with a face almost as grey as his hair. He mistook Edwin for yet another questioning official; an Intelligence officer in civilian clothes, maybe. Regler berated him in good English. "Sir, my wife is not fit to answer any more questions." When Frau Regler explained he was Philip Ashton's father, Herr Regler became polite, but unbending. "Your son was killed. He suffers no more. My wife will always suffer."

Edwin saw for the first time that she was in pain. She had not mentioned that she had been injured by the blast and he had been so concerned to learn about Philip that he had not noticed how still she was. He apologised for being so insensitive. He left disturbed and bewildered.

Edwin got Philip's bunk mate, Corporal Cobb, to get him some cigarettes from the N.A.A.F.I., and he took them to Frau Regler. It was like a gift of money, the currency of a shattered society, and she was grateful. She apologised for her husband's rudeness, and explained that they too, had lost a son at the very end of the war.

Herr Regler took Edwin into a blanketed-off part of the cellar and whispered, "My wife is my worry now. She will not get better unless she is taken into hospital." He had tried official sources, including the Military, but the hospitals were too full already.

No, this was not their home; they had an apartment which escaped damage. They had been turned out; it was needed as an office for the Control Commission. Regler had gone back to ask for the curtains, for bedclothes to give his wife extra warmth; but they would not let him take them. They said he should have removed them at the time. An English girl clerk was typing documents, that was all it was used for. He was very bitter.

Edwin reminded him that to prevent Germany over-running his country, he had lost two sons. Regler replied that he had lost four; and his wife might die. A teenage girl clattered down the stone steps in sandals. Regler took her hand and showed him her undernourished face. "This is Emmy. All we have left."

Edwin had questioned Corporal Cobb about Philip. He had a girl-friend, Erika. But Cobb was anxious that Edwin didn't get the wrong impression. If he met Erika he might. But Edwin kept at him until he learned she was a singer at the "Goldener Adler", a small beerhouse where there was slight relief from the slough of defeat. The local people went there for each other's company, rather than the music or the beer.

Edwin had to catch Erika between her songs. She was watching the time because the buxom proprietress was strict about her breaks. Although no-one seemed to stop talking to listen to her, or to the accordionist now giving selections from old Vienna.

Erika apologised for her poor English. She had known Philip about four months. They were friends, that was all. He was very nice to her, she hoped she was nice to him. She had been to see him buried. Her father should not object to a girl-singer in a bar being friendly with his son. She knew she could not sing very well. Earning money this way she did not have to sell herself. Philip had helped her too. How? By giving her cigarettes, of course.

It was time for her next song and she left Edwin without another word. Edwin tried to understand what she meant. She didn't seem the sort of girl Philip would be attracted to. Bleached hair, too much make-up. But then he asked himself how could he know whether she was or not. Philip never mentioned her in his letters. Then why should he? Oh, Philip, Philip. . . .

Edwin pressed Harkness. Behind his desk, in uniform, the Town Major epitomised enemy-occupation officialdom, but failed to daunt Edwin. "Major, the explosion was in your area; you must have held some sort of enquiry. Didn't any experts investigate and find the cause? For your own satisfaction. It killed one of your men."

"Of course. I had the Royal Engineers look-see. Naturally."

"And what did they find?"

"Mister Ashton, why on earth are you persisting? This is the aftermath of war. There have been many explosions. It won't help your son for you to know why this one happened."

Edwin was not to be put off. "Why do you refuse to give me the details?"

Harkness sighed intolerantly. "For the same reason that I haven't told the civilian population. The rumour is going round that it was a booby-trap. We didn't start it. It's a pathetic hope that underground forces are at work. To set up a free Germany."

"You know it wasn't a booby-trap, don't you? What was it? I demand to know. Or I'll go back and kick up a stink." Edwin was red-faced with anger.

Harkness had had enough. It would be quicker and easier to get rid of him by telling him. "It was an unexploded bomb. They must have triggered it off shifting rubble, or whatever they were doing at the time."

"You mean, it was one of our bombs?" Edwin was shattered.

"We found the tail fin. Regulation R.A.F. type. Yes, one of ours."

Dropped by one of our planes? One such as David had flown in over Germany. Perhaps a bomb he'd dropped had failed to explode and could still kill, who knows when?

Edwin wanted to talk to Erika again, and though it was pitch dark he remembered his way to the "Goldener Adler". Its pre-war neon-sign intermittently highlighted the surrounding ruins garishly. As he approached the entrance a hand came round his neck and clamped tightly over his mouth. Many more hands pulled him down to the gritty pavement. Several bodies pinned him helplessly whilst his pockets were rifled. He felt his wrist-watch loosened and saw a grimy hand pick up a half-brick from the gutter, only inches from his face. He lost consciousness as it cracked onto his head.

He must have lain there several minutes, before he was able to pull himself to his knees. He shook his head in an attempt to clear it and staggered painfully to the door under the "Goldener Adler" sign.

Berte, the proprietress with a voice to match her weight,

said she could guess what happened. Anyone venturing out alone after dark risked robbery. He gulped down the glass of schnapps she offered as a reviver and followed her pointed finger. "Through that door: toilet is on right. No soap, no hotwater, but may be towel."

Nobody took any notice of his dishevelled appearance as he limped through the beer-drinkers and pushed open the door to a bare-walled corridor. Nor was Edwin clear-headed enough to have noticed that Erika was not at the side-table where she sat between songs.

The door closed, quietening the accordion music which had dinned in his aching head. He made for the first door on the right failing to notice that it was the second door that was marked "toilette". He barged through the first door and immediately saw he was wrong. The room's only furniture was an unmade bed. Two naked bodies writhed on it, locked in love-making.

The man lifted his face from the girl's to shout "Bugger off". Edwin saw the anger on Corporal Cobb's face and the guilt on Erika's. He slammed the door shut and stood shaking in the corridor, his mind bruised worse than by any blow on the head.

The British sentry prevented Herr Regler from entering the Town Major's office building; the Military Police had their orders. Regler waited all morning and when eventually Major Harkness left the building to get into his waiting car he fell in step beside him. "Please, Major. Please. In God's name do something for my wife. Or she will die." In officialese Harkness reminded him once again that the British were not responsible for the explosion.

As the Major's driver smartly opened the door of the Humber staff-car, Regler said simply: "It was an R.A.F. bomb, Major. That makes you responsible?" Harkness paused, asked where he'd heard such a cock-and-bull story.

Regler chose his words carefully. "A soldier talked. He slept last night with –." He paused, so as to avoid naming his informant ... "with a young girl. She has told me, Major. He boasted to her he had seen the documents."

Harkness clipped his reply as he got into the Humber. "No such documents exist. It's another rumour. Responsibility has not been proved." He rested his hand on the car door, delaying the driver's closing it. "If you don't want to lose your job with the Red Cross, stop repeating civilian gossip. You understand?"

He nodded to the driver who slammed the door.

Edwin, packing his few things when Corporal Cobb came into the bunk, was about to tell him to get out when Cobb held out a photograph. "Philip and me; on leave; in Brussels. Thought you might like to have it."

Edwin showed no gratitude. "Thanks."

"I know what you must think, Mister Ashton."

"You're probably right." Edwin made to close the door, but Cobb stood his ground. "She wasn't only his girl, you know. Not just his."

"She told me different."

"Well, she would, wouldn't she? He needed a woman; like the rest of us do. We're all human."

"It couldn't enter your dirty mind that she might be telling the truth? Maybe she and Philip loved each other."

Cobb thought he knew what was upsetting Philip's father. "You wanted to take that back with you, that it? Yea, well, I suppose they did. Yea, they loved each other."

"Don't make anything up for my sake, Corporal. I was in the first lot. Just about your age, at the time. You're not telling me what it's about; I went through it, too."

"Didn't you need it, then? In your day? By God, you did if you went through anything as rough as we have?"

"You've had it rough? In Intelligence? He never mentioned it in his letters." But as he said it, Edwin realised Philip had never worried them with his own misfortunes, even when he was in the Desert.

Cobb elaborated vehemently, "D'you think we never heard a door bang in anger, then? Because we were non-combatant. We were up front, I'll tell you. Collecting prisoners, taking 'em back to grill 'em for information. If you think that didn't affect your Phil, you didn't know him; soft-centred as they come, he was. Know what he once said to me? After a twenty-six hour session with some Jerries? They knew something about the opposition up-front of us, we were told. They didn't, as it turned out. And after the rough time we'd given 'em and this proved a fact, Phil and me had a rare-old argument about it. – You may not believe this, Mister Ashton, but you want the truth and I'm giving you the truth – Phil said, it was us made 'em put Hitler in the driving-seat because of what

178

we did to 'em after World War One. We argued 'till he was blue in the face, but he believed that; he honestly believed it."

"How could he? He was a babe-in-arms then. After my war, that was."

"Well. I'm only telling you what he said." Cobb left Edwin looking at the photograph. Philip could have done so much, given the chance and the time to do it.

Edwin paid a farewell call on Major Harkness; the formality of saying "Thanks" for what he'd done. To his surprise Harkness said he had a messenger out looking for him. There was something he wanted him to do before he left.

The Town Major led Edwin to an upstairs room where a slip of a teenage girl was guarded by two Military Policemen. In a corner, much more distressed than his daughter, was Herr Regler. Emmy looked at Edwin without a flash of recognition. Her eyes showed fear and innocence in the same haunted stare.

Harkness held out his hand; the C.M.P. Sergeant put a wristwatch in it.

"This yours, Mister Ashton?" The Town Major's voice was official.

Edwin still looked at the girl. "Hello, Emmy." She could have been as young as twelve. The unexpected friendly greeting took her off-guard. She smiled, in case it might help her; but she didn't answer.

Harkness dangled the watch on its strap. "This girl, Emma Regler, sold this watch on the black market; caught in the act by British Intelligence. Regler; you know this was stolen from Mister Ashton. Robbery with violence."

Regler bowed his head, shook it slowly, murmuring apologies; he knew nothing. His daughter did not tell him anything.

Harkness spoke sharply. As Town Major he had to break these marauding gangs. Catching Emma Regler was only the first step. Who were the others? Who did she work with? Or even play with? Her father must know something about her.

Regler swore she never told him anything. Refused to. He made a pathetic plea for her. Look what the war has done to her. From six-years-old she had lived through a horror story: taken from her parents, forced to work on communal farms, suffered the terrible bombing, lived in fear of starvation, seen death many times; and watched some of those who survived the bombs turn into near-savages, fighting each other for sur-

179

vival. Was there any wonder ...? He shook his grey head slowly.

The Town Major had his job to do. He was not concerned with the cause. Nothing must obstruct his efforts to stamp out these gangs.

Harkness turned to Edwin. "Mister Ashton. You recognise this girl as one of your attackers?"

Edwin looked at the waif that was Emmy. Could she have helped strike him to the ground? Then he noticed her scuffed sandals, and the memory of them close to his face as he lay pinned to the pavement came back vividly.

"No. I don't recognise her. I was attacked from behind. I went straight down, and was knocked out."

"You're sure, Mister Ashton? Everything depends upon your word?"

Edwin did not take his eyes off Emmy Regler. She stared back. "Yes, I'm sure, Major. I'm sure I can't identify her as one of my attackers."

Harkness did not seem as frustrated as Edwin expected. He barked a command. "Take them home. Both of them."

Regler's eyes showed "Thank you" to Edwin as he walked past. Edwin dared not acknowledge his gratitude. Harkness spoke as they went downstairs.

"Your boy, Corporal Ashton ... He wouldn't have made a good officer. Got too involved ... Emotionally, I mean." The Major made it very pointed. "Funny thing how strong heredity can be."

Edwin was glad Harkness knew that he'd lied. And hadn't pressed him to tell the truth.

Edwin discovered he had still time to make one more call before his train departed. But when he arrived at the cellar, Frau Regler was sleeping. "Would you be insulted, Herr Regler, if I sent a few things over for her? When I get back to England?"

"We cannot afford to be proud; not at present. Thank you for your kindness. I told my wife what you did for Emmy today; for us all."

"We fought this war from necessity, Herr Regler. Whatever the situation now, that is true."

Regler tried to imply agreement. "I was never a Nazi. But I did feel a pride for my country. When Hitler proclaimed how great Germany was, we had cause to believe him. But it was not a reason to go to war, I never believed that. I did not say so out loud, you understand. I was not brave enough to do that."

"My son Philip believed this war was our fault because of the aftermath of the last war."

"Do you agree with him, Herr Ashton?"

"There's something in it; yes."

"But there is more to it. Whatever the world did to my country, it was no excuse to go to war again."

It was time for Edwin to go for his train, and as he left the cellar Emmy came dashing down the steps and bumped into him.

"Emmy," her father scolded. "Be careful. Say sorry and thank you to Herr Ashton."

Emmy did; and curtsied briefly before dashing past him.

The two men walked down the devastated street towards the station, still talking, finding more and more points of agreement all the time.

When they came to shake hands, Edwin said, "I think I found what I came to find out."

CHAPTER NINETEEN

November 1945

Edwin's return to Liverpool coincided with a domestic upheaval. Ian had finally convinced Freda that their house was too big for them. And the people who bought it from them wanted to move in quickly, as they were in temporary accommodation. Edwin had suggested to Freda, just before the cable from Germany shattered his thinking, that they could come and stay at the Ashtons until their new home was ready. They had moved in whilst Edwin was in the British Zone of Western Germany.

Margaret and Freda had both taken the news of Philip's death extremely badly. John and Ian tried to console them, but sadness pervaded the Ashtons' house. And they were all worried about Edwin. He suddenly seemed years older.

Tony remarked on his first day back at the printing works that he seemed very tired, and suggested he took a few days off. But he had to agree with Edwin's logic; it was better that he occupied his mind, teaching Tony the crafts of the trade. At home he would only sit and think of what might have been for Philip. Tony kept printing-craft questions flowing hard on the heels of the answers. Edwin noticed, gratefully.

At the end of the day, with the machinery shut down and the last of the staff leaving, Tony asked one more question.

"If you hear of a flat coming vacant, Uncle – I know it's unlikely – but if you do, would you let me know?"

"Yes. I will. I've got an idea Margaret and John are looking for a place of their own too, so I'll mention it to them."

"Time for a quick one, or do you want to get home?"

Tony produced a flask and dug two cups out of a cupboard. They sat sipping whisky in silence.

Then Tony said: "Eric Fraser's very happy with the work we're producing for him."

"He's no regrets about buying the business?"

"On the contrary. He was on the telephone today. He thinks it's a good investment. He did make pretty sure before he moved in, you know."

"With more than a little help from you. Quite a streak of your father showed there, Tony. You quite surprised me. All with the best intentions, I know; but it was very craftily done."

Tony smiled. "You're not saying there's too much of him in me, I hope."

Edwin smiled. "Well, no, I wouldn't go that far. What's this about a flat. Thinking of moving out? What's your Dad say about that?"

"He doesn't know yet. You can't talk to him; he's getting worse, you know. I think it's this chap Howells he's involved with. He's a pretty sharp operator. I warned Father from the start. There was something about the man I didn't like. But you can't imagine him taking a blind bit of notice, can you? Well, he's taken on his match, in Howells. Unfortunately, he never says a word to me about it; even when I try to draw him out."

"You never know, Tony. Howells could find your father's a force to be reckoned with, when it comes to putting it across anyone. But going back to Eric Fraser. Has he said anything ... about me?"

"In what way?"

"Oh. That he's saddled with me, can't get rid, anything of that sort?"

"Of course he hasn't. Why should he want to?"

182

"Because you're picking the job up very quickly. And you're not going to need me looking over your shoulder much longer."

Tony reassured him that irrespective of any contract clause, Edwin's experience would always be essential to the efficient running of the works. "And, in any case, I'll be back and forth, going to London."

Edwin harked back to the days when he first took the job. How he had visions of turning a back-street works into a big firm of printers. He soon found that he could never do it; not whilst he was kept down by Tony's father. He kept hoping that one day he'd run the place his own way. Now it had come; but too late. Ambition no longer burned in him.

Tony drained his cup and smiled. "And I'd always thought of you as a life-long Socialist, Uncle."

"I am. That's to say, I'll always vote Socialist. Always will. But I don't know what I am, really. All the things ingrained in me from a child – poverty, real hard times, the way my father had to work and live – seem to be drifting into a hazy past. You know, when I went back to see him, so proud to tell him I'd been made manager of a printing-works, I never expected he'd take it like he did ... I was some sort of traitor; I'd gone over to the other side. But I should have known he would Tony. I should have expected him to. I would've reacted like that myself, once. No, it's strange; I really don't know what I am now. Makes me wonder if I did then. When I was sure I knew."

Edwin set down his empty cup on his desk. "Well, it's no use sitting here holding an inquest on life, is it? Come on, it's been too long a day."

Tony felt closer to Uncle Edwin than he'd ever been.

Having the Mackenzies temporarily with them showed Margaret that all was not quite honey-and-roses. She proved she was right; she asked a seemingly innocent question, whilst Freda was helping her wash-up. "Are you going to carry on, at the hospital, after you've moved into your new house?"

Freda snapped back sharply. "Oh, he's been getting at you, has he?"

Margaret saw the picture. Ian wanted her to; Freda didn't.

"Well, love; you'd have to if you started a family."

"Would I? Why would I? You're still teaching, aren't you? And you've got John-George."

"Yes, but it's not the awkward hours you put in. No night duties, all that."

"Well, it's a job worth doing. And I'll cross any other bridges when I get to them: And only if I get to them."

"Oh. . . . Don't you want to have a baby?"

"Course, I do. What makes you think were not trying." But Freda sounded uncertain.

"You think . . . Is it . . . that possibly, you can't?"

"How do I know whether I can or I can't? Don't be so impatient on my account; don't try and talk me into it."

"All right, I was only asking."

"Well, I'd rather you didn't, if you don't mind." Freda threw down the drying cloth and left the kitchen before Margaret could protest in reply.

Things were far from honey-and-roses for Margaret either. Since the election John's political activity had slumped to practically nothing, but he still went out a lot. Never anywhere special, when he was asked.

Nowhere special was usually the Labour Club. But on the evening of Margaret-and-Freda's kitchen-sink fracas, John had gone to call on Marjorie. He just wanted to ask why didn't she come to the Club any more? Was it because she didn't want to see him?

"To be honest; yes, John. It is. I feel . . . Well, I don't want us to get involved in anything I can't get out of. I won't do that to Margaret."

John didn't want to talk about Margaret. "Anyway. I thought I'd just call in to tell you I'm not going to the Club any more myself. It was just an excuse to get out a bit."

"To get away from Margaret, d'you mean?"

"No, I mean . . ." John shook his head in dismay. "I don't know what I'm getting away from; that's the trouble. Boredom, I think; sheer bloody boredom. It's all so . . . all so domestic . . . and pointless . . . and oh, I dunno."

"What about that teacher-training course you were thinking about?"

"That means Margaret would have to keep on working. Until I qualify and get a job."

"Does she mind? I wouldn't have thought so. She likes teaching. I teach at the same school, so I know."

"No. It's me that minds."

184

"Oh, I see. That's the bone of contention is it. You wouldn't be the breadwinner of the house."

"What house? We're still living with her father."

"But supposing you and I ... got involved ... Wouldn't our conversations become boring, too? And get very domestic? Once we'd exhausted what's wrong with the world and put it to rights? In theory, I mean."

"Exhausted that subject?"

"Well, yes. If we talked about it every time we ... met. You'd find there's a limit to what we could discuss; and our differences would grow from niggles to arguments, and then to rows. And then we'd start to get on each other's nerves. Just like you and Margaret now."

"Are you saying there's no point in our talking? In enjoying each other's company, discussing political issues? Like we did during the election?"

"No. I'm saying it's no excuse you coming here and expecting it to be any different. I bet I'm right about this: you thought you were coming back from Belgium to the situation as you left it. Even better; to a second honeymoon! With Margaret rushing into the arms of her long-lost love, like they do on the pictures. And what happened? You learned about Michael; that took the glossy romance out of it, didn't it? And now you've settled into a routine and where has young-love's dream gone? What happens then? I know what happens; girls who reach my age, still unmarried, we know about it because we get the other end of the stick. From the bored husbands. They turn to us for a bit on the side; stolen fruits or a diversion, or something excitingly different for a change. And d'you know how soon that starts to bore them? I'm speaking from experience, a certain Labour councillor I could name, but won't. Not many months! Not many weeks, in some cases. And honestly, John, I don't want to go through it with you. Because ... in your case ... it might leave me, not just on my own again ... but hurt. So it's not on, love, unless ... unless you're here to tell me you've left Margaret and you have this burning thing for me that if I don't run away to Paris or wherever with you, you'll kill yourself. Now be honest."

John had never bothered to sum up the situation for himself. But Marjorie was almost right. "Well ... no. No, it doesn't add up to that, Marjorie, anything like, really."

Marjorie was in full fig. His disclaimer did not stop her. "You know how I got into this mess? The one I'm in, I mean;

185

left on the shelf, as my dear mother used to call it, not that she ever thought I would be, bless her soul. I'll tell you. I had one sweetheart in my last years at school. One and only one. George and I were crazy about each other, absolutely crazy. Neither of us looked at anyone else, ever. We saw each other every night, weekends, holidays. It was a foregone conclusion we'd get married. When we could afford to, whenever that day might come. He was as much out of work as he was in; more. But of course he got a regular job as soon as war was declared, didn't he. Full-time, oh yes; no chance of being laid-off in khaki, was there? We were still under twenty-one, and our parents decided we could wait 'till it was all over. Everybody was saying it wouldn't last more than six months, a year at most, anyway. Think of that, now, six years later. Well, he was posted out to the Middle East, but I didn't mind, because they were safer out there than we were here at that time, with the blitz going on. He wrote every day; every single day. And I tried to do the same. Then he went down with dysentry. And he ... he ... never came back."

"He died? Out there?" John had had no inkling of all this.

"If he had come back; and we'd have got married; could I have lived up to what he was dreaming of, looking forward to, expecting of me? I doubt it. Dreams, John; something to make us grit our teeth and hang on, keep us looking for rainbow's end, where the pot of life's gold is. Well, now we're here; at our rainbow's end. As much as we'll see of it. Is it anything like our dreams? Is it hell! ... I'm sorry. I'm going on at you."

"No. No. If it helps to say it, say it. It's ... interesting."

"There's nothing more to say, John. Except, I think you should go. For all our sakes, I mean. Margaret's, yours, and mine."

John agreed; and went.

When John arrived home he told Margaret he'd been a walk in the park. She snapped back that she'd promised John-George he would take him out later. John snapped back that she might have asked him first. Margaret reminded him that Ian was in the other room; they must keep their voices down. "And that's another thing," John did not lower his voice, "When are we going to have a place of our own?"

"When are you going to help me find one?" Margaret countered.

Edwin could hear them the moment he stepped inside the
186

front door. John stormed out of the living-room with John-George, saying "Come on, I'll take you in the park, eh?" Anger lingered in his voice.

Edwin told Margaret it would be better for them when they had a place of their own. He'd seen the marks she'd made against advertisements in the "Echo". Was she thinking of using her money from the sale of her Briggs and Son shares?

"Well, yes, I'll have to. But there aren't that many in the paper that we could hope to get. I wasn't going to tell you until I'd got onto something that might come off."

"What about that teaching-course John was on about? All forgotten now is it? Nine days wonder."

"I haven't a clue, Dad, really I haven't. And what's more I've no desire to ask him."

Freda briskly turned into the Ward corridor and came face to face with a girl patient wearing a hospital dressing-gown that was never tailored for late-stage pregnancy.

"Doris. What are you doing here?" Freda unwittingly sounded more astonished than pleased.

Doris looked down at her size. "What's it look like? Chickenpox?"

"No, I mean, why here, from over the other side of the river?"

"Oh. Simple. I left home; just after you'd been, we had a real bust-up. They're moving to Manchester anyway. So I'm back at my sister's; of this parish, as they say in the wedding ceremony; though God knows how I know that. So: this is where I have my monster. Sorry."

An authorative voice called "Staff Ashton?" from Sister's room.

Doris smiled at Freda. "Staff Nurse; you made it then. Course you did. Great."

"Yes. I'll come and see you in your ward, okay?" Freda made for Sister's door.

Sefton Briggs had papers spread all over his desk. George Askew was poring over figures and totals and ratios and cross-referring them in consultation with Harold Jacks, accountant and auditor. There were murmured comments, scribbled calculations and financial comparisons. Sefton, edgy pending their pronouncements, found comfort in the whisky

187

decanter. No, they wouldn't have one, thanks. Not this time of day, Askew added.

Jacks ventured a delicate question. "We have er ... everything here have we? All the figures? And facts?"

Askew looked towards Sefton for the answer.

"Course you have. No point keeping anything back from you two is there? You're on my side. Supposed to be. That's what I pay you for."

Askew and Jacks exchanged a glance and attacked the papers again.

Sefton gulped his whisky and poured another as they straightened their backs.

"Well? What's the verdict?"

"Er ... There's no doubt, it would seem," Askew deliberated, "from a litigation point of view, you do have a claim on Howells."

"You mean I should sue him?"

Jacks immediately added the rub. "Unfortunately, as he's been crafty enough to go into voluntary liquidation, it's not at all certain that your legal claim is going to be worth anything. Until we've investigated what assets remain to be claimed against."

Sefton looked into his empty glass. "And to think I put almost everything I had into that bloody building venture. Sold up the printing works, the shop ..."

"I did advise against selling the shop." Askew reminded him of his good counsel.

"Well, I was hamstrung from expanding it because I couldn't get the right staff. And I needed the extra. Oh, I can see it all now. Howells has really taken me for a ride, the bastard."

Jacks qualified the judgment. "Of course the present economic climate hasn't helped has it?"

"You mean this bloody Government. Aye, if the Tories had got in, it would've been a different story."

"Well ..." Askew was determined to avoid politics. "That we'll never know. Of course, you still have one or two properties that aren't involved in this, haven't you, Sefton?"

Jackson added his advice again. "I'd hang on to those, if you can see your way. Property may rocket up. Due to the shortage. And the post-war demand."

"I will if I can afford to. What have I left to live on?" Sefton began to count the items on his fingers. "The mortgage on the Ashtons' house. I gave 'em that as a gesture, you know. A promise I made to my late sister Jean. Not much of an income from it though, these days."

"Well, Sefton," Askew was surprised Sefton hadn't seen this for himself, "Isn't your brother-in-law now in a position to pay your mortgage off? From the proceeds of his shares in Briggs and Son, when it was sold to Mister Fraser?"

The reply seemed surprisingly un-Sefton. "He very probably can, but I'm not going to ask him. If I suggested it, it's bound to be taken the wrong way. And I don't want that. Not again."

"Pity," said Jacks. "The capital would be a useful injection of cash in your present crisis."

"Yes, well, no one's to know about this. I'll sort it out myself, thanks. Without any sympathy from the family."

Freda had been on late-duty and only Edwin was still up. Ian was on early call; Edwin told her he'd gone up over an hour ago.

"Are those letters that you're burning, Dad?"

Edwin was kneeling at the fireplace, his face flushed by the flames as he fed them from an old shoe-box. "They are, love."

"Dad, they're not . . . Mum's . . . to you?"

"And mine to her. From our courting days. You didn't want to see them, did you? You wouldn't recognise the two people who wrote them. They're written by someone you never knew, to someone else you never knew. We didn't start growing apart until long after you were born, Freda. Least, if we did, we didn't notice. Not whilst Philip and David and Margaret and Robert and you were . . . while we were creating you, I suppose you could call it. We did love each other, Jean and me, then. A marvellous love too, whilst it lasted. That's the only way to have children: I mean it's the only way you ought to have children, Freda, remember that; have them only in love."

Freda said she'd had a tough duty, and what he was saying wasn't going in. As she said "good night", he took a letter out of an envelope.

"Don't keep reading them, Dad."

"It's all history now love. All past and done with. That's why I'm burning them. Gone. For ever. Let bygones . . ."

Freda looked at him sadly and went up to bed.

Askew called again to see Sefton Briggs. "I've been through

the papers once more, and one thing still worries me. When you first discussed forming a company to build houses, what did Howells say about the land? Can you remember exactly?"

"He said he'd already bought the site. And was prepared to sell it at market-price to the company he and I were forming together. I remember that very well."

"And you took him at his word?"

"I didn't; I wasn't that gullible. One day in his office I asked to see the deeds. He took them out of his safe and showed them to me."

"Or what purported to be deeds. You didn't refer them to me, did you, for scrutiny or searches?"

"Well, of course I didn't. I didn't suspect they weren't genuine deeds for a minute. They looked like proper deeds. I presumed he'd had searches made, in our joint interests. You think they could've been forged or something?"

"Could be, Sefton. We know now that all his other companies and ventures were just juggling in the air. None of them are worth anything. That one your nephew, David Ashton, worked for, collapsed like a pack of cards."

"Probably why he fired David, if that was the situation. Yes, it fits doesn't it? I couldn't quite understand why he said he didn't like David. It was a put-up job, to get rid of him. If only we could have seen then, what we can now."

Askew was disgusted. "Yes, well I think you can take it he had no intention you should ever build any houses. It was a confidence trick and a clever one, Sefton."

Sefton Briggs took the blow on the chin; without flinching.

Helen chose what she thought was the right opportunity to break the news to Sefton. She'd had it in mind for some time but had deferred telling him because she knew Sefton had enough worries. And as he'd come to rely on her looking after him she was chary of broaching the subject. But she knew she must do so soon, or she never would.

Sefton had mellowed himself from a whisky bottle, now half-empty. So she began with "That's the last bottle from your stock in the side-board, isn't it?"

"D'you want a drop, before I finish the lot off?"

"No. But it seems a pity. Unless you're restocking shortly. You usually manage to, before you get that low."

Sefton thought of his low financial stock. "There'll be no replenishment." He slurred the last word.

"Sefton, I've been thinking. Quite a while actually. But now I've decided. I'm ... I'm going back to Australia."

It was received better than she could have hoped.

"That's entirely your affair, Helen. I've no right to ask you to stay on. I mean, I don't know what I'd 've done without you, when Mrs. Foster went but –. Yes, I do. I'd 've had to get someone else. Like I'll have to now; if I can. That's not to say I want you to go; I don't. Or that I don't care. I do. If I thought I could persuade you not to go, I would. But we Briggs are not persuadable – persuadable, is that a word? – Anyway we're not, are we?"

"I won't be going before Christmas."

"Oh good. I'd 've hated that. Been a lonely one if you weren't here."

"Come off it. With all your friends?"

"Friends? I've no real friends, Helen!"

"I've never known you at a loss for someone to turn to yet, Sefton."

"They're not friends. They're contacts. Quite a different kettle of fish. I wouldn't call one of 'em a friend, you know that? Not one. Not a single one."

Sefton reduced the level of the whisky again. For the first time Helen felt sorry for him.

Margaret was out with John-George when John arrived home. When they came in he reproached her. "You shouldn't keep him out this late, at this time of the year. It's been dark an hour. He could catch his death."

"He's well wrapped-up. Anyway, someone had to see those agents."

"Agents? What agents?"

"The estate agents I mentioned to you. About that house, in the paper; I showed you. Don't you listen to anything unless it's politics?"

The barb went home. "When did I last talk politics? I don't these days. Nothing like as much, anyway."

"Well, I wouldn't know, would I?" John-George toddled up-stairs as if to get away from hearing his parents hurt each other.

Margaret ignored John-George. "Just in case you're the slightest bit interested, I'll tell you. They've given me first re-fusal on it. For a fortnight. So all you've got to do is make up your mind. Do we want it or not. And I'll put the deposit down. And there's another decision, whilst you're at it. I've got until Christmas to put in my notice at school. If you're going to take that teacher-training course, say so. But if you're not, I'm leaving. So make up your mind please."

"Oh. I see. A pistol to my head, is it?"

Margaret looked up to John-George, playing precariously on the top stair. "Call it two pistols if you like. It's up to you. Heh, Johnny, you be careful; or you'll fall." And she dashed up to give him the safety of her arms.

John shook his head and turned into the living room. He was about to complain about women to Edwin; but he wasn't there.

Sefton seemed pleased to see Edwin, for once. "Let me have your coat. Nice of you to pop round. Sit down, that's the best chair."

"Thanks, Sefton. Actually, I'm dropping in on my way home to ... Well, ask er ... Well, ask if you'd agree to something. I mean, could we come to an agreement."

"I'm sure we can, Edwin. If it's humanly possible. What about?"

Strange words were passing between two men who had disagreed and distrusted each other continuously, since the day one had married the other's sister.

The next words were music to Sefton's ears; and the shock nearly made him give himself away.

"Well, Sefton, the truth is I've been thinking about the money from the sale of my shares. It's in the bank doing nothing but earning a bob or two's interest. I mean it's not doing anything worth while if you see what I mean. And what I'd like to do, if you agree that is; I'd like to pay you off. Pay off the mortgage on my house."

"Pay off ... your mortgage?" Sefton tried hard not to look pleased.

"Only what it's worth, now. No tricks. I'm not going to let you haggle over terms. Or we forget the whole thing."

"No question of that, Edwin. All we have to do is ..." Sefton held out his hand. "Shake on it. That's all. Isn't it?"

Edwin couldn't believe his eyes or ears. Was Sefton going soft in his old age? He'd put up no fight at all. None at all.

They clasped hands. Edwin thought Sefton was never going to let go.

CHAPTER TWENTY

December 1945

Edwin was rummaging through his memories in the attic: stuff no longer needed but banished to the top of the house to avoid the finality of the dustbin. His eye caught the repaired patch in the roof. Where the incendiary bomb came through. What a night that was; it was a miracle that the house hadn't caught fire. Robert and Tony Briggs got up there in time to put it out before it had done much damage.

He sat on an old tin trunk. What holiday memories that brought back. Those seaside days he mentioned in a letter to Helen, when she was still in Australia. A lot had happened since then. Or seemed to have.

He picked up a pop-gun from a heap of old toys and stuck the cork into the muzzle. He'd had one like it himself when he was a boy, but this gun had been Philip's. He pulled the trigger; it "popped" and he found himself thinking of Spain.

The Spanish Civil War. Yes, that had affected Philip, hadn't it. He went out a boy, came back a man. He felt more proud of Philip than he ever had before. Somewhere, Phil must know that; he must. Somewhere? Not under that wooden cross; he wasn't lying there. Where?

Margaret's voice carried from the landing. "What are you doing there, Dad?"

"Oh, just looking for something."

"There isn't anything up there is there? Only rubbish."

"Probably not, love."

Edwin found what he was looking for; a letter amongst a bundle of yellowing papers.

John and Margaret were already eating breakfast; they only conversed at the "pass the salt" level. Edwin joined them in the kitchen.

"Dad, what were you doing up there, this time of morning?" Margaret wanted to know; Edwin didn't want to explain. "Was a bit daft, wasn't it. Never mind. When's your mother and father coming, John?"

"Tonight. Soon as they can get a train, I suppose. Dad'll be working till normal knocking-off time, in spite of the Christmas holiday."

Margaret was at the sink. "I don't mind your Dad; we get on fine. But we could do without her grumbles; hardly a spirit of goodwill-to-all-men, is she? But we all know that, don't we?"

Edwin tried to mediate. "It's a time for our goodwill to all men too, Margaret. And to all women."

"Margaret's right. I wouldn't mind if someone told Mum it was. She can kill goodwill stone-dead, faster than anyone I know."

Margaret smiled wryly as she turned the taps on.

Breakfast at the Briggs was more formal. Helen still served it in the living-room as Mrs. Foster had done until she left. Sefton took it for granted. Tony didn't; he helped out.

Tony noticed his father hadn't shaved. Very untypical. "Not going to the office today, Father?"

"Not today," Sefton thought of the financial stalemate.

"Not much point really. You know, I've got to think seriously about being looked after when your Aunt Helen's gone back. And running this house. Like a barn it is, these days."

"Well, don't rely on me, dad. I've got myself a flat."

"A flat? You're going to move out, too? You didn't tell me."

"I'm telling you now. It's only just happened. What about the shop? That not opening today?"

"Closed until after Christmas."

"Not like you to give 'em that long a holiday."

"No well, it's for stocktaking. I've sold it. Lock, stock and barrel."

"You didn't tell me that."

"Well, as you just said, I'm telling you now. You don't have to move out, you know; just because your Aunt Helen won't be here to look after us. I'll make some arrangements, somehow."

"It isn't that, Father. I just feel ... Well, I want to be on my own. In my own place. Not that it's much to write home about. But it will be mine."

"I see. Want to take the car? I mean, this morning. I shan't be needing it."

Tony smiled. Was his father trying to court him to stay on?

"Thanks, but I've no petrol coupons."

"There's enough in the tank to get you to the Works and

back. Well, I'd better go and shave." Sefton went out sadly.

Tony knew his father was hurt; he chastised himself for not breaking it to him more gently.

When Peter and Janet awoke on Christmas morning they took as many toys as they could carry into Mummy's room, and were surprised to find a man in her bed. In the joyful rough-and-tumble of realising their Dad was home for Christmas, Sheila escaped to make coffee.

"Did you come with Father Christmas, Dad? Down the chimney?"

"That's right, Janet. He let me drive his reindeer."

The truth was less attractive. David had failed to hold down a job in London: more money, more prospects, the man had said. But you earned every penny by sheer slavery; David came to realise that they'd work him until he dropped and then fire him. The prospects were nil. The prospect of another Christmas away from his children was too much, and he'd taken the night train to Liverpool.

Sheila knew none of this background when, over coffee, she asked when would David have to go back? He couldn't tell her without giving the reason. So he said, "You got this week's money okay?"

"Yes. Thanks. I wrote to say so yesterday, as usual; I didn't know you were coming home, then. Thanks for sending it so regularly." David had never been so financially responsible as he had been since he went to London. It gave her hope that he was growing up; at long last.

"Wish it could have been more; I sent what I could. I've been living in one room, no bigger than our old place. Honest. Cost me a bomb at London prices, looked as if it had been hit by one. Much worse damage there than here; you've no idea. Anyway, you've done well to manage."

Sheila thought it best to tell him. "Well, we haven't actually. We've had to use the money you sent to buy food and they've both needed new shoes; several things like that had been let slide; you know while they were evacuated, so it's all come at once, you know."

David was anxious. "What about the mortgage? You haven't let that slide, have you?"

"No. Your Dad's paid off six months for us. At one go."

David shook his head with relief. "Thank God for that then. Thank Dad, too."

Sheila was gratified that he was so concerned.

The morning of Christmas Eve brought bad knews as well as more cards. A letter from the estate agents politely but baldly advised Margaret that the option on the property she'd shown an interest in had lapsed; and "the vendors had accepted an offer, fifty pounds in excess of the price quoted to her heretofore." She thrust the letter at John.

"Look at that.... Why didn't we do something about it? Put a deposit down or something?"

John shook his head. He didn't know why. Except they were so unsettled; his job, her job, the future. Margaret saw the uncertainty in his eyes.

"You've not given your notice in? At the Town Hall?"

"No. Not yet."

"Are you going to? You've got to make up your mind, you know. No one can do it for you."

"I've still got today. No point in doing it any earlier. Just in case.... Well, what's the point of rushing it?"

"John. Marjorie called to see me yesterday."

"Oh? What on earth did she want?"

"I don't know; I was out. She pushed a note through, asking me to get in touch. Would you know what she wants me for?"

"I haven't a clue. Haven't seen her myself for ages."

"Having a trial separation, are you? Of your friendship?" Margaret felt she'd been too sarcastic, but it was too late.

John got up as if he was going to hit her. But he took it out on the door instead, slamming it behind him so that the whole house shook.

Driving to work in the luxury of his father's car, Tony decided to call at the Ashtons to collect Uncle Edwin. John had already left.

"Very nice car this, Tony." Edwin noticed how smoothly it ran. "Your father still going to keep it?"

"I couldn't say, Uncle. He's playing his cards as close to his chest as ever; whether he's up or down makes no difference. He looked as if he'd had a bad night, at breakfast. But he didn't say anything."

Edwin pointed through the windscreen. "See that seat by the library steps? That's where I proposed to your Aunt Jean. Nearly forty years ago now, it is. Not a ha'penny to my name but the cheek to say 'Let's get married'. Her a Briggs, and me from the coalfields; not long before I'd been working down the pit. I was expected to look on your Grandfather Briggs as some tin god. And he'd come up from nothing himself, hadn't he?"

"You've given father as good as you've got. Over the years. Maybe you don't think so, but I do."

"No. I never really won a battle against him. Now he seems to have come a cropper. Neither of us has won the war; our private war I mean. I feel sorry for him; does that surprise you? I see they've got Howells for fraudulent conversion, it said in the paper. D'you think that might help your father? Or will it make it worse for him? Being associated, I mean?"

"Father isn't involved, except as one of Howells' victims. He's swindled him out of practically every penny; to see his face."

"Can't be every penny; there's the shop."

"He sold that, too. To invest in the Howells' project."

"So he's lost the proceeds from that as well." Edwin thought how easily he'd accepted his offer to pay off his mortgage. He'd needed the money badly; it was clear now. "Poor old Sefton."

Freda popped into the ward to see Doris whenever she had a chance. Doris noticed that she never touched her beautiful new-born son. And whenever she tried to talk to Freda about it, she quickly changed the subject. Doris wondered if she imagined this and decided to test her theory. She held the baby out. "Cop hold, Freda."

"What for?" Freda made no attempt to take it from her; almost any woman would automatically.

"What d'you think for? Wipe the floor with? To hold him and cuddle him. Feel what it's like to have a baby. So you'll know when you have one yourself."

"I'm not having a baby."

"I know you're not; you've told me often enough. But it'll give you a taste for when you are." Doris found herself going further. "Maybe it'll make you want to have one. Then you will."

Freda still hadn't taken the baby. "What on earth makes you think wanting one will do the trick."

Doris looked questioningly. "D'you mean, you don't want one?"

"I didn't say I didn't want one; I said it wouldn't make me have one."

Doris couldn't hold back now. "Are you saying you can't have one? You're . . . not able to?"

"Well. In a way. That's . . . the situation, yes. I can't."

"What d'you mean 'in a way', Freda?"

"I don't want to talk about it. It's . . . between Ian and me."

Doris hit on the truth immediately. "You mean, it's Ian. It's Ian can't have one? That's it, isn't it? Oh Freda. Love."

"Oh, we've got over it now. We've known for . . . quite a bit. We both had tests and . . . we've got to face it. That's all there is to it."

Freda tried desperately to sound as though it didn't matter.

Doris held her baby closer. "Course. Ian didn't have any when he was married before, did he?"

Freda smiled as if that was that. "You're having a ward-party tomorrow?"

"Course we are. You know all wards do Christmas Day. Funny, isn't it. Here's you wanting one and not having one. And here's me . . . The other way round."

Was Doris suggesting that her baby should be the child she and Ian couldn't have? Couldn't she see that wasn't the same thing as having your very own. Freda felt cold. "Well, I must get back to work. Take care, Doris."

Edwin thought it odd that Sheila should come to see him at the Works. Particularly as she and David and their children would be joining them for Christmas dinner the next day. He closed his office door and asked her what the trouble was.

"David's managed to get home for Christmas. Well, that's the best way to put it. I haven't dared ask him, but I've got a good idea what's really happened. That job in London was just like all the others. Either it was no good, or it wasn't any good for him. Oh, he's not shouting the odds like he used to; you know, telling me what he's told 'em to do with their job, like he used to go on. All that's past, thank goodness. He arrived with his clothes all creased, and he looked so sad. He's right down on the floor and. . . Honest, Dad, in spite of what's past and gone, it hurts me to see him like that. It really does."

After all that Edwin's son had done to Sheila, she still felt for him. "I marvel that you don't say he's only getting what's been coming to him all these years."

"Maybe that's it. But I can't stand by and watch him try to

198

take it; I just can't. What can I do? I mean for David?"

"I don't know: but there is something I can do, love. And I'm going to. For your sake and the children's as much as for his. I'll just happen to pop in on my way home. How about that, eh?"

"Oh, if you could. . . . See you then."

As Sheila left, Edwin returned to production figures but he couldn't concentrate on them. Suddenly he swept the papers from his desk.

Tony came in as they fluttered to the floor. Edwin's face registered surprise at his involuntary action. "Oh hello Tony. Just . . . letting off a bit of steam, that's all."

"Oh? What about?" Tony had seen Sheila leaving.

"D'you know how old I am, Tony? Damn near three-score-years. So I've only ten to go according to the Bible. And what have I done with 'em so far? My first seventeen, a bare existence in a family struggling to survive. Then the First War, four terrible years. Then between-wars: twenty years of striving to earn enough to bring up five kids. And did they respect me for it? Maybe they did; I doubt it, personally. Even my wife saw me as something different from the man she really married. Now we've had over six years of this last lot. Jean gone, Robert gone, Philip gone. For ever . . . and ever."

Edwin's arms were folded on his desk-top. He lowered his head onto them. Tony put a hand out and gripped his shoulder. But could do no more.

When John Porter arrived home, he found Helen looking after John-George. Margaret had telephoned to ask if she'd come for an hour but no, she hadn't volunteered where she was going so Helen hadn't asked her.

When Edwin "happened to pop in" after work, Sheila made a domestic excuse to leave him alone with David.

Edwin welcomed him warmly. "Glad you could get home for Christmas, David."

"Yes, well . . ." For a moment, Edwin feared he was going to flannel through again; to say he'd managed to squeeze in a short holiday-break in spite of the pressures etc. etc. But Sheila was right, he had changed.

The more David explained, the more Edwin realised his son had matured. David concluded with tears down his cheeks. "I'll do any job, Dad, anything I can get my hands on, so long as it brings in a decent wage. For Sheila and the kids' sake, that's all I ask. It isn't too much, is it?"

"But you haven't told her? That you're out-of-work again?" No one knew better than Edwin what "out-of-work" meant. What it did to a man's morale.

"I've tried to. Ever since the moment I walked in; God knows how many times. There must be something wrong with me. Is there, Dad? Tell me straight."

"I don't think so, David. Now you're trying to think of others a bit more. Like you were just saying about Sheila and the children. You see, the day's going to come when I won't be here for you to run to, you know that. I've been thinking hard these past few weeks and I've decided I want you to have a better chance than I ever had. But it's the last you'll get, David. If you mess up this one, nobody's going to want to know. Including me. If you understand that clearly, I'll go on."

"I understand, Dad. Honest I do."

Tony arrived home with his father's Christmas gift: a bottle of Scotch.

Sefton looked at the golden liquid; then at Tony, detecting pity. "You must think things are bad for me."

Tony smiled. "Well, aren't they?"

"They are, yes; but they could be worse. They can always be worse, never forget that, Tony."

"Why didn't you tell me, Father? I'd 've liked to have tried to do something. To help, I mean."

Sefton looked at him, a rare fatherly look. "To be honest, lad, I didn't think you'd 've wanted to. It shows how wrong I can be. Come on, we'll have the first snifter out of this before dinner." As he unstopped the bottle, Helen returned from the Ashtons, and Sefton invited her to join in a toast: "To the future; our future. Hoping it'll be better than the past."

John was coming downstairs from putting John-George to bed when Margaret returned. She didn't say where she'd been; avoided his questions by asking where her father was? had Helen gone home? who was in the kitchen? When John said it was his father she went to greet him, but John caught her arm. "I resigned, Margaret. Wrote it out and handed it to Temple."

"Oh. Good." Margaret went into the kitchen and found

Harry Porter there. He explained why he was alone. "Celia insisted on going to John's Aunt Hilda's, and I wanted to accept your invitation. D'you know Celia and I have never spent Christmas apart before, since the day we were married?"

"Be a real holiday for you, without her, won't it?" Margaret knew she could say that to Harry.

His answer surprised her: "No, it seems . . . very strange, somehow. Don't know that I'm going to like it. Habit I suppose. Very strong, you know, habit can be."

Harry told Margaret that he'd sensed that John had been waiting anxiously for her to come home. Her sharp reaction made it quite clear there was anxiety on her side, too.

"Oh has he? Well it's up to him to say what it's about. I've something more to do than wet-nurse him."

Harry saw the tell-tale signs he knew too well. "Margaret, I don't want to interfere, but whatever it is that's . . . coming between you and John. Don't let it drag on. Whatever it's all about. Nothing's worth what you could lose. I know what I'm talking about; I've had plenty of experience. Years of it."

"Make the best of a bad job? Is that what you recommend? Accept what there is, and be satisfied?"

"Is it a bad job? I doubt it, if you look at it properly, squarely. Set-off the rough against the smooth. If that's making the best of it. Yes; do. I've come to that conclusion."

John-George's toy-trumpet fanfared Christmas-morning reveille at the Ashtons. Margaret complained across the pillow to John that it was a stupid present to give him. It started a new argument, even before they were out of bed.

By the time breakfast was over, Margaret could stand the continuous buglering no longer. She took the trumpet into custody for the duration of the holiday. With the Mackenzies and the Briggs for dinner, she had enough to cope with, without that racket in her ear.

John said he was sorry; he just hadn't thought.

On their way to the Ashtons, Sefton asked Tony not to mention his financial problems.

Tony said that his own son didn't know anything to mention. "Oh, and by the way, Uncle Edwin's asked Eric to sell him ten shares in the Fraser Group of Companies."

"Oh? That's how he's investing the rest of the proceeds of his Briggs and Son shares, is it?" Sefton raised an eyebrow.

"Well, not all of it, father. And it's not for himself. They're for David. He's coming into the business to learn printing and publishing."

"Oh. Good. Give the lad a sense of responsibility, that should. It's all he lacks, in my opinion. When he realises it's partly his own property he's handling, he'll rise to it, you'll see. Edwin's made a very good move there. And magnanimous. Quite magnanimous."

His father? Complimenting Uncle Edwin, thought Tony. Things are beginning to change.

Margaret got everything going in the kitchen, then went upstairs to change. Edwin followed her surreptitiously, and tapped on her bedroom door. "Happy Christmas to you and John," he said, taking out an un-Christmassy package from inside his jacket.

"Thanks, Dad. What can it be?" she said, squeezing the manilla envelope, but detecting only what seemed like folded papers.

"Open it and see," Edwin enjoyed her bemusement. He crossed with John on the landing as he came up to put his best suit on. "I've given Margaret your joint present, John."

John entered the bedroom and pointed at the envelope. "What is it?"

"Your guess is as good as mine." She extracted a sheaf of documents. They looked at the legal verbiage. Margaret sat down on the bed from the shock.

"My God. It's the deeds. He's given us this house." Neither of them could get used to the idea as they hugged each other.

David and Tony snatched a word of shop-talk at the festive-burdened table. Although rationing was still in force, no war-time Christmas dinner had looked like this. "D'you like the idea of coming to work with us, David?"

"I'm looking forward to it. More to the point, what do you think?"

"Even your Uncle Sefton approved. That's saying something."

"I won't let you down, Tony."

"If you did you'd be letting yourself down."

David spoke quietly and sincerely. "It's about time I paid back what I owe. All round. To the whole family, if you like."

Harry Porter and John snatched a few words of father-son

202

talk. "John, you won't mind if I slip back home after dinner?"

"If you want to, Dad. I thought you were staying on."

"Well I would, if your mother was here. I feel a bit mean, coming on my own. You know, we've always spent Christmas together; it seems all wrong, somehow, this year."

John didn't understand. Then he nodded. "That's all right Dad, I understand."

Edwin didn't want to make an after-dinner speech and Sefton was quick to offer his oratorical talents. He began nostalgically reminding them of other Christmases, of those loved-ones absent who had been at this same table in other years. "And are still here with us, in spirit; in our hearts and –"

Margaret suddenly pushed back her chair and dashed out crying. John chased after her.

Sefton was puzzled. "Did I say something wrong? What did I say?"

John followed Margaret into their bedroom and put his arms around her. "He doesn't think what he's saying, love."

"No. It was me. I just suddenly felt full to the brim. Uncle Sefton's right. When people die, they do live on ... in our memories. We keep them alive ourselves, or should do. But these past months I've only been thinking about myself, my own troubles. There's been no room for Mum and Philip, and Robert. And there should be. I still love them as if they were here."

John put his arms round her. "Margaret, don't cry love. You're thinking about them now. And I am. They are alive, in us. The thing is... It's changed us; we're not the same as when we got married. And it's no use us trying to be the same. You mustn't expect us to be."

"You mean, after Belgium, don't you? And the things you and Marjorie can talk about? And you and I can't."

"And there was Michael. Doesn't that make you a different person?"

"Yes. Suppose so." Margaret was so close to him, she was whispering. "I went to see Marjorie. That's where I was, seeing her. She wants you, John. But only if I'll let you go. That's what she said, John."

"D'you want to let me go?"

"If you want her, I wouldn't stop you. But I told her ... that I want you. On any terms, I want you."

"Marjorie needs someone, too. All right, someone like me, whatever that's worth. But that's only my feeling for her. I'd like to do something to help her. But I can't. Because I want you. And Johnny. That's for me."

Margaret couldn't find a reply. John kissed the tears on her cheek as John-George came in to see what they were doing.

Margaret's sudden exit seemed to signal a general break-up. Ian was due for his Christmas Day duty. David asked could he give Sheila, the kids and himself a lift. Tony offered to take Freda to her hospital's party; and Aunt Helen; and run Harry to the station, too. Sefton said he would stay on a bit.

Suddenly the kisses and goodbyes were over, and Edwin and Sefton found themselves clearing the table.

Edwin wasn't sure that Sefton would tell him, but he asked, "You were in for a bob-or-two, weren't you Sefton? The Howells business, I mean."

"Aye. More'n a bob-or-two."

"Not . . . all you'd got?"

"Well, no, not quite the lot, you know. But . . . a bit too close for comfort."

Edwin waited for Sefton to elaborate but he didn't. So he pressed. "How did it happen? To you of all people?"

"Happened because I made a mistake. A bad one. And I've paid for it. In hard cash. Simple as that."

"I made a bad mistake, too, Sefton. Not in business. Something Jean could have put me right on . . . if I'd let her."

"Is that why you've bought David the Fraser shares?"

"And given Margaret this house. I've done that too."

"I see. That mean you'll be moving out?"

"Something smaller, Sefton. All I need now."

"I'll have to find me a smaller place, too."

Edwin raised his eyebrows, but did not comment. "D'you know Sefton, I was burning some old letters the other day. And I started reading 'em. Couldn't help it. And, d'you know, I didn't know the people who'd written 'em. I'm not exaggerating. Jean's to me; mine to her. It reminded me of when I went back home. To the shadow of a pithead. Where my roots were, for God's sake. But there was nothing left in me that made any sort of . . . contact. You know what I mean, Sefton?"

"I feel like that with our Tony sometimes. No real contact."

"Another letter I found. One I wrote and never gave you. Very formal it reads. My resignation; twenty-five years ago."

"Twenty-five years, Edwin? I don't remember you even hinting you were thinking that way. Not 'til years later."

"Times were too hard for the luxury of resigning. I couldn't afford to let you suspect. I'm a bit ashamed of that to this day."

"Maybe we'd both have done better apart. Better than all that not seeing eye-to-eye. My fault, mostly. I've never been able to change what I am, that's the trouble."

"I did, Sefton; by God, I changed. Anyway, let's not get morbid. We've got to look ahead. With hope. We've no other choice, have we?"

Edwin saw it was time for the King's traditional Christmas speech and switched on the wireless to give it time to warm up.

"Doesn't seem John and Margaret are coming down. Only an audience of two this year, Sefton. Time was we hadn't enough chairs to go round. . . ."

"Aye, time was. Wonder if he'll say anything about first Christmas in peacetime?" Sefton folded the tablecloth inexpertly.

"Wonder where he was when war was declared? I was in the garden with Philip. The summer flowers were a picture that year, remember?"

"September 1939, Edwin. Sounds like a generation ago now."

They sat down; the last evidence of the family gathering stowed through the hatch into the kitchen.

"Aye," Edwin reflected. "The end of an era. The start of a new one."

The wireless came to life; the drums rolled into the National Anthem. Edwin Ashton leaned back in his chair and, as the King began to speak, his mind travelled back down the years, remembering the Ashtons as they were before events overtook their lives; and the family found themselves at war.